THE HIGHEST PRAISE FOR WILL HENRY,
"THE GREATEST WESTERN HISTORICAL
NOVELIST OF THEM ALL."*

"Humor, romance, gutsy adventure, realism, and accuracy. That's the West of Will Henry."

—Don Coldsmith,
author of The Spanish Bit Saga

"Will Henry combines the best talents of a natural storyteller with an inspired poet's glorious use of the English language."

—Elmer Kelton,
author of *The Man Who Rode Midnight*

"Henry and his alter ego Clay Fisher have established a godhead of frontier lore that has changed the course of the Western. His prose skirles off white-ice mountain peaks and stings the nostrils with the scents of burning wood and spent powder."

—Loren D. Estleman,
author of *Bloody Season*

"His work . . . comprises some of the best writing that the American West can claim."

—Brian Garfield,
author of *Wild Times*

* Dale L. Walker, author of *Will Henry's West* and syndicated columnist

Bantam Books by Will Henry

JOURNEY TO SHILOH
PILLARS OF THE SKY

PILLARS
OF THE
SKY

◆ ◆ ◆

Will Henry

**Originally published under the title
TO FOLLOW A FLAG**

DOMAIN™

BANTAM BOOKS
NEW YORK • TORONTO • LONDON • SYDNEY • AUCKLAND

PILLARS OF THE SKY

A Bantam Book / published by arrangement with the author

PRINTING HISTORY

Originally published under the title To Follow a Flag
Random House edition published March 1953
Condensed in Zane Grey's Western Magazine *under the title*
"Frontier Fury," September 1952
Condensed in Toronto Star Weekly *June 1953,*
under the title To Follow a Flag
Bantam edition / September 1956
New Bantam edition / February 1970
Bantam Domain edition / February 1991

DOMAIN and the portrayal of a boxed "d" are trademarks of Bantam Books,
a division of Bantam Doubleday Dell Publishing Group, Inc.

ISBN 0-553-28878-4

Published simultaneously in the United States and Canada

Bantam Books are published by Bantam Books, a division of Bantam Doubleday
Dell Publishing Group, Inc. Its trademark, consisting of the words "Bantam
Books" and the portrayal of a rooster, is Registered in U.S. Patent and Trademark
Office and in other countries. Marca Registrada. Bantam Books, 666 Fifth Avenue,
New York, New York 10103.

PRINTED IN THE UNITED STATES OF AMERICA

RAD   0 9 8 7 6 5 4 3 2 1

Contents

◆

Introduction

♦

by Dale L. Walker

There comes the moment, about halfway into *Pillars of the Sky*, when Bvt. Lt. Col. Edson Stedloe's field column gets its first glimpse of Kamiakin, the Yakima war chief, at the ill-fated parley on Tohotonimme Creek, Washington Territory, in May 1858.

This moment—and there are such moments in all of Will Henry's Indian novels, from *No Survivors* to *Black Apache*—is filled with awe, a word the author himself employs to describe his emotional response to these warriors of the horseback tribes of the Old West.

The "hostile messiah" Kamiakin, as the reader sees him through Will Henry's indelible word portrait, is six feet three, broad-shouldered, hawk-faced with a great mouth "that appeared to hinge somewhere behind the small, flat ears," an undershot jaw "as long and sharp-hooked as a steelhead trout's," a nose "made unlovely by God to begin with and subsequently laid half over toward his left cheek by a deep lance slash."

Kamiakin's powerful body, clothed only in an elkskin breechclout, moccasins, and a cartwheel warbonnet, is forked over the back of an Appaloosa stallion, its withers draped with a gaudy, bloodred three-point blanket.

Kamiakin, or Kamaiakan (1810?–1877), principal chief of the Yakimas and the confederation of tribes of eastern Washington, was in life no less a mesmerizing figure than Will Henry depicts him in fiction. As early as 1840 Kamiakin won recognition as the leader of a peaceful faction of his tribe that remained neutral during the Cayuse War of 1847–48, following on the murders of missionaries Marcus and Narcissa Whitman and twelve of the men working at their mission on the Walla Walla River.

But by the mid-1850s the influx of white gold-seekers and such ham-handed, without-warning episodes as the invasion by a military party (under Capt. George B. McClellan, later the Union's early commander of the Army of the Potomac) to survey a railroad route through tribal lands, made it impossible for Kamiakin to remain neutral forever.

Governor Isaac Stevens of Washington Territory negotiated a number of peace treaties with the Yakimas but embittered Kamiakin and his people by announcing that he intended to purchase Yakima lands, threatening violence if the tribe would not sell them.

In September 1855 Kamiakin declared his intention to keep whites out of tribal lands and began attacking all trespassers—settlers, prospectors, soldiers—the result being a series of small military expeditions in what became known as the Yakima War of 1855–56. This obscure conflict ended after Col. George Wright, a sensible officer, convinced Governor Stevens to withdraw all military forces from the Walla Walla Valley.

The campaign of *Pillars of the Sky* (which is sometimes called the Palouse Rebellion, so named for both the Palouse River and the Palouse Indians living near its banks who participated in the fight) followed the momentary peace nurtured by Colonel Wright.

After the Palouse expedition, the final spasm of rebellion, Kamiakin exiled himself to British Columbia, returning to southeastern Washington Territory in 1861.

He died at his camp at Rock Lake in 1877.

Kamiakin was described by contemporaries as imposing,

intelligent (he had been educated by Catholic priests), of proud and noble bearing, well over six feet tall, and an eloquent speaker.

In truth, we do not know how the real Kamiakin looked at that climactic moment north of Fort Lapwai in the spring of 1858, but Will Henry has solved that problem for us. He draws from a deep well of research and reading, of traveling to the historic places, seeing, listening, restaging in his mind the events that occurred there.

But he is a fiction writer and as such can take certain license—filling in what we do not know, elaborating, embroidering, *painting* with words these re-creations of times and events and people long gone.

Those who love history and read history will not countenance the twisting of it even by a fiction writer. What is known, provably known, ought not to be tampered with—by anybody —we insist with unassailable common sense.

Reading Will Henry's reconstructions of historical events in his novels will show he sides with the lovers of history, loves and respects history himself, but does not pretend to be *writing* history.

Only a writer of fiction, and a superb one, can give us such a sense of the time and place in which historical events are occurring as this: "The early May evening lay over the restless surge of the swollen Snake like a calming, blue-dark shawl. Overhead, the fat Washington stars bloomed thick and white as Shasta daisies."

Or, "In the leprous gray of the fog-patched morning, Red Wolf Crossing loomed dreary and desolate as the devil's dooryard. The bleakly carved banks of the booming Snake cut like a ragged war-ax slash through the long hills."

Only a fiction writer of Will Henry's caliber can depict what it must have been like to see those fabulous Indian pony herds of "butter-bright buckskins, blood bays, burnished blacks, glaring whites and blazing paints," and their riders, a "cascade and plunging foam of snow-tipped eagle-feather bonnets," a "flash and sun-glitter of pennoned lance," wearing "garish cobalt, ochre and vermillion greasepaint."

His treatment of Kamiakin, if a slightly larger-than-life portrayal, is vivid but soundly grounded in fact, as is the entire backdrop, and much of the detail, of the Palouse campaign depicted in *Pillars of the Sky.*

The essential framework of the conflict between Kamiakin's force of 1,000–1,200 Spokane, Coeur d'Alene, Yakima, Palouse, and Nez Perce tribesmen and the 4 officers and 154 men (the number in some histories of the campaign is 5 officers and 152 men) of the First Dragoons and Ninth Infantry is handled meticulously in the novel.

The key decision that lay behind the conflict *was* the American force's leaving the Colville Road and marching to Red Wolf Crossing into treaty lands; there *were* two mountain howitzers in the army's force; Father Joset, the Jesuit priest from the Coeur d'Alene mission, *did* play a role in the confrontation; the Nez Perce chiefs Timothy, Vincent, and Lawyer *were* principal players in these events of the spring of 1858; and the outcome of the battle is pretty much as the author has it.

Will Henry gives himself some fiction breathing-room by making Chief Timothy a loyal army scout, forever ready to "follow a flag" (which was the original title for this 1953 novel) when, in fact, the real-life Timothy was camped at Red Wolf Crossing when the army force arrived and, always a friend of the whites, lent his fleet of canoes to ferry the soldiers and their equipment across the Snake.

The author's commander of the field force, "Edson Stedloe," in historical fact was Maj. (Bvt. Lt. Col.) William Jenner Steptoe of the Ninth Infantry (West Point '37), a good officer, twice breveted for gallantry and meritorious conduct in the Mexican War, and, in 1858, commander at Fort Walla Walla, Washington Territory. The origin of his expedition across the Snake was the petition for military assistance he received early in 1858 from some white settlers living at Colville who feared for their lives and property because of the cattle-stealing raids by Palouse tribesmen in the Walla Walla Valley and the killing, allegedly by Indians, of two gold miners at Colville.

Lt. Wilcey Gaxton in the novel is modeled after Lt. William Gaston, commanding E Company in Steptoe's force and fatally wounded in the battle; Will Henry modeled Capt. Oliver Baylor after Bvt. Capt. Oliver Hazard Perry Taylor, commanding Steptoe's C Company, who died of his wounds after the battle; and Colonel Wrightson of the novel is Col. George Wright, Ninth Infantry, who waged the retaliatory campaign against Kamiakin's force after Steptoe's retreat.

Even the "Capt. J. Mullins," whose name is found on the map of the Colville Gold District in *Pillars of the Sky*, is based on a historical personage. Lt. John Mullan, Second Artillery, later renowned as the builder of the wagon road between the Dalles, Oregon Territory, and Fort Benton, Montana Territory, was Colonel Wright's engineering officer during the post-Steptoe expedition in the summer of 1858 and did, in fact, make the maps of both the Steptoe and Wright campaigns.

1st Sgt. Emmett D. Bell of H Company, First Dragoons, is pure Will Henry invention, of course, as are Calla Lee Rainsford of Lynchburg, Virginia (and how the author etches her on our brain: "graceful as a willow wand in moving water . . . oddly pagan look of an Inca altar carving"); Sgt. Erin Harrigan; and that giant, simple, amiable, loyal Kentuckian, Bull Williamson, who loves to sing "On Top of Old Smokey" to the accompaniment of Emm Bell's mouth harp.

Bell, Harrigan, and Williamson are Will Henry creations, but there were over one hundred fifty enlisted troopers in Steptoe's expedition into the Walla Walla Valley, and among them, without a doubt, were soldiers *like* Emm Bell, Erin Harrigan, and Bull Williamson.

Timothy and Kamiakin in *Pillars of the Sky*, Chief Joseph in *From Where the Sun Now Stands*, Crazy Horse and Gall in *No Survivors*, and Black Kettle in *Yellow Hair*—all the Indians in all the Will Henry novels, are grandly but fairly drawn. They are neither (to use Will's own words) "rote-carved figurines pared to fit his romantic notions of Horseback Hiawathas" nor can the author be accused of being "some sort of Caucasian communist-apologist for, lo, the Poor Red Man."

Says Will, "Indians have always been larger than life to this author," and he admits to re-creating them in his fiction a bit larger than life because they *were* a bit larger than life.

He also says this: "No non-Indian can see the Indians as an Indian would. But he can try. In fact, he must try. It is no good to write another book filled with the eternal white prejudices."

Such scenes in *Pillars of the Sky* as those with the looming Yakima, Palouse, Nez Perce, and Coeur d'Alene warriors sitting patiently astride their Appaloosas just across the river and waiting without fear for what the white man brings—these scenes and images have never been written better than by Will Henry.

The reason for this can be found in Will's own third-person admission: "Given his own choice of lives, as surely as vermillion and ochre are the paints of war, Will Henry would have been born a horseback Indian of the high plains, riding wild and free and forever far away from the haunts of the white man, racing the sun and the wind and the rain beneath the spotted eagle's cry until the day that Wakan Tanka called him home. . . ."

Author's Note

In the state of Washington, midway along the arid Idaho border, there is a pleasant little city called Rosalia. And in Rosalia there is a monument; an ugly, barren, four-sided spire of native granite.

Rosalia is a busy place, filled with busier people. The times are pressing, and the talk is of important things. Of winter rain, of drilling weather, and of good, hard, Washington wheat.

And the monument? Well, it is forgotten. Like the century-dead names graven into its bronzed flanks. Names like Lt. Col. Edson Stedloe, Lt. Wilcey Gaxton, Capt. Oliver Baylor, and 1st Sgt. Emmett D. Bell.

Forgotten, too, is the name of the dark-faced, un-smiling Nez Perce chief, whose steadfast following of a foreign flag has been repaid with the peculiar coin of oblivion reserved by white history for its red-skinned heroes.

Indeed, men will forget. And space and time fail to remember. But think of that name, Rosalia, along with the winter wheat and the drilling weather and the welcome rains.

Think of it often. Remember it well.

It was *Timothy*. . . .

PILLARS
OF THE
SKY

1

◆

The Colville Road

At the top of the long rise the white soldier eased his rawboned bay to a halt, sat him, hipshot, while his squinted gaze studied the fall of the wagontricks toward the distant river. His silent red escorts let their slant eyes join his in frowning consideration of the flood-swollen Snake.

First Sergeant Emmett D. Bell, H Company, First Dragoons, wrinkled the hawklike bridge of his sun-black nose. He spat disgustedly into the settling dust of the Colville Road. Behind him the three Nez Perce Indian scouts took note of the sergeant's attitude. Two of them grinned loosely, the third, a dark, piñon-lean Indian wearing the scarlet and ermine choker of the hereditary Nez Perce chief, flashed his companions an arrowsharp scowl before returning his expressionless gaze to the broad back of Sergeant Bell. Presently the big soldier turned, his soft voice oddly at variance with the hardness of the face which housed it.

"Well, Tamason, yonder's the Snake. And yonder's our main crossing, there, where the road dips down off the rim."

"Yes, that's the Snake, Ametsun." The Nez Perce had

1

taken what he wanted of Bell's name and made of it a good Indian word; something that sat properly in a red mouth rarely shaped to call a white man friend. "That's the Snake, and that's the crossing there where you have marked it."

After the deep bass of the chief's mission-school English had ceased, Bell nodded thoughtfully. Presently he grimaced and spat again into the roadway. Contracting the beaded blackness of his gaze, the Indian spoke quickly.

"Twice now you have spat, Ametsun. That's a bad sign. Don't you like what you see?"

"You know damn well I don't, Timothy." Bell used the Nez Perce's Christian name. "I don't like what I see ahead and I don't like what I see behind."

Timothy grunted, shifting his pony to bring him abreast of Bell's mount. Seeing the sharp look his move drew from the white man, the chief's frown deepened. "I come close to talk, Ametsun, only because in these days I don't know that even my brothers' hearts are good."

"You're making sense." Bell's frown compounded the chief's with grim interest, his quick-thrown side glance flicking to the other two Indians. "What's on your mind?"

"You spoke just now of what lies ahead. Is it the Snake being in high water that worries you, then?"

"You know better than that. That crest won't hold over a day or two, and the column can use the rest."

"Three days, perhaps," amended his companion. Then, after a pause, "You are thinking of what I am, then? Of something beyond the Snake?"

"Depends on what you're thinking of." The soldier's eyes narrowed, watching the Indian closely.

"Of a name," said Timothy simply.

"Palouse?"

"Palouse—"

"All right then, we're both thinking of Chief Kamiakin."

"We are both thinking of him," echoed the Nez Perce softly.

For the first time Bell straightened in his saddle, threw a quick smile at his red comrade. "Well, by God, Tamason, it's a relief to know somebody else in this stinking outfit has got brains enough to be worried. Come on. Let's get back to the column and give the colonel his 'all clear' to the crossing."

"Wait—" The Indian had his bronze hand on Bell's bridle. "You spoke as well of not liking what lay behind you. How did you mean that, Ametsun?"

"Come along up here," grunted Bell, turning his gelding up the ridge. "I'll show you quick enough."

Joining Bell on the ridge, Timothy followed the long arm with which the white man pointed out the climbing swell of the prairie to their rear. "Now you take a good look down there, Timothy"—the sergeant's instruction was not so brief that the Indian couldn't catch the muted bitterness in it—"and tell me what you see."

"I see the flag, Ametsun. Then the oak-leaf chief and all the pony-soldiers following after it." Timothy shrugged, wonderingly. "Truly, is there more to see?"

"Nope, that's it." The bitterness was stronger now. "The dear old Stars and Stripes up front on schedule. Backed by Brevet Lieutenant Colonel Edson Stedloe"—the acid in Bell's tones etched the continuing roll call deeper still—"with four company officers and a hundred and fifty-two enlisted men. Five gentlemen by grace of an act of Congress. And a hundred and a half ignorant heroes by the grace of not having got through grammar school, or being on the dodge from the sheriff back home. Christ!"

"Amen," echoed the Nez Perce, solemnly.

Bell looked at him sharply, half suspecting Timothy had meant the benediction to be funny. Studying the Indian's blank face, he decided he had not. You take a pure savage like Timothy, one who had been ground, exceedingly fine, through old Marcus Whitman's missionary mill, and you had a case on your hands that was just about as far from funny as you could get.

"It is the soldiers behind us you don't like?" The Nez Perce's low question broke in on Bell's sidestepping thoughts.

"That's it," grunted the white man. "And you know it better than I do. Hell. With Kamiakin over there in the Bitter Roots heating up the Yakima and Spokane and Palouse tribes with a mess of lies about us planning a military road through their treaty lands, and about how Colonel Stedloe's coming to Colville for war instead of peace, how else can a man who knows Indians feel?"

"You are sure those are lies, Ametsun?" The question was put with childlike directness and Bell had to drop his eyes before it.

"I don't rightly know, Timothy. But that's neither here nor there. What's *here* is a full-out field column toting along two mountain howitzer companies and three of crack dragoons. And it's supposed to be heading for Colville for a peace pow-wow with the red brother! And what's there is an out-and-out hostile Palouse chief who's been predicting to the Yakima and Spokane right along that we'd come just the way we're coming —armed to the eyeteeth and loaded for bear. Anyway you want to pull that boiled dog apart there's going to be big scrapping over the bones."

"No!" Timothy's contradiction came softly, the slit eyes behind it looking far away. "If Colonel Stedloe follows his word to march only along the Colville Road, there will be no fighting. I have heard this among my people, and you may believe it, Ametsun."

"Hallelujah!" breathed Bell in mock relief. "We're saved. I saw those field orders and they route the column square up the old Colville Road. That's thirty good miles north of Kamiakin's sacred stomping grounds. Looks like the Old Man's soldier boys might get to Colville yet."

"They will get there if they stay on the Road," was all Timothy said, before turning his pony to follow Bell's.

The early May evening lay over the restless surge of the swollen Snake like a calming, blue-dark shawl. Overhead, the fat Washington stars bloomed thick and white as Shasta daisies. Ashore, the camp's cookfires coruscated the surface shift of the river with their myriad sequins. On the lamplit patch of bare ground in front of the command tent, Sergeant Bell's "five gentlemen by grace of an act of Congress" had dined at length and well, were comfortably disposed to idle discussion of their prospects in Colville.

"I don't know, Colonel, sir. Colville's a gold town." It was young Davis Craig speaking. He was, by Bell's hard-bitten estimation, one of the two good heads in Stedloe's command. "I should imagine Chief Kamiakin would have suspected the good faith of our peace talks a great deal less had we held them back at Fort Wallowa."

"Nonsense, Craig!" Colonel Stedloe was entirely satisfied with his own grasp of the Indian mind. "You miss the whole point. Kamiakin is a documented murderer, a complete renegade with no less than five white killings charged to him within the past year alone. Now, the first thing any indicted criminal wants is a change of venue. Precisely my idea in holding these 'peace' hearings in Colville. 'Scene of the crime' sort of thing, you see? The murdered men were all prospectors from the Colville district. Kamiakin knows that as well as we do. Naturally he'd be uneasy about any hearings conducted up there, and from that standpoint we shall have the entire advantage of him. Don't you agree, Winston?"

"Well, sir, I don't know." Captain Harry Winston, Stedloe's second in command, was a heavy man, as deliberate in thought as in motion. And he was the second of Sergeant Bell's "two good heads."

"Like Craig says, we know those Colville miners went into those ore-rich Palouse and Spokane lands, exactly in the same manner in which they've already succeeded in breaking down the boundaries of the Coeur d'Alene reservations. I would suspect, sir, that if you've got any crime at all up there in Colville, your bill of indictment is more apt to read 'white conspiracy to defraud' than anything else."

"Well, well!" The colonel's words moved under an easy cloak of fatherly good humor. "It appears I'm faced with a disintegration of command in the field! Any of you other gentlemen care to call the question on your C. O.? Baylor? Gaxton?"

"Not me, sir." Lieutenant Wilcey Gaxton, a pale, twenty-four-year-old West Pointer, eighteen months in the Department of the Pacific, nodded nervously. "If the devil pumped all night he couldn't get that water of his high enough to keep me out of Colville, this trip."

"Just *what* is your big secret up there at Colville,

Gaxton?" The sharp-grinned query came from the black-bearded Baylor, the others quickly joining him in a rapid-fire round of good-natured proddings.

"Gentlemen, gentlemen—" The young officer tried for a lightness to match that of his companions, but trailed instead into a stammering confusion of embarrassment.

"A woman, by God!" Baylor's handsome face lit to the sudden flush. "Damn your cotton-picking soul, Gaxton, if you've gone and imported one of your sweet-smelling magnolia blossoms on us, I'll—"

The captain's meant-to-be-humorous ribaldry was stemmed by the patient voice of Colonel Stedloe. "Wilcey, you haven't brought a woman out here."

The statement, neither challenge nor question, was simple declaration. The colonel, a Southerner of the old school, had no real thought that young Gaxton, himself a Virginian, could dream of such a transgression. Stedloe was, in effect, letting his own calm phrasing deny the possibility of such a situation.

The lieutenant, in turn, wasn't having such an easy time of it. But his colonel's elastic faith in Mason-Dixon manhood was more than equal to the awkward moment. His courteous nod dismissed the subject painlessly. "Don't look so desperate, Wilcey. I know you too well to press such a question. And now, gentlemen"—the paternal tones were briskly exchanged for the crisp diction of the colonel-commanding—"I think we'll let that do it for tonight. I've something of a surprise for you in the morning and I'd like you to have a good night's sleep ahead of it."

As his youthful staff traded raised eyebrows, the colonel concluded. "If there's nothing further, I bid you good evening."

Apparently there was not and the young officers, despite their faintly aroused curiosity, quickly arose to take their leaves. As they did so, Stedloe motioned to the boyish Gaxton. "Wilcey, send a man to find Sergeant Bell. Winston tells me the insubordinate devil sent one of his Indians on up the Colville Road this afternoon. Damn it all, I sometimes wonder who's running this command, me or Sergeant Bell!"

Facing Colonel Stedloe in a sagging "at ease" which qualified as such only because he was technically still standing up, Bell covered his position with his usual bluntness.

"You sent for me, Colonel?"

"I did." Stedloe's tone wasn't annoyed yet, just short enough to let Bell know it soon would be. "What's this Winston tells me about you sending one of your scouts on up to Colville this afternoon?"

"Yes, sir. Timothy."

"You've heard of authorizations, I presume?" Now the annoyance was putting in its scheduled appearance.

"Didn't think any was called for, Colonel."

"Oh? How so, Sergeant?"

"I'm in charge of the scouts on your own order. Reckoned the Colville Road could do with a good scouting and sent my best man up to see that it got it."

Stedloe had an excellent set of upper teeth, and a guaranteed habit of tapping them with his fingernails, broad chin in thoughtful palm, when his temperature was rising. He was tapping them now.

"Did it ever occur to you, Sergeant, that colonels commanding field columns sometimes have orders and ideas not completely conveyed to line noncoms?"

"Does that mean you're not going to Colville?" Bell ignored the form of the question to get at its sense. After a moment's hesitation, Stedloe passed the bluntness of the sergeant's demand to put one of his own in its place.

"I dare say you'll find out what I mean, Sergeant. Right now, I'm asking the questions. And what I want to know is why you felt called upon to send that Indian up to Colville?"

Bell thought a minute, then let his answer come slowly. "I don't like to leave an Indian sitting around doing nothing. They get sour. I reckoned we'd be held up here a day or so and I figured he could improve his shining hours a hell of a lot better in scouting the Road than in building up his bottom-bunions squatting around an idle pony-soldier camp."

"Anything else, Sergeant Bell?"

"Yes sir." For the brief time it took him to say it, Bell's gray eyes sobered. "I've got a four-bit hunch, Colonel, that all isn't as happy in the hunting grounds of Kamiakin's Palouses as you might care to imagine. And I ride my hunches dead-out."

Lieutenant Colonel Edson Stedloe, whatever his limitations, was no martinet. Contrary to the grimly regulation attitude of his staff, he himself not alone tolerated but actually enjoyed Bell's refreshing lack of deference toward commissioned personnel.

In this instance he agreed, in theory, to the sergeant's economic employment of his scout's spare time, while in the same breath advising the confounded noncom, in fact, that there would be no layover at the main crossing of the Snake. With the dropping of that little howitzer burst, he retired to his tent to get on with the really important business at hand; the laborious writing of his endless operational reports.

Long after Bell's lounging shadow had been lost to the feeble arc of the command-tent lamp, the colonel's stubby quill scratched the dull litany of its progress across the yellowed sheets.

> "Snake River Crossing, Wash. Terr.,
> May 12, 1858.

Major: On the 2nd instant I informed you of my intention to leave Fort Wallowa with about 130 dragoons and a detachment of infantry for service with the howitzers, and to move directly where it is understood the hostile party of the Palouse chief, Kamiakin, is at present. Accordingly, on the 6th instant I left there with companies C, E, and H, First Dragoons, and E, Ninth Infantry; in all, four company officers and 152 enlisted men.

As advised to you in mine of the 2nd instant, the announced purpose of this movement was to seek a council with the hostile Indians at Colville, and there to mediate their differences with the whites of that settlement. However, learning that the hostile Palouses were in the vicinity of Red Wolf Crossing of the Snake River in Nez Perce lands, I have reconsidered my earlier plans and now intend to march directly for Red Wolf Crossing. I have not thought it advisable to previously acquaint my staff with this fact since there exists among them some unwarranted feeling of doubt as to the real intent of the reportedly aroused Indians.

However, my own intelligences assure me that the Spokanes and Yakimas will not unite with the Palouse chief Kamiakin (who is personally wanted on half a dozen white murder charges) and that there is no danger of a general uprising at this time.

I shall accordingly issue the revised order tomorrow, the 13th instant, and the column shall move at once on Red Wolf Crossing. I am satisfied the new route will heighten the originally desired effect of intimidating the various restless tribes into accepting our direction for an immediate hearing at Colville. I shall keep your office advised with regular field dispatches but you may assure General Clarkson of an early and peaceful settlement of the complete matter.

I have the honor to be, very respectfully, your obedient servant,

MAJOR W. W. MACKAY,	E. S. Stedloe
ASST. ADJ. GENERAL,	Bvt. Lt. Col.
U. S. ARMY	United States Army
SAN FRANCISCO.	

Once well away from Stedloe's tent, Bell removed his canteen and tipped it skyward. For five full seconds he held it thus, saluting its exalted position with reverent genuflections of his prominent Adam's apple. When at last he brought the container away from his smacking lips, it was an aroma infinitely more redolent than soft mountain water which assaulted the evening air. Twenty strides later, passing Lieutenant Gaxton's tent, Bell was perfectly aware of the young officer's hail, but chose nonetheless to ignore it.

"Sergeant Bell!"

This was an order, now, not a greeting, and Bell halted his dragging footsteps.

"Yes, sir?" The sergeant, pausing in his loose slouch across the fire from the officer, didn't offer either to salute or sit down.

Lieutenant Gaxton looked up frowning. And with ample reason. What he saw would have stiffened the neck of the least proper of Congress's gentlemen.

First Sergeant Emmett Bell crowded six-feet-two without the benefit of his thick dragoon bootsoles. His arms, heavy as wagon tongues and half as long, hung the best of the way to his bent knees. His complexion, rare in a sandy-haired man, was as dark and sunlined as a Prairie Sioux's. The patent slovenliness of his dirty blues, together with the dust-red bristle of his short beard and the more than faint aroma of fusel oil which impregnated his entire person, completed the picture of the factual frontier cavalryman—drunk, dirty, and disrespectful.

Gaxton turned his eyes away from the waiting noncom and coughed heavily. At the hollowness of the sound, Bell's jaw twitched. Before he could speak, Gaxton motioned him to sit down, cleared his voice with difficulty. "Sit down, Emm. There's something I've got to tell you. Been wanting to for a long time. And don't say anything about this damned cough. I know it isn't getting any better, but Randall says it's nothing to worry about."

"Well, that makes either you or Randall a cold-deck liar," grunted Bell, sinking to his haunches. "You've got lung fever, Wilse."

"Damn it, Emm, Randall said I'd be all right."

" 'Randall said' hell! I know that bark. The way you've been baying the past six weeks would make a coonhound hoarse."

"It's a funny thing, Emm"—the reply came only after a long look between the two—"but I never could get past you. You could always give me a headstart and then be waiting to help me across the finish line. I guess the only time I ever did beat you was with Calla—"

"Forget it!" Bell jumped the short words. "Let's not go to turning over wet hay. What did Randall tell you?"

"Six months."

Bell, busy packing his pipe, was not too busy to throw a guarded sidewise glance across the fire. One look was enough to let a man know Surgeon Randall had protected his prognosis with plenty of time. The pallor of the face, the bright flush of color over the cheekbones, the snakelike glitter of the eyes, it was all there. Bell had seen too much of it among the Nez Perces and Coeur d'Alene Indians. A man hacked away with that sick-dog bark for a few weeks and then one day the back of his hand came away from his mouth with that bright smear on it.

"Listen, Wilse. You're playing around with a rifle-squad salute and a led-horse with nobody in your saddle but a black blanket."

"Not me, soldier!" Gaxton forced the laugh, bringing the cough again. When the spell passed, he smiled weakly. "I'm saving myself for that graduate plot at the Point."

"You won't make it without lungs." Bell ignored the attempted bravado. "Don't be a hero, Wilse. Randall can wangle you a transfer down south. Tucson would be the spot—"

"Maybe after Colville, Emm. But I've got to make it up there." Bell missed the tenseness in the interruption, snapped back irritably.

"Oh the hell with Colville. What's so damn important about Colville? There's nothing up there that somebody else can't take care of for you."

"That's where you're wrong, Emm." The tension in the sick man's voice was at last straining through the soggy mesh of Bell's bourbon filter. "That's what I wanted to talk to you about. Calla's up there."

"Oh, God—not Calla." The words came out of the big man like they were being cut from him with a dull knife.

"Yes. God forgive me, Emm—"

"God may, Wilse." Bell's interruption had the flatness of dead anger in it. "I never will."

With the words Bell was on his feet, the scarecrow hulk of his shadow hanging over the smaller man. He stood a moment, thus, the odd, faded gray of his eyes darkening. A pineknot shifted in the fire, sending a dance of sparks upward. Their brief flight cast a ruddy glow over the hovering face, held it there long enough to show the wide mouth soften, the opaque eyes uncloud. "Good night, Wilse." The words came with the hand that reached out to pause on the silver-barred shoulder.

When the lieutenant's eyes swung up to the touch, he was alone in the paling circle of the firelight.

"Emm, wait! I didn't tell you why Calla came out. Emm, you damn bullhead, I—"

The rack of the coughing broke the young officer's plea, and when the spasm had subsided there was no other sound in answer to it. Bell had gone.

The white-faced man by the fire slumped weakly back. Presently he coughed again, wiping his mouth with the back of his hand before moving to stir the graying ash of the flames. The fitful flare of the disturbed coals lit the back of the reaching hand, briefly limning the bright red smear upon it.

In front of the tent he shared with the remaining three first sergeants, Bell found a small fire still burning. Squatting alongside its glow, he sat for ten minutes staring out across the black and moonless rush of the river.

The shift of the firelight seemed to play deceiving tricks of softness and sentiment with the immobile lines of the graven face. Yet, perhaps, the illusion was not entirely one of seeming. Nor of deceit. For in the end what man may turn his mind at long last homeward without the weary mileposts of memory marking their paths across his features?

Bell took the oilskin packet from inside his shirt, unfolded it slowly, brought the dingy envelope to view. With equally distracted precision he removed the single page of the letter and spread it on the firelit sands. He read it with his lips moving, as a man not seeing it but knowing it by heart.

Refolding the letter, the sergeant returned it to the envelope. For a moment he studied the addressed side, his lips moving across the treasured legend.

> Miss Calla Lee Rainsford
> c/o Gen. Henry Clay Rainsford,
> The Sycamores,
> Lynchburg, Va.

After another moment he turned it over to the flap side, revealing the soiled embossing of the letterhead:

UNITED STATES MILITARY ACADEMY
WEST POINT

The Class of 1854
—

Second Lieutenant Emmett Devereaux Bellew

This time Bell's lips didn't move until long after his eyes had left the envelope, and then only as he spat acridly into the smoking firebed. "To the Class of Fifty-four," he announced grimly, tipping the canteen. "And to First Sergeant Emmett D. Bell thereof."

The morning of the 13th came on sweat-hot and glass-clear. Accordingly, the members of the advancing column got their first real bath in a week. The fact it was taken in perspiration and under full field dress detracted from its effectiveness not a jot. By early forenoon every man in the command had sweat a quart and Bell, at least, had drunk one.

The merciless sun to the contrary, noon halt found the men in excellent spirits. Stedloe's dramatic announcement of the shifted course of the command, and his cryptic reference to its real purpose, had filtered through his enthusiastic staff and on down to the greenest buck in the outfit. Bell, scowling at the picnic-outing atmosphere of the whole thing, thought of Timothy's grim warning about staying on the Colville Military Road and cursed bitterly. The idiots. The poor, blind, stupid, white fools. Bucking blithely ahead into treaty-forbidden red lands as though Kamiakin and his angry Palouses were so many beef-fed, reservation boot-lickers!

The sergeant's forebodings notwithstanding, the afternoon march began as briskly as had the morning's. But late afternoon, with ten miles still facing them to the Nez Perce crossing at Red Wolf, found the column's blistered bottoms beginning to drag. Stedloe, in no great rush and exercising his good professional eye for such enlisted symptoms, called the halt at 4:00 p.m., a matter of perhaps five minutes before First Sergeant Bell would have felt compelled to call it for him. The remaining long hours of daylight were spent looking to the lathered horses, policing the spotless company streets, and furbishing the colonel's precious howitzers.

An hour after dusk, Bell, feeling the better for his supper of three pipes of shag-cut burley and a half canteen of bourbon, was lying with his back to the welcome slope of the tentwall. For lack of a better recreation he was adding his usual silence to the regulation campfire converse of his fellow noncoms—that endless and oathful rehash of the glories of past campaigns, a painful few of which were military, the bulk of them amatory.

Presently the chevroned orators had run through their short supply of new twists to put into the tails of their tired old lies and had, by mutual consent, turned the floor of the following silence over to the rush and stir of the passing river and the rusty sawings of an out-of-tune cricket under the nearby sidewall of their tent.

"Sarge—"

Though the least number of service stripes among them would have trebled Bell's, the others reserved this address for their red-bearded junior. There had never been any particular thought given this inconsistency, and Bell gave it none now.

"Yeah, Mick?"

"Play us a tyune, boy." Keg-chested, airdale-hairy Sergeant Erin Harrigan put the request in his turfy County Donegal brogue. "I can't abide the dev'lish black mutterin' of that miserable river."

"Nor me, the sawin' of thet cricket, theah." Bull Williamson rolled his tiny eyes toward the tent, protecting the reference by forking the first two fingers of his right hand and holding them away from himself and toward the cricket. "Back home they say a cricket singin' in the house means a death in the family. Play us a tune like Mick says, Sarge. I got the fan-tods."

Bell looked at the giant Kentuckian, disgustedly. To Sergeant Bell's way of seeing things the burly hillman, both in bulk and brilliance, was humanity's closest approach to a Hereford. The fact this bovine behemoth chose to attach his dumb-brute devotion to First Sergeant Bell did nothing to endear him to that restive-tempered individual. Nonetheless, Bell assuming it was given unto each of God's likenesses to bear some impossible burden through life, wearily accepted Bull Williamson as his.

"All right, Bull. What'll it be this time? Old Smokey or Bluetail Fly?"

"Atop of Old Smokey!" Williamson brightened like a child who's been handed a nickel with no strings. "Play it slow, Sarge, so's I can do the words of it."

"God in Heaven! Not that dirge again!" For the first time the fourth man entered the conversation. Demoix was a fiercely mustached, ex-hussar of the French Grand Army whose fifteen years as an American regular had done little to dim his memories of the matchless continental cavalry. With the emphasis on the sabre, *naturellement!* This loyalty, along with his Gallic preference for settling all personal differences with the handiest piece of edged steel, had won him vast respect and scant love among his chevroned fellows.

"Shut up, Frenchy." Bell, putting his faint, frosty grin on top of the remark to assure its being accepted as a request and not an insult, knocked the pocket lint out of his harmonica, ran a wheezy scale or two, settled down to the serious work of "Old Smokey." On the second dolorous chorus, Williamson, eyes closed, thick body swaying, began to sing.

"On top of Old Smokey, all covered with snow,
I lost my true lover from a'courtin' too slow.

Now come all young ladies and listen to me,
Don't hang your affections on a green willow tree.

For the leaves they will wither
And the roots they will die
And leave you forsaken, and a'wonderin' why."

As the oddly beautiful voice of the huge Kentuckian faded, Bell rapped the reeds of the mouth organ against the calloused heel of his hand, shook his head in wonderment. "If the poor dumb ox could only think like he can sing." The remark hung, suspended, in the little silence following the ceremony of the cleaning of the harmonica.

"He's got you to do his thinkin' fer him," said Mick. "And that's a good thing."

"Good for what, in God's name?" demanded Bell irritably.

"And you have him to do yer singin' fer you," continued the Irishman, ignoring Bell's question. "And that's a good thing, too."

"Maybe," grunted Bell, knowing Mick was alluding to his, Bell's, habitually close-hard mouth, "but all the same that voice gives me the creeps. God never meant an animal like that to have that voice."

"Aye," muttered Mick, uneasily. "In the body of a murderin' bull, the blessed heart of a bird."

"Et un ame de boue!" added Demoix, angrily.

"Tut now, little man." The squat Harrigan clucked reprovingly at Demoix. "I've warned you about spoutin' that heathen tongue of yers. Now you'll be forcin' me once agin to be askin' Monsewer Bell what you said."

"And a soul of mud," translated Bell, unsmilingly, not waiting for the threatened request.

Any further digging into the commoner clay of Bull's spirit was interrupted by the hip-swinging approach of Stedloe's orderly.

An ambitiously proper soldier, needle-neat and not yet twenty, Corporal Roger Bates was listed "all business and no belly" in Bell's caustic catalogue. He ate clean, kept clean and slept clean and was, by his own oft-stated conviction, "officer material" of the most patent caliber. He drew up at the sergeants' mess with all the dignity possible to a size twenty-eight chest in a forty-two shirt.

"Colonel Stedloe to Sergeant Bell," he announced, dramatically. "And will the sergeant please report at once!"

Bell, glancing up, demonstrated that disconcerting habit common to quiet men, of looking squarely at someone without apparently seeing him at all. Williamson and Demoix bent their attentions to a speculative regard of the river. This left Harrigan, the hairy one, moved by all the compassion native to the Celtic breast, feeling compelled to relieve the silence.

"Faith now, lad. Will you never learn? Now you just

watch yer Uncle Erin this one more time. It's the last I'll be showin' you of how to address yer superiors in this man's army."

With elaborate patience Harrigan arose and drew off from the fire, to return a moment later in a perfect, mincing mimicry of Bates' running-walk approach. Hitting a rigid brace in front of the reclining Bell, he bellowed delicately, "Git up off yer big dead ass, you drunken slob! The Old Man wants to see you on the double."

"Thank you, Sergeant Harrigan." Bell's sober salute was a minor miracle of deadpan earnestness. "Please accept, through me, the sincere gratitude of the entire service. The United States Army may well be proud of such memorable devotion to dire and dangerous duty as you have only now displayed in getting through to this command with Colonel Stedloe's message. I congratulate you, sir!"

"Oh, bless you, General Bell, sir." Harrigan's words broke pathetically. "Remember me when the next Commission Board is sittin', sir."

"That I will, Sergeant. You're very clearly officer material. As any fool can plainly see."

Corporal Bates stood a moment, torn between his throat-choking urge to blast the remaining three rascals, and his indecision as to just what First Sergeant Williamson meant to do with the barrel-swinging butt of that issue musket. By the time it became evident that the huge sergeant had it in heart and hand to try the battered walnut against the quivering indignation of the Bates buttocks, it was already too late.

Corporal Roger LeRoy Bates, Headquarters Company, Ninth Infantry, took off after the retreating form of First Sergeant Bell, bearing black murder in his burning heart.

Because, during his four years on the northwest frontier, Bell had painstakingly learned the guttural intricacies of the Chinook dialect used by the five main tribes, the Nez Perce, Coeur d'Alene, Yakima, Palouse and Spokane, and had demonstrated a repeated ability to get along with the quirky red men, Stedloe had long since turned the post scout-force over to him. The Indians composing that force, all Nez Perces, found in the gaunt sergeant's shortness of tongue and temper, and tart readiness of acid humor, a common bond of hard-core understanding. As to Bell's side of the unwritten bargain, he was as lonely as most men of his patently dangerous disposition and hence glad enough to accept the frank regard of his Nez Perce admirers.

Going now toward Stedloe's tent, Bell's mind was running ahead of his lagging gait. If he didn't miss his guess, and a man seldom did when he was guessing nothing tougher than Colonel Stedloe, the Old Man would be just now getting into a proper sweat about the absent Timothy. And about the cussed river being so bank-brim full. The colonel's was a mental mill which ground excessively slow, though, withal, extremely precisely.

Damn it, sir! Stedloe was a Southerner and always put that "Sir" in there, enlisted man or not. About that Indian you so insubordinately sent up to Colville. I've been thinking, you know. I say, do you definitely trust the rascal, Sergeant? You do? Well, sir, I don't. And you may as well know that to begin with. As if a man didn't know that "to begin with" about any officer on the frontier! And another thing, Bell. Didn't that Indian tell you this infernal river would be up twenty-four hours at the longest? Well, sir, here we are two days and a blind man can see it's still on the rise. I tell you, man, I don't trust the beggars. And I don't care to hear another of your lectures about their sterling character if treated as confounded equals. Now then, Bell, you're to take a squad on up the river and locate a suitable crossing, if and when you find Red Wolf impassable. You can start before dawn and . . .

"Sergeant Bell reporting, sir." Bell's reaching stride had caught up with his ranging thoughts, bringing him to a halt outside the lamplit square of Stedloe's tent. "Corporal Bates said you wanted to see me."

"Well, come in, man. Don't stand there talking to the tent. It won't answer you!" There was that in the barely covered warmth of the greeting which made of it more invitation than order, and which hinted, further, at the fact that First Sergeant Emmett D. Bell occupied something of a unique position in his colonel's personal regard as well as in his impersonal command.

Bell bent his six-foot-two awkwardly through the half-open flap, came to what was supposed to be attention within. "Yes, sir. What was it the Colonel wanted?"

"Damn it, sir, I want to know about that missing Indian!" Bell bowed politely to his inner thoughts, complimenting their prescience while his eyes idly wandered the wall of the tent two feet above the colonel's head. "Twenty-four hours is ample time to get up to Colville and back. And another thing—"

"Begging the Colonel's pardon, sir"—Bell's plea, though phrased in respect, was delivered with the automatic rote of well-worn patience—"but twenty-four hours is hard-short time for even a Nez Perce to get back from Colville and catch up with this column. And, yes sir, I do trust that Indian completely. And coming to the river being still on the rise, I was the one who gave it twenty-four hours. Timothy gave it three days.

"If the Colonel will excuse the suggestion, I'd say the Snake doesn't run on any man's schedule, red or white, and that if Timothy's a bit late in reporting back from Colville, he's run into something that wasn't written in the colonel's field orders, *sir.*"

"Sergeant!" There was that in the stiffening of Stedloe's back which warned Bell he had just stepped past the boundaries of his sub-rosa privilege of informality.

"I'm sorry, sir. It's just that I'm absolutely sure of Timothy and not sure at all about that damn river."

"All right, Bell."

"Thanks, Colonel. Anything else?"

"As a matter of fact, yes." Stedloe's voice stopped threatening, turned thoughtful. "You've said you trust Timothy, but what about the other two?"

"Jason and Lucas?"

"Whatever you call them."

The hoarfrost of Bell's questionable humor touched the edges of his reply with characteristic brittleness. "I wouldn't trust either of them any farther than I could pitch a buffalo bull by the tail. By the same token, Colonel, I'd put my last dime on Timothy and expect eight cents change."

Stedloe nodded, pressing on into the realm of Jason's and Lucas's reliability as though he hadn't heard Bell's answer. "Do you suppose we could depend on them to guide the column on up the river until a crossing is found, or do you recommend holding up here until Timothy returns?"

"I'd wait for Timothy."

"Sergeant"—again Stedloe's nod was automatic rather than understanding, and his next question jumped ahead without apparent regard for the present conversation—"are you aware of the current rumor that the Nez Perces, as a tribe that is, wish to embroil the army with the hostiles of Kamiakin's federation, thus seeking to come out top dog on the Territory Indian pile?"

"I've heard some talk."

"Well, what do you think of it, then?"

"Take some and leave some." Bell shrugged, deprecatingly. "Timothy has as much as told me some such bull-chips are being thrown into the tribe's fires. Hell, there's always white-haters and soldier-scalpers in any outfit of horseback Indians, Colonel."

Stedloe was quiet for several seconds, during which time he eyed Bell carefully. When he spoke again his low words managed at last to ripple the set line of the sergeant's scowl. "Bell, have you heard anything to confirm our intelligence reports that Brigham Young's Mormons are sending rifles to the hostiles? Or that Father Joset is issuing them ammunition?"

"From what I hear, the first half of that report is plenty correct." Bell's grunt was as curt as the look he backed it up with. "But the last part's uncut hogwash. Father Joset and that Coeur d'Alene mission of his are the best friends the army's got on this man's frontier."

The column commander chucked his head, for the moment thoughtful again. "Sergeant, how many active followers do you suppose Kamiakin has behind him? I mean in the field right now."

"Timothy tells me Joset's Coeur d'Alenes claim Kenuokin —that's their name for Kamiakin—has better than a thousand bucks out with him. And that a good part of them are Yakimas and Spokanes, with even some 'badhearted' Coeur d'Alenes thrown in."

"All right, Bell. One thing more. Have you gotten any information about Kamiakin's reported threat to start his uprising if the troops come toward Colville in strength? Or if we choose to come by any other course than the old Military Road?"

Bell, by this time agreeably surprised by Stedloe's considerable information, and disagreeably aroused by his apparent refusal to pay any attention to it, took the bit in his teeth.

"Yeah. My information says he'll do it. Timothy says he'll do it. Father Joset says he will. But that's a plug you'll have to bite your own chaw off of. I've been over that ground with you and the staff twenty times in the past two weeks." Bell could sense the colonel's back go to ramrodding again as the bobtailed words hit into him. But the big noncom only held his eyes on the tentwall and straightened his melting stance the least bit. After a pause that walked around the floor of the little tent as stiff-legged as a courting camp cur, Stedloe spoke.

"All right, Bell, I don't share your convictions but they'll be considered."

Eager to be away from the tent, stuffy alike as it was from the humidity of the May night and the opaqueness of its owner's outlook, Bell's breakaway query came quickly. "Yes, sir. Thanks, Colonel. Was there anything else?"

"Yes, Sergeant. I want you to take a squad and head on up the river. Check on Red Wolf Crossing and if it's too high, find me another and report back. Start two hours before daylight. This damnable river may be up a week."

Bell made another thought-curtsey to the accuracy of his original forecasts. "Begging your leave, Colonel, there's no point in such a scout. There's no feasible crossing between here and Red Wolf, and there's none beyond. And Colonel, sir"— the gaunt enlisted man's request came with uncharacteristic tact and gravity—"may I remind you of something about that particular crossing?"

"Of course, man!" Stedloe's reply showed a slight hone along its sharpening edge. "You know I rely on your knowledge of all this terrain."

"Yes, sir. Red Wolf Crossing is right in the middle of the Nez Perce reservation. Square as a war buck's bottom in a Springfield sight." Bell let the statement fall, flat-out, not troubling to put the least cushion of "sir or salute" under its harsh drop. Stedloe, wincing, nonetheless folded his silver oak leaves to give the remark tacit permission to pass unchallenged.

"Well, if that's the best we can do, Bell, it's still good enough. The Nez Perces are friendly. I don't get your point."

"Oh, sure," agreed the red-bearded noncom. "They're friendly enough. That's half the battle, anyway—" He addressed the suspended drawl to the tentwall above Stedloe's head, knowing its lack of conclusion would draw the latter's fire.

"Now what do you mean by that? Damn it, Bell, quit talking to the tent and say what you mean!"

"I mean there's two sides to every river," shrugged the gaunt sergeant, not offering to add anything to the cryptic gesture. It was hot in the tent and Bell's overtime drill with the canteen was beginning to bear down on him.

"Sergeant Bell."

"Yes, sir."

"You'll give me a direct answer or go on General Report."

"Yes, sir." Bell, wearily aware of Stedloe's rancor, rewarded it by forcing one dangling hand halfway to the sweated dirt of his forehead. "I meant what I said, sir. Two sides to a river. Our side and the other side."

"Well?"

"Well, our side's Nez Perce."

"Hang it, Bell, I know that."

"Yes, sir. Begging your pardon, sir. The other side's Palouse."

"Of course. I'm aware of that, too, Sergeant. What *is* your point, man?"

"The Snake's the deeded boundary of the Palouse country, sir. That makes everything past Red Wolf Crossing, east, treaty land. And Colonel, you can't rightly put troops across it."

"I know that, Bell. That cussed Stevens deal in Fifty-five. Is that what you're referring to?"

"Yes, sir, that's it."

"Well, plague take it, that agreement was never ratified. Nothing to it but a makeshift arrangement certified by a civilian territorial governor. I've decided that under the circumstances we can ignore it."

"Sir, when an Indian signs something, he's made a deal. He isn't waiting for the U. S. Government to tell him he has, ten years later." Bell mustered the best brace he could manage, hoping to make it cover the bluntness of his demurrer. The blank look behind Stedloe's quiet challenge let him know he hadn't mustered or managed quite enough.

"Well, sir?"

"Well, sir, Kamiakin was the top chief of fourteen who signed that paper of Governor Stevens."

"So?" The colonel's demand rose as short-bristled as a huffy hound dog's roach, his ordinarily soft brown eyes hardening with the sudden set of his smooth chin.

"So, if you stick your head across the Snake at Red Wolf you're apt to pull it back with a Palouse hair-cut." Bell had his own lean jaw out, now; stood waiting, belligerently, for the senior officer's outburst. When it came, it was considerably quieter than he had anticipated. And somewhat stiffer.

"You're a big man, Sergeant Bell. And a good one. It's a shame you and I can't agree as to which of us is wearing the oak leaves. Orderly!"

Corporal Bates' eager face was inside the tent flap before the call got well out of Stedloe's mouth. "Yes, sir! The colonel called?"

"Put this man under arrest, Corporal." Stedloe's words had the resigned, tired quality of an order which had been too many times repeated in the past. "Insubordination, as usual. And tell Lieutenant Fanning to ready a detail to take him back to the post tomorrow."

"Yes, sir!" Bates' triumphant smirk was as thick as top cream on a chessy cat's whiskers. "Do you wish him under guard until he leaves, sir?"

"I suppose." The column commander paused, shooting a brief look at the sagging Bell. "Make it 'house arrest,' Bates." Stedloe paid his little jest the courtesy of an anemic smile. "The corporal of the guard can spend the night as Sergeant Bell's guest. I wouldn't want our noncommissioned chief of staff to be put out in any way."

"Thank you, sir!" Bates snapped into his incomparable brace. "Come along, you!"

The command was enhanced with a dramatic shove of the corporal's musket in the small of Bell's back, the big man moving half a step to accommodate it. "Careful, sonny. You've got to be gentle with a drinking man's kidneys. One more shove with that popgun will have me messing up the colonel's floor, and there goes your commission."

Stedloe looked up, irritably. "Oh, for God's sake, relax, Bates. You don't need a musket to put this man under simple arrest. Get him out of here."

Outside, Bates yelled for the corporal of the guard, turned his prisoner over to that worthy with patent relief. Starting away from the colonel's tent, Bell listened with the abstract disinterest of long practice to his new escort's cob-rough curiosity.

"Well, *big man*, what've ye done, now?" Bell had a way with squad corporals and such lesser forms of military life, a way not precisely calculated to win him any post popularity polls. "I take it for granted ye're on report for insubordination again, but what's the details this time? Did the Old Man bust ye back to a buck or only route ye back to Wallowa with a squad?"

"Stuff it," Bell grunted.

"Ye're a lovable bastard, ain't ye? A man tries to give ye a good word and gets the back of yer bad hand fer his trouble. If I was the Old Man I'd give ye a stiff rope and a short drop."

"Shut up." With a short growl Bell lengthened his stride, turning abruptly for the main company street.

The weary camp was quieting down as the big noncom and his disgruntled guard headed toward Bell's tent. Here and there a last bed of cooking-coals was still flickering fitfully and within Captain Baylor's quarters light from a smoky whale-oil lamp was wavering over the final yawns of a bored-stiff card game. On the picket lines, the artillery mules tossed at the last of the chaff in their nosebags, while beyond them the scattered shadows of the dragoon horse herd grazed the thick-misted swales of the river bottom.

Drifting up behind the solitary figure at the fire outside the noncoms' tent, Bell settled alongside it with all the racket of a perching hawk's ground shadow. Behind him, the corporal of the guard paused with ready musket.

The nodding figure at the fireside came awake, its red-rimmed blue eyes burning resentfully behind the straggling brush of the scowling brows. "Damn yer red-lovin' soul, Sarge! It's enough to give a decent Christian the Nez Perce shakes, the way you featherfoot it around!"

"Never mind the Nez Perce shakes, Mick. I've brought you something a sight stronger. Where's Bull and Frenchy?"

"In the tent poundin' their hairy ears. What do you mean, 'somethin' stronger,' boy?" The squat Irishman, eyeing the alert corporal of the guard, put the query nervously, knowing from long-suffering experience that when his red-bearded junior put the wide-mouthed frost of that certain, light-quick grin on a remark, the coming humor was apt to freeze up faster than scum ice on a February waterhole.

"Palouse palsy," said Bell shortly. "Roust the boys out. The colonel's pulling out at daybreak. Aiming to cross over at Red Wolf without waiting for my Indian to get back from up Colville way." Bell paused, nodding and poking a disdainful thumbjerk at his uneasy escort. "And don't pay any mind to sonny-jim with the Springfield, there. The Old Man's still trying to teach me manners."

With the newly aroused Williamson and Demoix staring, owl-eyed, under his terse words, Bell spent the next few seconds conveying the failure of his attempts to stall Stedloe short of Red Wolf Crossing, together with his own grim forecast of what that failure was apt to mean to all of them before they were twenty-four hours older. He had meant to put the spark to one of those impromptu councils of war by which regular sergeants, the professional military world over, were wont to rectify the tactical blunders of their commissioned superiors. The angry fuse of his bombshell sputtered miserably and went out.

With the tired aplomb of the career noncom, the three soldiers took the news back to their clammy blankets, assigning it at once to tomorrow's big backlog of little concerns. In a matter of seconds the dissonant trio of their snores was in full nasal sway.

Shrugging disgustedly, Bell pulled his own blankets from

the tent and rolled up by the guttering smoke of the fire.
Shortly the heavy tones of his exhalations were adding their
rich bass to the carefree quartet of old campaigner snores. Grimacing hopelessly, the forgotten corporal of the guard squatted
down across the smoke from Bell. In ten seconds his chin was
on his chest and in fifteen the pointing musket slid, unnoticed,
from his nerveless fingers. Following the muffled "cal-lumphf"
of the weapon's arrival in the inches-deep camp dust, there was
no further sound to disturb the happily chorusing snores.

Bat-blind officers, pig-ignorant men, flooded-out Snake or
heated-up Palouses, there was one thing any seasoned soldier
could do. Any time. Any place. And that, by damn, was sleep!

Bell came hard awake, suddenly prodded by the instincts
which could put a man to sleeping like a log and still shuck him
out of it, gingery as a frightened cat.

The first, campwide sweep of his narrowed eyes recorded
three things: first light of the four o'clock false dawn was tipping the tent rows; a sudden rash of oil lamps was dimpling the
interiors of the staff canvas; a confused ruckus of muffled talk
and moving figures was clotting up down by the river. With the
last intelligence, his long legs were under him, and he was
standing shoulder-hunched and gut-strung, his tense gaze boring toward the fogbound Snake.

"For the luvva Pete! What the hell's goin' on?" The querulous voice of the slowly waking corporal of the guard signaled
his belated reaction to the disturbance which had aroused Bell.
His lament was broken off by a renewal of the commotion
down by the river, but before any further questions could be
framed as to its origin, a group of excited soldiers hove into the
hastily stirred up firelight of the company street, half carrying,
half dragging the body of an unconscious man. One look at the
naked slimness of the figure was enough for Bell.

"Timothy, by God!" His cry of recognition was seconded
by the bug-eyed corporal.

"It's the damn Injun!"

Bell was running, then, leaping through the darkness toward the loud talking soldiers. He burst among them and
seized Timothy's body from its bearers. "Give me that Indian!"

The barking command came like drumfire. "Where the hell did you find him? How long ago? What's the matter with him? Come on, goddammit, don't just stand there!"

"Fished him out'n the river, Sarge. Just now." One of the troopers pried his startled tongue loose. "He hollered from the other side, first. We could just make out by the starlight that he was mounted. When he put the horse in the river we lost both of them agin the black of the water. About five minutes later Joe seen the Injun flounderin' in the shallows on this side. Me and Joe we jumped in and fished him out. He's plumb drownded, I reckon. The horse, too. Least we never seen the horse come up on this side at all."

"You worry about the horse, soldier"—Bell put the Nez Perce's slack form over his shoulder as easily as though it were that of a red, rag doll—"and get the hell out of my way!"

As he started with his burden across camp, he was confronted by his recent, armed chaperone. "Where do ye think ye're goin', Bell? You're under arrest. Remember?"

"Surgeon Randall's quarters," was Bell's bobtailed reply. "You think I'm not?"

"I think ye're not." The corporal set himself in the big man's path, his words and face suddenly tight.

"Well, take a little more time to think," nodded Bell, accompanying the advice with the twisting, upward snap of his free, left fist. The blow took the corporal low in the abdomen, doubling him over and forward. As he fell, Bell's hand wrenched the musket from his grasp. Half turning, he let the stricken noncom fall past him, cracking the back of the man's head crisply and expertly with the weapon's stock.

Tossing the gun to one of the gaping soldiers, Bell growled quickly, "Dunk him in the river. When he comes to, give him this and remind him he had me under arrest. Tell him to pick me up at Randall's tent. And tell him, next time he points a gun at somebody, to keep his finger on the trigger."

Under Assistant Surgeon Randall's expert eye it developed that Timothy was suffering more from weariness than water. The medical officer brought him around quickly enough and after a subsequent, long peg from Bell's omnipresent canteen the Nez Perce was ready to talk. What he had to say would have lifted the short hairs off any white man's neck and Bell, contrary to any impression which might have been fostered by the chronic mask of sunblack and traildirt that coated his rocky face, was a white man.

Five seconds after the first, deep-grunted phrases broke haltingly from the exhausted Indian's mouth, Bell was shouldering aside the flaps of Stedloe's tent to rap out the grisly news.

And five minutes after that, a general command council was in white-faced session.

It was a scene for any professional soldier to remember, and Bell never forgot it. The cleared ground in front of the colonel's quarters was glaringly lighted by the hurriedly built-up coals of the supper fire. On the three open sides of this shifting illumination crouched Stedloe's four company officers, along with the unattached Supply Quartermaster, Second Lieutenant Henry Fanning, as well as Bell's three fellow sergeants. The column commander sat in his camp-chair just outside the tent opening, while on the ground in front of him, facing the ring of officers and noncoms, squatted the shivering, blanket-wrapped figure of the nearly naked Nez Perce chief. Bell, overlooked in the first confusion of the gathering, hung the tall silhouette of his standing shadow on the tentflap to Stedloe's left.

It was 4:15 a.m., Friday, May 14th.

There was one brief touch of relief occurring just before the council got under way. The insatiable Corporal Bates, recognizing an historic opportunity when providence pushed one under his eager nose, took advantage of the moment of awkward silence following the sleepy-eyed assembling of the officers to remind Stedloe that First Sergeant Bell was illegally present, being in effect under guard arrest for insubordination. It was Bates' natural and obsequious expectation that this astuteness would be rewarded by a quick compounding of the insubordination charge against Bell, as well as by a kindly pat on his own curly head from the grateful C. O.

What he got was a chevron-curling look and a tight-lipped aside from Stedloe to "get damn well back to attention and stay there." The distraught C. O., looking up in time to catch the flash grin snaking across Bell's wide mouth, growled warningly, "Don't mistake me, Sergeant. You're still under arrest. You're here to back this Indian up, and nothing more."

"Yes, sir," said Bell, straightfaced. "You'd better let Timothy talk now, Colonel. He's no more than about three gulps from passing out again."

Stedloe nodded and turned uncertainly to the waiting staff. "Gentlemen, this Indian of Bell's can, I feel, impress you better than I. I'm going to let him tell this in his own way. What he will have to say will confront all of you with a tactical and moral decision quite beyond any you may have studied at the Academy. That is, it will if you can bring yourselves to accept it. I myself am still unable to agree to the reality of his report and I want to hear every word of it again. You will therefore kindly refrain from interruptions until the Indian has finished speaking."

Stedloe suspended his warning long enough to cover it with a running look around the intent circle of his listeners, then concluded with a nervous gesture toward the Nez Perce. "All right, Timothy—"

The crouching scout hesitated, his beaded glance loping after Stedloe's around the hushed ring of graven-faced officers. Licking his uncertain lips, he shifted his black eyes to meet the steady, gray ones of Sergeant Bell.

Bell's big hand found the thin, red shoulder. "You tell them, Tamason. Like you told me and Colonel Stedloe. That's all. Remember, you are a chief. These are common ones."

The Indian reached gratefully up and patted Bell's red-haired paw. *"Gu'tgut,"* he murmured, low voiced. "It is just that I am so tired, Ametsun." And with that, pulling in a long breath and fixing his slant gaze in the heart of the fire, Timothy told his story.

It was short. Brutal. Naked.

"At sundown, yesterday," the Nez Perce began, "I went up the Colville Road as I was told to do by Ametsun Bell. As I went, I kept my eyes southward instead of on the wagon tracks in the road. Down toward the Bitter Roots. Down toward Kamiakin's country. This I did, too, because Ametsun Bell had told me to do it that way.

"Still I saw nothing." The scout's deep voice hesitated, his habitual frown deepening as though he were trying to remember precisely the fall of each of his horse's hoofprints. "All the way to Bitter Root Meadows, I saw nothing. Then the night came and I saw them. South of the meadow, all the way toward Colville. Signal fires.

"After that I opened my eyes very wide and walked my pony very slow. I saw two war parties, black against the night sky. And then I saw four more. I quit traveling and hid the pony. Then I waited for the sun." Timothy paused a moment, then added with a sober nod, "It does a Nez Perce no good to be traveling in the dark on that side of the river."

Bell hid his little grin as he leaned further forward to catch his scout's continuing narrative. But before the Indian could resume, Baylor, the irrepressible, broke rank and order.

"My God, Colonel, is this red rascal trying to tell us he's been all this time cooling his haunches halfway up the Colville Road? I suggest, sir, that—"

"And I suggest, sir"—Stedloe was that *rara avis* among West Pointers, a C. O. who rode his staff with shorter stirrups than he did his troops—"that you keep quiet or go to your tent."

While the black-bearded Baylor blunted the edge of his sharp-honed tongue with his clenched teeth, Stedloe gestured abruptly to Timothy and the Nez Perce took up again.

"I waited for the sun, as I said. And it came very bright with bad sign. From every hill within a short day's pony ride the mirrors were flashing and the blanket smokes were climbing. So I waited some more. In an hour, maybe two, a line of wagons rolled down the road from the way of Colville. I rode out to them, and they were from Colville. I told them of the bad signs. I asked them to go back. But the wagon chief said, 'It is only old Victor and some Coeur d'Alenes. We passed them at dawn. We are all right. Besides,' here he pointed at a young white woman and a big black woman who were in his wagon, 'these are army women going to Fort Wallowa. They won't try anything with army people.'

"Ametsun—" Interrupting his story, the Nez Perce

palmed his hand helplessly toward Bell. "What was I to do? I am an Indian. They wouldn't listen."

"You've told me this, Tamason." Bell kept his words low and short. "Now you're telling it for the officers. *They* will listen."

The lean scout looked at Stedloe's staff, nodded thoughtfully, speeded the barking gutturals of his schoolbook English. "I went quickly then to look for Victor. We are old friends. At noon I found him. And his heart was bad. His young men were moving to join Kamiakin and he, their old chief, was just going along to try and persuade them not to do so. But it was already too late. The scouts had come from the Snake, saying that the oak-leaf chief and the pony-soldiers were coming from Fort Wallowa in great numbers, and that they had swung straight south last night, away from the Colville Road, to march directly for the treaty lands of the Yakimas and the Spokanes and the Palouses. Kamiakin's prediction had come to pass and there was no holding the young men, now.

"I came away from Victor, riding fast to find Ametsun Bell and the soldiers, here, to warn them of this big trouble. As I rode, I saw it. Black smoke to the west, behind me, where I had met those wagons."

The thin Nez Perce shrugged, pulling his blanket closer. "There is little more to tell. When I came up to that smoke, there was no noise there and nothing moved. All seven of the white drivers lay dead among the burning wagons. The young white woman was gone. The big black woman was gone.

"The men were all without their hair. The way it had been taken from them, high up and toward the front of the head—you know how they do it, Ametsun—told me which tribe had done it. Any Nez Perce could tell, easily. No other band takes it in just that way. Those were Palouse scalp-cuts up there.

"Kamiakin stole those two women from that Colville wagon train!"

2

◆

Red Wolf Crossing

At the close of his simple accounting of the thirty-six hours which had seen him cover 145 miles, eluding constant hostile war parties both coming and going, then ride his dying horse up to the roaring bank of the main Snake and swim that father of evil waters in full flood, the Nez Perce chief looked slowly around the speechless circle of his white listeners.

"I have said this now, and you can believe it. I have promised to follow the flag. The flag is my life," he concluded expressionlessly.

Despite the chief's words, the reaction of the officers was one of incredulity, if not outright disbelief. Stedloe himself, in his careful, methodical way, paved the path for their quick challenges and suspicions.

Bell, watching the white commander, thought he knew what was passing behind those deceptively soft brown eyes. Stedloe had heard this story twice now and had had several spare minutes over the others to think about it. He was probably, Bell figured, beginning to realize Timothy's report and to put the responsibility for the Colville Road massacre right where it belonged. Right where Bell himself had told Timothy

32

it was going to belong when the two had sat on that hilltop three days before to watch Stedloe's heavily armed column approach the Snake. Right, as a matter of fact, in the very middle of Brevet Lieutenant Colonel Edson Stedloe's lap.

The correctness of the tall sergeant's suspicion notwithstanding, Stedloe and the others were now beginning in nervous earnest to cross-examine the silent Nez Perce. The colonel, as was his right-of-rank, set the pace. And he set it at a stiff clip.

"Well, now, Timothy," the column commander led off, "there are several points I wish to be cleared up on. In the first place why didn't you come back and warn us, last night, right after you encountered the first war parties? As our chief of scouts, it would seem to me you should have been more quickly aware of the identity of those parties. Do you ask us to believe it took you nearly twenty-four hours to determine they were Kamiakin's? Do I understand you are asking us to believe that Kamiakin and a large force of hostile Palouses fooled you so easily?"

Timothy nodded seriously. "Indeed," he grunted, "you may believe just that. Kamiakin is a great raider. One of the best in that very bad business. And his personal force was not a large one. I counted their pony tracks where they left the wagons. They were few. Not more than thirty braves. Such a small force, all picked warriors and led by a brainy fox like Kamiakin, could easily have lain along the road and not been seen—even by a chief of scouts."

"All right, then, Timothy"—the belligerent Captain Baylor took over the grilling—"suppose that much is true. How do you expect us to swallow that story about Victor having warned you of Kamiakin's presence along the road? And of Kamiakin's knowledge of our big force approaching?"

The Nez Perce nodded, blank-faced. "I've told you what Victor said to me. I don't lie."

"Suppose you don't." Baylor was irritably short. "Don't you realize that by admitting you even talked to a suspected unfriendly like Victor, you make us suspicious?"

"No. I think Victor's heart is good toward you."

"Well, Timothy"—the patient-faced Captain Winston entered the questioning for the first time—"even if Kamiakin is up there with a big force of Palouses, how are we to rely on your word, alone, that he means us harm? You know we don't trust Victor."

"You don't trust me. You don't trust Victor. Whom do you trust?" The Nez Perce was entirely serious, but the restless Baylor, missing the patent heaviness of the Indian's mood, or again, perhaps because of it, chose to turn facetious.

"Whom would you suggest, chief?"

"Father Joset." Timothy's reply was as instant as it was soft. "He is a Black Robe, and a white man. I have carried three letters from him to Colonel Stedloe. In each of these letters he said Kamiakin would go out if the soldiers came in force to look for him."

At this point Bell had a disturbing vision of himself locked up in the Fort Wallowa guardhouse for the next year at least. For there was just one way Timothy could have known what was in those sealed dispatches—and Bell was it.

Fortunately, Stedloe was so eager to cover his own tracks, he failed to see Bell's. He was onto Timothy at once, his voice and manner as near to querulous as Bell had ever noted them. "That will do, Timothy. If it comes to Father Joset's letters, their main burden was consistently the same—the repeated fact that your precious Nez Perces were plotting to get us into a real war with Kamiakin's Palouses. As long as we're quoting the good Coeur d'Alene priest, what have you to say to that?"

Confronted by the new charge, Timothy answered it as calmly and frowningly as he had its predecessors, the openness of his agreement surprising even the forewarned Bell.

"I have heard the story, and more. I believe parts of it. A chief's heart is heavy to say that of his own blood, but we are a big tribe. Not all of the Nez Perces are keeping their tongues straight with you."

At this point Bell, whose roving glance had noted the silent approach of Jason and Lucas, Timothy's gargoyle henchmen, caught the slit-eyed exchange of looks between the two newly arrived Indians at their chief's mention of disloyalty among his own people. Cataloguing the incident for future remembering, the big sergeant put his attention back onto the suspended drama about the fire.

Taken aback by the Indian's frankness, the white officers were hesitating, were experiencing some difficulty in reloading for the next fusillade. The plodding Captain Winston shortly touched off the first round.

"Timothy, assuming you've told us the truth so far, how are you so sure it was Kamiakin and the Palouses who committed the murders up there?"

"By the hair-cutting," grunted the red scout. "I've already told you that."

"How about Kamiakin, himself?"

"I know his pony. A bad lance-slash in the right front foot. It makes a mark like buffalo. Split in two pieces, like that."

"Do you mean to say that the Nez Perces, for instance, couldn't have scalped those men to make it look like the Palouses did it?" Bell, watching the heavy-set Winston, knew Stedloe's second in command was not baiting the weary red man and was, as a matter of fact, asking the only sound questions so far put forward. At the same time his first-hand knowledge of Indian ego—always touchy where the question was called on personal veracity or scouting ability—was telling him it was about time for Timothy to be getting on his dignity. He was right as rain.

"Nobody can cut hair like a Palouse. Not even a Nez Perce. I've said that twice now. It won't be said again." With the slow-worded, guttural statement, the chief turned his gaze back to the glow of the fire and left it there. The seconds dragged from three, to five, to ten, before Stedloe broke the halting silence.

Frustrated alike by his own and his officers' palpable failure to shake the Indian's grim story, the colonel abruptly took the discussion off on a final, fretful tack. Watching him, Bell knew, by the nervous hurry with which he piled his challenges one atop the other, heaping them up without giving Timothy a chance to tear them down, that his original hunch had been right. He knew his Stedloe pretty well. The Old Man was a reasonably good egg as far as Academy hatches went. But right now he was tolerably close to cracking his shell.

"Well, Timothy, I don't like the sound of this whole thing. Naturally, we can check on the murders of the wagon drivers.

But even if we find a massacre up there we would still have to take your word, and your word alone, for those missing women. I simply haven't got time to send a courier to Colville and back to substantiate your claims. And frankly I don't think it's necessary. You must understand that it is the Army's business to know who is on the various white posts. There are twenty white families up there and every man, woman and child of them is known to us. Had there been any newcomers, strange white ladies, colored servants or whatsoever, Major Morrison would have reported them in his last week's dispatch. What are you trying to do, man? Get us to go chasing off into the Bitter Roots to start your Nez Perce war with Kamiakin's Palouses? Run after some white spirit lady who has suddenly appeared in the middle of Washington Territory from nowhere? I'll send a squad up to Bitter Root Meadows to look for that supply train, but until I myself get to Colville I'm afraid I just can't accept your statements about Kamiakin and this white woman. Do you understand that?"

At this point Timothy stood up. As he got to his feet he half staggered from weakness, and would have fallen save for Bell's quick step forward to support him. After a moment, the chief disengaged himself from the sergeant's bracing arms and stepped forward into the full light of the fire. None of the officers spoke as the deep-bronzed Nez Perce dropped the sodden issue blanket from his shoulders to stand naked but for his breechcloth, before them. Reaching a thin, red hand into the doeskin pouch of the garment, the Indian removed something from it and flung it upon the ground.

"I brought you this," he said slowly, the vibrant bass of his voice accusing the white silence. "For I know your hearts are bad toward my word and the words of all my people."

A dropped pin would have shattered the following stillness like the crash of an eighty-foot pine.

On a village street in Virginia or a plantation porch in Georgia the object might have fallen unnoticed. But on that naked stretch of firelit frontier dirt two thousand miles from St. Louis the mutely crumpled pertness of the tiny Eugénie hat struck with stark and glaring shock.

"Good Lord!" Captain Baylor's hushed words were the first to break the stunned silence. "A white woman's!"

"And a lady's, too, I'd say." Captain Harry Winston spoke with his usual flat literalness.

"A *Southern* lady's," corrected Bell, softly, stepping out of the tent shadows and picking up the little hat. "Am I right, Lieutenant Gaxton?"

The question, accompanied by the enlisted man's slate-gray stare, landed across the firelight in front of the fish-pale Gaxton.

Before the young officer could answer, Colonel Stedloe was on his feet. "That will do, Bell. I'm asking the questions, here. Give me the hat. Lieutenant, what have you to say?"

Bell's big paw tightened around the pathetic smallness of the hat.

"I've got the hat, Colonel, and the question that goes with it." The sergeant's pike jaw closed on the refusal with an audible snap. "Lieutenant Gaxton, there, has got the answer. And if it earns me the guardhouse for the rest of my natural life, I aim to hear him come out with it."

"Corporal of the guard! Orderly! Orderly!" Stedloe's terse call and Corporal Bates' eager response thereto, were interrupted by the low intercession of Gaxton's shaking voice.

"Bell's right, sir. You can't blame him. Nor his Indian. What they've both had to say is true. That's Calla Lee Rainsford's hat, Colonel. Old General Rainsford's daughter, sir."

"You can't mean that, Wilcey!" Stedloe's loyal Southern mind was refusing the thought that Gaxton, no less a Virginian than himself, could be guilty of such a heinous breach of chivalry. "She was your fiancée, was she not? May I ask why in God's name, sir, you brought her out to this country."

"I can't tell you, sir." The color of young Gaxton's face was toad-belly white, even in the deep glow of the flames. "She and I had agreed on some very personal business. God help me, I urged her to come out. We both felt it absolutely necessary under the circumstances."

"What circumstances, Wilcey? By the Lord, sir, don't tell me you led that poor girl into coming out here to be married? Or that that's your idea of absolutely necessary circumstances!"

"No, sir, I did not—" Gaxton's denial was a struggle of misery and nerve-break. "We were no longer engaged. You see, sir—"

"Begging the colonel's pardon, sir." Bell's blunt reminder put words to the common thought of the restive officers. "I would suggest that Lieutenant Gaxton's private life with this lady doesn't discount the fact she is possibly still alive, and certainly in grave circumstances if she is."

"How's that, Bell?"

The even, white-toothed way in which Stedloe asked it, let the sergeant know the commanding officer had reached the outer edge of that sharply cleared area dividing his natural liking for the rebellious noncom, and his West Point heritage of commissioned untouchability.

Nonetheless, when First Sergeant Bell set his size-eleven dragoon boots to overstep a simple line of authority, he didn't mean to put them down just halfway across the mark.

"You've got seven white men murdered up there on the Colville Road, and a white girl and a colored woman taken captive by Kamiakin's Palouses. I'd say that suggested some more academic course of action than cross-examining Lieutenant Gaxton's well-known Mason-Dixon morals."

"Oh, you would, would you, you insubordinate devil—" Angrily embarrassed by the longjawed noncom's calling of the obvious question, Stedloe now rapped out his vengeance in long-delayed earnest. "Corporal, get this man out of my sight and keep him there. If I see him once more before Fanning takes him back to Wallowa I'll cashier you along with him."

"Yes, sir!" Both Bates and the corporal of the guard outbraced their best braces.

"I'll confine him to quarters, Colonel, sir, with an armed guard posted all night," Bates promised with ill-concealed glee. "You won't see him again, sir. Thank you, Colonel, sir!"

Thus for the second time that evening Bell found himself on his way to his tent under the armed and triumphant auspices of the corporal of the guard. At the particular time there could be no doubt as to the corporal and the colonel being in complete agreement as to the immediate and inactive future of First Sergeant Bell.

But time is only time, after all.

It was still only 4:30 a.m. and Colonel Edson Stedloe had yet to figure a way to contact and punish the Palouse murderers, not to mention the ticklish retrieving of their white captive. Accordingly, from the standpoint of his understanding of his colonel's character, or lack of it, the sergeant might easily have been forgiven his conviction that the C. O. would hesitate to assault any such long-odds adventure without the backing of First Sergeant Bell.

Bell's crystal ball of cynicism bore unusually early fruit. Twenty minutes after his banishment from the command fire, presumably to a lifetime in leg-irons, a clearly disgruntled Corporal Bates trotted up to an equally disappointed corporal of the guard with an order for the prisoner's release. And two minutes after that he was standing once more in the muggy confines of the colonel's tent.

Facing Stedloe for the third time in as many hours, Bell sensed at once that the game had been named, the deck cut and dealt, and his own hand laid out cold.

Without any further ado, Stedloe picked it up and showed him his cards.

"Sit down, Bell. Have a cigar."

Bell swung his bony face up from its regard of the dirt floor in front of his boots. What the hell? This wasn't the army. The goddamn C. O. offering a line sergeant a smoke? Well, hell, that was this crazy Stedloe all over. He ran a command like no other officer in the lousy service. Bell's bemusement showed itself in the odd quirk of his wide mouth.

"I beg your pardon, Colonel?"

"Sit down man, and have a smoke. That is, if it won't come between you and that precious eight-ounce burley cud of yours."

Bell flushed as he ducked his head out the tent flap to park the quid of long-shag in the middle of the ten-foot-distant fire. Wiping his mouth, he reached for the proffered panatella, saluted with the free hand. "Thanks, Colonel."

Bell was the first to get his vocal pontoons in place. He rushed headlong across them, jumped ashore on the other side, big feet first. "Colonel, for God's sake don't send me back to Wallowa. Put me on report for the next ten years if you will, but let me handle these Indians for you until you get to Colville. I—"

"We'll get to that," the older man advised, quietly snapping the thread of Bell's plea in mid-skein. "Right now I've got something I want to make sure you understand, Sergeant.

"Yes, sir."

Bell sensed the keenness with which Stedloe was watching him and for the first time in the colonel's service felt uneasy, and suddenly ashamed. Stedloe was actually one hell of a gentleman and a damn fine officer. One of those rare ones from the Point who understood and genuinely loved his men. He was the kind who had probably stood about forty-ninth in a class of fifty at the Academy, but who ranked Number One with the dogfaces of any command he had ever held.

"Sir"—the towering sergeant's outsized feet seemed all at once in need of considerable shifting—"I want you to understand something, too. I'm downright sorry I spoke up to you tonight in front of the staff. I haven't been in the ranks all my life and I'm afraid my temper can't seem to remember that fact. I'd just like you to know that when I crack out at my superiors it's not because I'm an officer-hater. It's just that I get mad. And when I get mad I always seem to remember where I'm from, and forget where I am. I don't suppose all that makes any sense to you, sir." Bell finished lamely, like a man will when he's trying to tell somebody the whole of something without letting him in on any solitary part of it.

"On the contrary, Sergeant," Stedloe's reservation brought Bell's glance sharply upward. "In the light of what Wilcey Gaxton has just told me, it makes a great deal of sense. All the same, I'll appreciate it if you can manage at least to remember to *act* like a sergeant while you're so rated in my command."

"Yes, sir." Bell kept his gaze on the ground, but his gray eyes clouded over and his long jaw pulled hard-down. "What did the lieutenant tell you, sir?"

"That you were a Point graduate and a commission-jumper."

"Yes, sir." Bell buried his eyes deeper still into the puddled dust of the tent floor. "Anything else, sir?"

"Yes. That he had spent the past six months trying to persuade you to turn yourself in."

"Is that all, Colonel?" Bell's eyes swung up defiantly with the flatness of the demand.

"That's what I'm asking you, Bell. Is it?"

The rock-faced sergeant wasn't the first hard apple Stedloe had fished up out of the catchall barrel of frontier enlistments. And the gentle-mannered C. O. had a fine eye for firm fruit. Fine enough to know that the stonier the flesh, the softer the core.

"Well, Bell?"

"The lieutenant slopped me a lot of hogwash about what a mess I had made back home. It all had to do with a girl we were both mixed up with back there and—well hell, Colonel, Wilse was always full of a lot of damn-fool, schoolboy notions about the honor of the service, too." Bell switched subjects as a man will when he's losing ground too fast. "Stuff like that never rubbed off on me. Not when I was at the Point, nor later either. If you know as much of my past as you let on to, you'll know I'm no purebred Southern gentleman like Wilse."

"I found that out, too. First cousins, aren't you? Your mother was a Gaxton, the old colonel's younger sister, I believe Wilcey said. Ran off with some Yankee scoundrel. Up into the Dakotas, or something like that. A minor scandal of some sort, if I remember rightly."

"You remember rightly enough, Colonel!" For the first time Bell's heat-lightning grin flashed. "They didn't get around to seeing the parson until I was nearly old enough to shoe. By that time my father had run off with a Sioux squaw and my mother had gone on down to St. Louie to work and support me. First female Gaxton in four generations to draw more than a deep breath without a dozen darkies to help her do it, I understand. After she died I wound up back at Mulberry Hill and was raised there with Wilse. Old colonel put me in the Academy in Fifty-one, two years ahead of Wilse. You know the rest, apparently."

"Yes." Stedloe nodded slowly. "After graduating third in

the class of Fifty-four, you enlisted as a buck private under an assumed name and worked like a field hand for four years to become the besotted ruffian you now are, sir."

"Yes, sir." Bell grinned inwardly at the colonel's magnolia-fancy Virginia rhetoric. "It wasn't easy, sir."

Stedloe ignored the remark, but his terse concluding words turned the harsh lamp of sudden understanding full-up in the big sergeant's groping mind, to explain his apparently aimless covering of Bell's personal background.

"You understand, sir, that it is my duty to put you in immediate charge for desertion? And that I will not hesitate one minute to carry out that duty?"

"Yes, sir."

"Well, sir, you see that you remember it. Because, as of ten minutes ago, you were under technical arrest for that selfsame charge. And because, as of right now, you are paroled to Lieutenant Gaxton.

"And because"—the dark-eyed C. O. leaned suddenly forward—"as of twenty minutes from right now, you've got your chevrons back and are heading a picked forward patrol for Red Wolf Crossing."

Bell came away from the subsequent abrupt briefing in Stedloe's tent with his mind spinning tighter than a hard-thrown top. The revelation that the colonel knew of his past life, of Wilcey, the Point, of Calla and all the muddled rest of it, would have been enough in itself—with maybe about twice more than enough left over. But on top of that the aroused C. O. had hammered the rest of it to him.

Briefly, an emergency patrol was to be readied to take the field at once in an effort to contact Kamiakin and whatever of his forces had Calla Lee captive. That was the main of it and Bell took it that far in good stride. But the details relating to that patrol, its composition and proposed course, bothered Bell plenty.

He mulled them over, now, as he made long strides for the assembly ground.

Even in the short space of his journey through the dawn-graying company street, the sergeant saw and heard enough to let him know big trouble was overdue to bust its cinch in the

Colville column. Company officers and noncoms were already barking and bellowing orders across the growing daylight, and all four companies were beginning to fall into ragged parade dress on the cleared ground between the camp and the river. Without being able to catch a glimpse of their owners, Bell recognized the vocal trademarks of his three fellow stripe-sharers echoing delightedly above the general din: first, the poodle-sharp accents of Demoix's Bordeaux baritone, then the whiskey-burred, terrier tones of Harrigan's matchless Donegal tenor, and finally the swamp-hound bass of Bull Williamson.

Cataloguing the familiar details of the hurried assembly as he went along, Bell put his mind back on the nature and content of Stedloe's "forward patrol."

The group was to be what the C. O. proudly and extemporaneously described to Bell as a "flying column." Exactly, this force was to consist of ten picked men and mounts from each of the four companies, all four company officers and first sergeants figured in addition. The balance of the column would cross over the Snake and follow this forward element as rapidly as possible, Second Lieutenant Fanning commanding this reserve. Failing an earlier contact of Kamiakin, the forward group would hold up at the Palouse River and wait for the following reserves. Rejoined, the entire force would press forward with all speed toward the Ingosommen, the treaty line of Kamiakin's Palouse domain.

The troopers from Company E, the mounted infantry outfit in charge of the two mountain howitzers, would use double hitches of mules in order that the artillery would not retard the speed of the reconnaissance patrol which, as a matter of course, from Stedloe's loving viewpoint, they would accompany.

Expressing amazement that the cannon would even be considered for such an action, Bell had been brusquely informed that where Lieutenant Colonel Edson Stedloe went, there went his two, completely worshipped, high-wheeled howitzers. None of the staff, the colonel had scowled, had ever appreciated the supreme morale-rupturing value of wheeled artillery in use against ignorant savages. Those two guns were worth a regiment of trained rifles in any man's Indian campaign, by the Lord, sir!

So much for the composition of the advance patrol, and for its nebulously rash purpose—the seeking and finding, far out ahead of the main force, of the renegade Kamiakin, and the engaging of him and his wild-eyed followers "in amicable council relevant to returning the captive white girl without unnecessary hostilities!"

It was that last which had given Bell a dose of premonitory shivers. *"Without unnecessary hostilities!"* Good God in goose-simple heaven, what were they thinking of? Appalled by the genuine idiocy of the entire conception, the gaunt sergeant had restrained himself from blowing up square under Stedloe's patrician nose only with the certain knowledge that any further outburst on his part would result in his being left with Fanning's group of main reserves.

The one raw-open flaw in Stedloe's resolve, at least the one to strike Bell instantly in thinking of the staff's earlier treatment of the Nez Perce, was the sudden apparent reliance of the entire command upon the recently and bitterly suspect Timothy.

Upon volunteered information from the scowling chief that his people were encamped near Red Wolf Crossing and could supply canoes enough to get such a small force as the forward patrol immediately across the Snake, it had been dashingly decided to start the patrol at once for Red Wolf, cross it over and strike with it at the earliest moment toward the Palouse River—a simple matter of ninety long miles over entirely hostile, badly gully-cut and brush-choked country!

It didn't take too much stretching of Bell's short opinion of Stedloe's staff, to cover its members being taken with the hoopla and heroics of such a galloping and gallant assignment, complete, of course, with captive white princess and faithful Nubian slave woman. But that his trusted Timothy had concurred in the insanity, let alone having evidently in part promoted it, struck Bell with a swift-rising chill of premonition.

Despite this foreboding, the confusion of the patrol's stumbling departure was ample to occupy his time for the ensuing fifteen minutes.

The aroused camp teemed like some fire-alarmed antheap. Troopers, noncoms, officers, horses, mules, baggage and ammunition animals, shouted, scurried, bawled, whinnied and brayed as though the encampment had been ridden into by five thousand unannounced Comanches. Bell, his H Company dragoons picked and mounted in the first ten minutes, sat his bony bay and waited for the uproar to resolve itself into a lined-out column. His tired mind tried to marshal some order out of the storybook shenanigans of the past hour, but at the end of two bitter-minded minutes, he gave it up.

No matter how a man turned and balanced the figures, the answers always came out in dark, red numbers.

Out there beyond the Snake, or the Palouse, or the Ingosommen, were Kamiakin and the combined forces of the Spokane, Yakima and Palouse hostiles; a force which the infallible Father Joset had numbered at better than a thousand seasoned braves. And when the old Coeur d'Alene priest said "seasoned braves" he wasn't talking about tipi Indians or mission mascots. And he wasn't talking about oldsters or squaws or barebutt kids.

He was talking about man-grown bucks, with not a reservation-bred bootlicker in a copper-colored gross of them!

So much for what was "out there." And what about what was "right here?" Right here under Bell's arrogant, high-bridged nose? Right down there on that river-bottom flat? What in God's good name was there down there?

The big sergeant's Indian-wide mouth lifted just the least bit at the left corner. Like a wolf's mouth will lift when he has smelled a tainted bait and is sneering at the damn-fool human who left it there for him to feast his deathful on.

Bell could tell them what was down there.

Forty men, already tired from a week's hard ride. Four company officers, two of them so far separated from twenty-five years of age they couldn't see to that birthday standing on a three-year stepladder. And taking all four of them together, they totaled three years less than ten on the frontier!

Then, a command head who had spent better than half his scant four seasons in the Department of the Pacific riding M. P. detail on old Brigham Young and his half-hearted Saints' Rebellion down in the Salt Lake Valley. And if that weren't enough to make you retch, you could take a look at what this "forward patrol" was toting along in the way of self-defense.

In that regard you'd better take the colonel's devastating howitzers, first off. And the best place you could take those high-wheeled beauties, insofar as any effect they might have on the hostiles, mental or physical, was to the nearest river bluff. Dumping them promptly over, of course. With the artillery out of the way, you could reassure yourself with the knowledge that those short-pattern musketoons with which seventy-five percent of the main column were armed could, on a clear day and with good light and no wind, speed a ball nearly as far, if not as accurately, as a sick squaw could wing an egg-size rock.

Naturally, you had to be fair and admit that the new Sharps carbines with which Bell's H Company had originally been armed, and which were now snugging comfortably in the saddleboots of the forty-man, forward patrol, were nice, long-shooting guns, and dead accurate as a regular sergeant with a four-ounce quid of long-leaf burley. But just in case that got to cheering you too hard, you could remember just as fast that when you got through leaving half the ammunition ration at Red Wolf Crossing with Fanning's reserves, you would have along a fine, fat issue of twenty rounds to a trooper!

Bell shook his head angrily.

Looking at the now-completed assembly of the patrol column, his shadowy gray eyes scanned the ranks of the waiting soldiers. The cursory examination done, he waved his gloved hand to the silent troopers behind him and started his bay moving toward H Company's assigned position at the head of the column. As he went, the mirthless, flitting grin which was his habitual expression of maximum merriment, went with him.

There was your final laugh, by God.

In a full field command of 152 enlisted regulars you couldn't even pick out forty of them who had done a full hitch. Eighteen of the top separated "cream" in Stedloe's slapdash emergency force were no-beard boys; first-hitch bottle babies who had never fired a shot in anger in their stable-sweeping lives.

Little enough surprise that a noncom of Bell's hock-leather cut could handily restrain his eagerness to see how they would react to a gut-bucketing charge of rawhide hostiles, firing five shots a minute from under the grass-cutting necks of their flattened out, paint ponies.

In the leprous gray of the fog-patched morning, Red Wolf Crossing loomed dreary and desolate as the devil's dooryard. The bleakly carved banks of the booming Snake cut like a ragged war-ax slash through the low hills. The rain, a misty drizzle all night, had thinned out and stopped, leaving the bare earth and sodden scrub drifting with a ground smoke of humid steam.

On Stedloe's prompt order, Bell set out with his scouts in search of the Nez Perce village. As usual, Bell rode first. Behind him jogged the pot-paunched, crock-headed caricature of Timothy's scrawny roan, while flanking the still-faced chief came his mute, red shadows, the subchiefs Jason and Lucas. No time was wasted casting about downstream. Bell knew his basic Indian handbook and had read well the paganly fastidious chapter on community sanitation. He acted, therefore, on the dead-certain assumption that Timothy's tribesmen would be encamped up-current of any traveled crossing like Red Wolf.

After a forty-minute push through bottomland sop, Bell heard the sudden, frantic yammer of the Nez Perce camp curs. Minutes later he was nodding gravely over the thick smoke of a wet-wood fire, his short-cropped head sharply cocked to the animated gruntings of the Nez Perce headmen.

The word in the Indian camp was uplifting. Notably so to the small hairs at the nape of a white neck.

The principal headman, a cousin of Timothy's, was the original possessor of a paganly enchanting Nez Perce name. But after reciting the seven or eight melodious Chinook syllables which comprised it, Bell's chief of scouts pointed at his dignified kinsman and grunted, "Lawyer."

Bell extended his big hand and the elderly Nez Perce took it eagerly. "Chief Lawyer. Chief Lawyer," he repeated, his child-bright smile and warmth of grip an assurance that any friend of Tamason's was, without reservation, welcome among the Red Wolf Nez Perces.

Sensing that the Indian either did not, or did not care to,

speak English, Bell replied gravely in Chinook. "Ametsun Bell. *LE-nta-mama.* Of the two of us, you are my father."

Delighted with the little compliment, Lawyer motioned Bell to squat by the fire. This the white man did, being seconded in the action by Timothy, Jason and Lucas. Immediately two of their host's squaws hovered over them with a fragrant cooking pot of breakfast stew. Bell graciously declined his portion when, upon the act of ladling it out, he stirred up the unmistakable hind leg of a spotted puppy. Lawyer proceeded to come at once to cases.

"You have come to talk about the Palouses. About the Palouses and that red dog with the foam at his mouth, Kamiakin. Is this not so, Ametsun Bell?" The old chief addressed his guest in the full flower of the Chinook dialect and Bell, properly, made him answer in the same complex tongue.

"That is so, Father. He has slain seven more white men and stolen a young white woman. There is big war on the Colville Road. The Ingosommen will run red with Palouse blood into the Snake before the snow flies another time."

"That is a long time. What is it you want, now? Of me? Of Lawyer? I know nothing of Kamiakin."

"The oak-leaf chief from Fort Wallowa is behind me with many pony-soldiers and two of the big guns which speak twice. We were told the Palouses were here. Were camped here at Red Wolf."

"They were, my son."

"How long gone, then, Father?"

"I will tell you," said Lawyer, quickening his words and leaning across the fire. "Now, listen—"

Until early evening of the previous day, the old chief intoned swiftly, a village of Kamiakin's Palouses had been squatting directly across the river from the Nez Perces. Ametsun Bell could raise his eyes from where he sat and see the many rings of their cooking-fire ashes. That had been a real village. Three hundred lodges, anyway. Maybe five, possibly six hundred warriors. And a bad chief with them. What chief? Perhaps Ametsun Bell had heard the name, Malkapsi? Aii-eee! Indeed, indeed. A real bad one.

Well, shortly before dusk three scouts had come. They had

ridden in from the north, from the side of the river up which the oak-leaf chief was marching. They had at once crossed over and disappeared into the Palouse camp. Minutes later, no longer than it would take a big bitch to whelp a small puppy, those Palouse tipis had begun to come down, and by real darkness there was not a Palouse within long coyote call of Red Wolf Crossing.

No, Lawyer could not say what news the Palouse scouts had brought. Yes, it did seem unlikely that they could so soon have known the oak-leaf chief had meant to come this way, so far from the Colville Road. More likely they had simply scouted the pony-soldier camp at the Colville Crossing, had noted its size and ridden to warn Kamiakin somewhere to the east. Over there toward the Ingosommen. In the Bitter Roots. Probably there was nothing more to it than that. But then who was to really know? Who could ever tell about those cursed Palouses? And that mad dog, Kamiakin? No one, really. Not anyone. . . .

Bell bore this disquieting report back to Stedloe along with fifty of Lawyer's braves and two dozen of the huge Nez Perce cargo canoes. Apparently, both delighted with the transport vessels and undismayed by Bell's intelligence, the colonel roused up his resting troops and with the wordless and watchful-eyed aid of Lawyer's canoemen got his patrol across the twisting Snake in a really creditable two hours.

It was now 11:00 a.m., Friday, May 14th.

An hour was taken at this time to prepare a hot ration for the fagged troopers. They wolfed it down, remounted, fell into column and were moving toward the Palouse a few minutes past high noon. Weary as they were from the forced march to Red Wolf and the laborious canoe crossing of the bankful Snake, the entire command appeared in excellent spirits. The belated sun was boring a sweltering hole through the heavy ground mists and eastward, toward the land of the Palouses, a fair blue sky was beckoning.

Even as the blazing midday dropped behind and the long miles rolled beneath the clip-clopping gait of the shod horses, the temper of the sun-sodden troopers rose rather than fell. It was as though the objective ahead were a forty-eight hour furlough on full pay rather than the likely prospect of riding unexpectedly up on the red rumps of a thousand of Kamiakin's hostiles. Indeed, no matter what else a man of Bell's caustic mind might choose to say or think about Stedloe's gallant lads, their morale was higher than the price of ice in hell.

Outriding the slowing trot of the column's head, together with Jason and Lucas, Bell ceased wiping the cascading sweat from his smarting eyes long enough to wonder why.

Every sign Timothy had taught him to read, had been reading wrong since they'd left the oppressive river mists of Red Wolf Crossing. And every minute of his own four-year backlog of Indian outpost duty was rising up in retrospect to hammer at him that something was rotten as a dead dog salmon with the whole dress-parade smartness of the column's advance.

For one thing, the tracks of the moving Palouse village, broad and clear at the outset, had shortly split into a dozen different trails, fanning out past the forefront of the advancing patrol like so many crazy coveys of flushed quail. And despite the fact that the big Indian camp could not have had more than a twelve-hour start on the army force, there wasn't a living sign that any Palouse was presently within sixty miles of Red Wolf Crossing.

Secondly, though the country toward the Palouse River was as open and easy to read as a hardshell Baptist prayer book, letting Stedloe's uniformed troops stand out like a colony of blue herons strutting a bare sandbar, not a local Indian had appeared to ride with the column and wheedle blankets and foodstuffs as was their invariable custom.

Lastly, Timothy, who had departed alone from the Snake to scout the country ahead of the patrol's advance, had failed to report back and Jason and Lucas, riding with Bell, had been grunting uneasily in Nez Perce for the past hour. The sum of their translated gutturals was to the effect that their chief's long black braids were no doubt already drying over the smokehold of Kamiakin's lodge.

His lean jaw setting like green mortar in a too-hot summer sun, Bell cursed inwardly and at bitter length.

Thus, sawing raggedly between the sergeant's contained profanity and his Nez Perce companions' uncontained dark prophecies, the afternoon wore into early evening, and the early evening in its turn into a picketless and open camp on the banks of Smokle Creek midway between the Snake and the Palouse.

The morning of the 15th brought a gray, cloud-driving dawn and an early, high-spirited start. The "flying column" was making remarkable time, its excellent progress auguring well for the success of the projected contact with Kamiakin. The tempers of its commander and his company officers cheerfully reflected this optimism.

Noon brought the usual short halt, along with clearing skies and a warmly brilliant sun.

But 2:00 p.m. and another ten miles of roughening trail produced a chilling change in the weather. This was remarkable for the fact that it occurred without the least dimming of the dancing May sun or the faintest suspicion of a cotton cloudpuff in the bellclear of the Washington afternoon.

Jason caught the first sign of the weather shift when his roving eye picked up a sunflash from the steepening hills to the column's left. Seconds later Lucas reported a similar phenomenon about two miles beyond the column's head and off to its right. Bell's eyes, good as they were, were no match for those of the Indians'. Accordingly it took him a shade longer to read the falling, copper-hued barometer. But within the next ten minutes he, too, had seen and catalogued the continuing increase of the foreign flashings.

Nodding abruptly to his Nez Perces, the sergeant wheeled his bay and galloped him back to the head of the column. Here he pulled the animal sharply up, saluted Stedloe and Captain Baylor and delivered his bad news, point-blank.

"Begging the colonel's leave, sir!" Bell's overdone salute and patent sarcasm lifted the escape valve on the sour head of steam the column's blithe advance had been building in him the past two days. "Sergeant Bell takes the liberty of assuming the colonel might be interested in learning his column is being escorted into the cut-up country ahead, by an undetermined number of heavily armed flankers."

The baiting of Colonel Stedloe, with his literal, clearly limited speed of thought, was a generally safe enjoyment. Baylor, quick-headed and hot-minded, was a horse of a trickier color. While Stedloe was still translating Bell's cyptic report, the captain was heatedly demanding a civil expansion of details.

"Goddamn you, Bell. If you've spotted some Indians, let's have it, right out. Save your humor for the sergeants' mess. When you're talking to me you keep your eyes on these bars!" With the words, Baylor slapped his shoulder insignia, angrily. "Now, what the hell do you want to say?"

"Indians, Captain." Bell had never liked Baylor, didn't aim to start "sirring" him at this late date. "Just like you said."

"All right. How many of them?" Baylor continued to lead the exchange, Stedloe's struggling mind still being several strides off the pace of the situation.

"A hotel-size slopjar of them, I'd say," drawled Bell, laconically.

By this time the following column was beginning to pile up behind the halted group at its head, and the remaining company officers to leave their places in the line and ride forward. Before Baylor could proceed with his questioning, Stedloe had regained consciousness sufficiently to take over the lead. By now Craig, Gaxton, Winston and Assistant Surgeon Randall had ridden up to determine the cause of the delay.

"Gentlemen, Bell has discovered Indians ahead." Stedloe waved vaguely in the direction of the distant Bitter Root Mountains. "You're just in time to hear what he has to say."

"Not just 'ahead,' Colonel," Bell corrected, softly. "We're belly-deep in them."

"Well, Sergeant"—the hominy-and-grits accents were those of the young Carolinian, Davis Craig—"so we're belly-deep in them. What we want to know is, who's *them?*"

"Palouses and Spokanes, Lieutenant, sir." Bell let his respect for the quiet-eyed youngster get immediately into the altered tone of his reply. "They're riding abreast of us about two miles right and left, ahead of us about the same distance. My guess is they're behind us, too."

"How many have you actually seen?"

"A dozen small bands, maybe fifty, sixty bucks."

"You figure there's more of them?"

"No figuring to it, sir. I know there's more."

"You think they're deliberately following us, Bell?" It was Captain Winston, now, adding his thoughts to Craig's.

"I don't know, sir. I doubt it. They seem to be passing rather than tailing. They're all heading north by east. Not riding hard, but all the same getting ahead of us."

"What do you think they're up to?"

"I don't know."

"What do your Indians say?" Craig was back in the questioning, again.

"They think they're bypassing us to get between us and Kamiakin, short of the Palouse River."

"Well, Bell," Stedloe broke in, impatiently, "do you agree, sir?"

"Not necessarily, Colonel." The gaunt sergeant frowned thoughtfully. "I can't guarantee you what they've got in mind doing." Bell paused, letting his glance sweep all of them as a man will when he wants his next words heard. "But I can tell you one thing. We're being flanked, headed, and probably tailed by several hundred interested Indians. Every bunch the Nez Perces and I spotted were Palouses or Spokanes. Wearing charcoal-paste and full feathers. And leading extra horses."

"Well, Sergeant, let's have it." Lieutenant Craig's terse query backed the keenness with which his eyes held Bell's "What does that tell you?"

"Their intentions," the big noncom grunted.

"Well, damn it to hell"—the explosive Baylor let out the belt of his impatience another long notch, kneeing his horse up to Bell's and jutting his chin demandingly—"what are their intentions, soldier?"

"*Unfriendly,*" grinned Bell, deliberately letting the remark stand alone in the little center of silence.

Following Bell's disturbing report, Stedloe dutifully formalized the column's halt by calling an impromptu council of war with his young officers, while the tired men dropped out of ranks and threw down on the handiest piece of Palouse Treaty dirt to joke and speculate on "Sarge's disappearing Indians."

The perverse fact of the matter was that following the stalling of the column, not a solitary feather bonnet or dyed horsehair tassel had so much as fluttered among the screening brush of the ragged hills around it. While waiting for the staff meeting to break up, Bell cursed the craftiness of the hidden hostiles. They hunted just like loafer wolves, letting their intended prey see just enough of them to keep it on the nervous move; then, when it stopped to take a really good look at its pursuer, dropped out of sight as though they had never been trailing it in the first place. Well, that much of it was all right—but Bell knew the rest of it. After just so much of that cat-and-mousing, just enough of it to get the victim to thinking he was safe when he stopped, they'd move in. After maybe the fifth or sixth, or fifteenth or sixteenth, of those harmless halts—look out. The crowding hills would look as still and vacant as though an Indian never lived in Washington Territory. And then, *whang-eee!* the first arrow or rifle shot would drill a laughing trooper and that hill-scrub would erupt war-whooping Palouses like measles at epidemic time.

The dark stream of Bell's thoughts was at this point further muddied by the hurried crossing of Corporal Roger Bates. The dour sergeant followed the orderly back to the head of the column to receive the results of Stedloe's field conference.

By this time Bell was hock-deep in the mire of his disgust, too fed up even to shoot Stedloe with his customary dead-center glare of defiance as the column commander briskly brought him up to date.

An admirably speedy command decision had been reached. Net findings: to ignore Sergeant Bell and his Nez Perces' report, and to march on at once. A mere hundred or so curious local Indians riding their flanks and points were nothing to deter forty picked dragoons and two mountain howitzers from continuing their avowed 'peaceful' mission of intercepting and counseling with Kamiakin and his errant Palouses.

Accordingly, the patrol resumed its gay advance, halting only when nightfall and the Palouse River conspired to get in its way.

It was into this euphemistic and brightly firelit camp that a slim, mahogany-dark bearer of grim tidings, shadowed by a squat Coeur d'Alene chief, rode shortly after 9:00 p.m.

As was his habitual and improper custom, Timothy went straight to Bell, passing within twenty feet of Colonel Stedloe and his cheroot-puffing, post-supper assembly of command to do so. The properly incensed C. O. sent Corporal Bates galloping after the Nez Perce but by the time the eager orderly had reached Bell's fire, the sergeant, tagged by the two Indians, was already on his bent-kneed way to the command tent.

Bell had heard all he needed in the first string of grunts from his Nez Perce chief of scouts, together with the latter's blunt revelation of his Coeur d'Alene guest's identity, to let him know Colonel Edson Stedloe's advance patrol was standing eardeep in red trouble. And in a fair way to strangle for keeps if it made so much as one false move in the deadly situation surrounding it.

The scene following Bell's introduction of the two Indians into the midst of Stedloe's officers, and the stark disclosures there made by the red men, burned itself as indelibly into the sergeant's memory as had Timothy's report after returning from the Colville Road massacre.

The Nez Perce chief led off by saying he had scouted clear to the Ingosommen in the preceding day and night. There he had noted the gathering of a considerable number of Indians but due to the presence in the vicinity of the constantly arriving war parties, had been unable to get close enough to ascertain whether or not Kamiakin had arrived with the captive white woman.

He'd also had to wait until almost dawn before beginning the ticklish business of working his way out of the area surrounding the growing camp. So great had been the activity of the incoming hostile traffic that by midday today he had succeeded in covering but half the route of his necessarily circuitous retreat. At that time he had had the great fortune to cross trails once more with his old friend Victor and a small band of Coeur d'Alene older chiefs sent southward by the omnipresent Jesuit, Father Joset, to locate the hostile headquarters with the intent of attempting to persuade the young men of all four tribes to forego any attack on the white soldiers.

He, Timothy, had inveigled Victor into accompanying him back to the column so that the weight of the Coeur d'Alenes might be added to his own in apprising Colonel Stedloe of the very grave danger in which his small, isolated force now stood. Victor's fellow Coeur d'Alene oldsters had gone on into Kamiakin's warcamp to announce that their headman had accompanied Timothy to the oak-leaf chief's camp to talk peace.

With this low-grunted introduction, the Nez Perce stood back for Victor.

The Coeur d'Alene moved forward, raising his right hand, palm out, and passing it slowly around the circle of white officers. It was the peace sign. By its use Victor meant his white brothers to understand that his heart was good toward them and that his tongue would have no fork in it when he spoke to them.

"E'tca-mxtc lxam." The old man nodded, somberly. "From my heart I will tell it to you, and you can believe it then."

Studying the Coeur d'Alene from his vantage point in the darkness beyond the command tent, Bell's big mouth curled ever so slightly at the corners, indicating his pleasure.

Victor was a short, powerful Indian who, despite his frost-white hair and stooped posture, possessed a vigorous and intent dignity. He was a Christian Indian, Bell knew, one highly trusted and spoken of by Father Joset. The Catholic missionary's word, together with Bell's own way of sizing up a man was enough for the big sergeant. Satisfied Victor would talk without a split in his tongue, he waited tensely for him to continue.

"A'x-otck, to begin with"—the Coeur d'Alene's snake-bright eyes glittered slowly around the little half moon of white officers—"I told Tamason I feared Kamiakin meant to do this thing. And now he has done it. It was Kamiakin who burned those wagons and who took that white woman. He did this because he had told his young men that you would come with many soldiers to make war, and not with a few soldiers to make peace, the way you said you would."

Victor paused to let the point of his lance-thrust settle into the thick hide of the white silence. As Stedloe's staff shifted uncomfortably, he continued, now speaking more rapidly.

"Thus when you came as Kamiakin had predicted, with many pony-soldiers and with the big guns which shoot twice, you made liars of the Black Robe and of us old men who had told our young warriors Kamiakin would be wrong and that you would indeed come with good hearts and not very many guns."

At this point Bell caught Timothy's quick glance and returned it with a silent nod. So far it was as Bell had said it would be when the two of them had looked toward the Snake, and then back onto Stedloe's long column of men and the menacing, awkward-wheeled howitzers.

"But even so," Victor continued, "the young men would not have made war had you stayed on the Colville Road. They would have talked peace with you still. Even as they had agreed to."

It was Timothy's turn to note and return Bell's scowl. Here was the thing the Nez Perce had said in reply to the sergeant's prediction of trouble beyond the Snake. Yet even as the two were acknowledging the accuracy of the Nez Perce's forecast, Stedloe was on his feet challenging Victor.

"You don't speak the truth," the white commander interrupted irritably. "We had not yet left the Colville Road when Kamiakin attacked that train and murdered those seven men. At least, we had only just left it. We have heard that scouts came and told Kamiakin we were leaving the Road before he attacked. But we don't think that's true. We don't think the scouts would have had time. Kamiakin began his war before he could know we were marching toward his country."

"Perhaps that is true." The Coeur d'Alene's answer was soft. "I have only the story as I told it to Timothy. The way he told it to you. But what I say is also true. After they burned the wagons many of the young men lost their hearts. They thought maybe the scouts had lied. They wanted to go home, then. They were afraid. They wanted to run away. We old chiefs made them feel this, and they were starting back to their homes. And more than that. They were angry with Kamiakin because they were afraid, when they found out from the white woman that she was the woman of one of the pony-soldier chiefs. They made Kamiakin agree to give them the woman so that they might bring her, unhurt, into Colville to show you their hearts were good and that they wanted to talk peace with you."

"Oh, hell!" Captain Baylor's choleric interjection burst loudly. "The damn dirty murderers kill seven innocent white teamsters and then they want to come in and talk 'peace.' Good God, Colonel, what are we doing sitting here listening to this lying red—"

"Shut the fool up!" Bell whispered at Stedloe's elbow, his gray eyes smoking.

"Captain Baylor!" Stedloe's command echoed the sergeant's anger. "I want to hear this Indian out. When he's done you can exercise your profanity to your heart's desire. Meanwhile, I'll thank you to keep entirely quiet. That goes for all of you." His mild brown eyes were snapping. "Go on, Victor. Captain Baylor apologizes for his lack of courtesy."

Bell looked at Colonel Stedloe, making a mental reservation to loosen the tight cinch of his respect for him a good foot-and-a-half. For all his sad hound's eyes and wilting mustachios, the Old Man was "all present and accounted for" when he needed to be.

"The way I was telling it"—the Coeur d'Alene resumed only after touching his left hand to his brow toward Stedloe in the sign-language gesture of respect—"the young men would have brought the woman to Colville. But then you did it. Then you made liars of all of us who were for peace. And this time more scouts came from the Snake, telling the same story as the first ones.

"You were taking all these soldiers and these two big guns and you were coming far away from the Colville Road and you were marching into the land of the Palouses and the Spokanes and the Yakimas as Kamiakin had said you would.

"There was no holding the young men, then. The woman was given over to Kamiakin and more scouts rode to all the tribes. The warriors have been gathering for three suns now. They are over there on the Ingosommen right now. Like leaves on the ground after the first frost. That many of them. All armed. All big for war."

The Coeur d'Alene stepped back a pace, as though he had said what he had come to say and was waiting to see how it had been heard.

"Ask him about Miss Rainsford." Bell side-mouthed the words to Stedloe, and the latter nodded.

"What about the young white woman, Victor? What does Kamiakin want with her? Is she unharmed? Well? In good spirits?"

"She is well," grunted the Coeur d'Alene. "And she will stay well if you do the right things."

"What things?" queried Stedloe, patiently.

"Do not move from here. Let me go to Kamiakin and say you will talk peace with him, here, tomorrow. Let me tell him if he brings the woman in, unhurt, the old murder charges against him and against his people will be forgotten. Let me go and tell him this."

"Good Lord, man!" The colonel's honest surprise jumped out impulsively. "I haven't the power to make any such offer. Do you mean to tell me Kamiakin is holding that poor girl hostage for his own pardon? And for the pardons of all those guilty of white murders among the Yakima Federation?"

"Yes. That is what he has told his young men. At first he took the woman only thinking to bargain with her in some small way, or to get a little ransom. But when he found out she was a soldier chief's woman, he thought he had the real power at last. That's what he said, anyway."

"Well, God in heaven, what does he say now?"

Wilcey Gaxton's suppressed voice cleared the bars of Stedloe's restraining hurdle with nervous haste. The colonel ignored the disobedience and listened with the others for the Coeur d'Alene's answer.

"Now he says this." Again the slight pause to let the emphasis of the change sink in upon the white audience. "Now he says they do not need the woman, for you have ridden into his land with but few pony-soldiers. All the others are far behind on the Snake. Now he says he can kill you and your few men up here like little salmon trapped in shallow water. Now he says he can do this and when he has, more warriors will come to Kamiakin. *Haastaq!* Like that. There will be a real big war at last."

"My chiefs and I don't believe this," said Stedloe, slowly. "We don't believe he has all these men that you and the Black Robe say he has. We don't believe so many would follow such a crazy chief."

"He has them. And they will follow him, too." The Coeur d'Alene's voice dropped flat and dead. "For in these past weeks many scouts have been coming among all our peoples from over there around the big lake. From those cursed Snakes over there. These lying dogs have told our people that Brigham Young, the Mormon chief at the big lake, has promised plenty of guns and ammunition to all his red brothers who will stand against the white soldiers of the grandfather in Washington."

While Stedloe's staff chewed the bitter cud of this sudden twist, the Coeur d'Alene concluded abruptly. "And so, *x'ol!* To finish the story. Kamiakin will keep the white woman and the black one, too, and tomorrow he will kill the oak-leaf chief and these few soldiers with him. *LqLa oL'q!* The Palouses will strike and they will win. That's all."

When the Coeur d'Alene stepped back this time, he passed his hand in front of his mouth and downward in a cutting motion, signifying he was chopping off his words and had finished.

Stedloe courteously thanked him and summarily dismissed him, requesting him to wait at the Nez Perces' fire until further word. As the Indians drifted away, the colonel turned at once to his officers, wasting no additional word or gesture in putting the problem at their disposal.

"Gentlemen, I don't know what to tell you. If this Indian is telling one half the truth, we are in the most difficult of situations. If, on the other hand, he has been sent here by Kamiakin to delay us while the latter gets safely into the Bitter Roots with Miss Rainsford, we have an equally hard tactical decision as to the numbers of the reported hostile concentration.

"Were it not for Miss Rainsford I should know our course and would order an immediate retirement upon Fanning and the reserves. As it is, I don't know what to recommend. As an old friend of General Rainsford's I have been quite close to Calla Lee since her childhood. Accordingly I won't lead you with my own feelings. I want your military opinions, only, and guarantee you, as usual, that this command will abide by a majority decision.

"All right, gentlemen—"

Baylor, his black eyes murky with temper, spoke first. "I don't believe a damn word this Indian says, Colonel, and I believe he's here for the simple reason of gathering information about us. From the Indians we have actually seen I'd say there's no more than a hundred or so to reckon with. My vote is to seize this Indian and use him to guide us to Kamiakin's camp. We can approach under cover of darkness tonight and attack first thing in the morning. In any event, this lying red scoundrel should not be allowed to leave this camp!"

Wilcey Gaxton, the fever in his sick body staining his pale face, arose with a heated second to Baylor's rash plan. "Colonel, I agree with Baylor's idea of a night march and surprise attack. I won't rest under any less arrangement, and for obvious reasons I request to go in first when we hit them."

Stedloe chucked his head, turned thoughtfully to Captain Winston. "Well, Harry, you're my steady head here. What do you say?"

"I say like the Indian." Never a waster of deference nor dignity, the bulky Winston moved straight into the matter. "Sit tight and don't do a thing. Don't move a muscle. Forward or backward. Send word to Kamiakin by this Indian that we want to pow-wow in the morning. Tell him Colonel Wrightson and six hundred regulars are due in Fort Wallowa this week. And tell him why."

Bell, who had just perked his ears to the startling news of Wrightson's approach with a major force, as well as to the implication of a direct purpose behind that approach, now swung his squinted gaze to the puzzled knot of brow-raised officers. By God, there was more going on in this Colville column than any dogface or noncom on the post had been told or gotten wind of. And more, apparently, than most of the officers themselves were aware of. As the thought formed in the sergeant's mind, young Davis Craig was demanding the formal answer to it.

"Why is Colonel Wrightson coming up here with a full regiment? Is there something afoot that wasn't in those Colville orders, Colonel?"

"Yes, damn it, sir. What the hell *is* Winston getting at?" It was the irascible Baylor seconding Craig's demand.

"Well, gentlemen—" Captain Harry Winston's phlegmatic voice carried the onus of the answer away from his superior's half-opened mouth. "For security reasons Colonel Stedloe and I deemed it best to keep the matter to ourselves." Stedloe's A.C.S. thought a moment, went on carefully, "Under the present circumstances there's nothing to be gained by further caution. This column was designed for an armed reconnaissance of the entire hostile region, with emphasis on Kamiakin and his suspected murderers of our Indian agent, Boland. The information we gathered was to be ready for Colonel Wrightson's force which, joined with ours, would arrest and try every hostile Indian charged with white atrocity in northwest Washington Territory. Those guilty, after field trial, were to be hung on the spot as examples.

"Departmental headquarters in San Francisco issued general orders to this effect last February 19th."

"Then the whole business of a peace council at Colville was a contemptible lie." Lieutenant Davis Craig spoke with naked disgust. "And Kamiakin was entirely right in his assumptions we came in war and not in peace. Damn it, sir!" The young officer's outburst was directed at Stedloe. "General orders or no general orders, I don't like bottom-deck dealing!"

"Save your temper, Craig." Stedloe's admonition was sharp without being resentful. "The whole business was not 'a contemptible lie' as you so dramatically put it. Had Kamiakin come into Colville with good intent, we intended to advise him to surrender those of his people against whom murder charges existed, and to guarantee him they would receive fair trial."

By this time, used as he was to the whirlpool confusion of the army's Indian policy, Bell felt himself beginning to lose contact with the whole drift of the situation. It was no wonder the poor red devils couldn't make heads or tails of how they stood with the white brother. Every time some well meaning missionary or Indian agent would give him a piece of issue beef, the army would slap it out of his mouth and then step on his fingers when he reached his hand to pick it up off the ground.

Further ruminations along this tortuous line were broken into by Craig's rejoinder to Stedloe's remarkable statement of official obfuscation.

"Well, good God, Colonel!" The young lieutenant was still hotter than a baker's apron. "That offer would include Kamiakin himself! Surely you wouldn't expect him to come into Colville for any such idiotic bait as that!"

"That'll do, Craig," Colonel Stedloe had his paternal manner firmly back in hand. "What we're after here is a reasonable decision as to our present danger—if any. What's your opinion, sir?"

"I vote with Captain Winston." Craig, after a sullen stare, subsided. "Sit tight and have Victor arrange a council with Kamiakin tomorrow. Advise him at that time of Wrightson's approach and purpose. Tell him his only chance for leniency is to turn Miss Rainsford over to us at once."

"All right, Davis." Stedloe used the Christian name to let Craig know all was forgiven.

"Well, Colonel"—Baylor brought the point of the meeting to hard bearing—"that leaves it on your oak leaves. Two for, two against. What do you say? Do we face the red bastards down or tuck our tails and run?"

"I've got to think about it, Baylor." Stedloe's voice trailed off in the direction of the wandering indecision in his glance. "If only we could *know* that this Indian is reporting the truth as to the hostiles' strength. If we could know just that. If there were some positive way of ascertaining it—"

At this point in their peregrinations the colonel's fretful eyes fell on the slouching figure of First Sergeant Bell.

The noncom's slate-gray glance pounced on the commander's warm brown one like a duckhawk on a wounded drake. His big hand shifted to his sunburned forehead in the least of flicking salutes. None of the officers caught the gesture save Stedloe but the relief in his cornered grimace was patent and instant.

"Gentlemen"—the good, crisp authority of the senior officer in command took belatedly over—"I'll ask you to give me a few minutes alone. Meantime get double pickets out at fifty and one hundred yards. Picket all the stock and put every man to sleeping on his carbine. Corporal Bates will have coffee ready in ten minutes."

There were no demurrers to the dismissal, the officers departing to leave Stedloe alone with Sergeant Bell and the four Indians, who had seemed to appear out of the pure blackness the moment the still-arguing staff filed away from the fire. Timothy came to a feather-footed halt directly behind Bell; Victor, Jason and Lucas floated like formless red shadows in his wake.

"Begging the colonel's leave, sir." Bell's deep voice dropped in on the muffled tread of the last of the retreating officers. "I'd like the colonel's permission to make a suggestion."

"Eh, what? Oh, you still there, Bell? Well, well, out with it, man. What's on your mind?"

Stedloe's studied surprise summoned up the big sergeant's caustic flick of a grin. The old boy wasn't far from 100% as C. O.'s went. He'd sure never ask an enlisted man for his opinion of a tactical decision in front of the staff, but if there were a spare noncom left over after the junior officers had had their say and fallen flat on their collective faces, that noncom could rightly expect to get himself heard. At any rate he could if he shaded six-two with his filthy socks on, had a red-bristle beard and smoke-gray eyes and called himself First Sergeant Emmett D. Bell.

The sergeant was not, ordinarily, a saving man. There were nonetheless two things he seldom wasted—whiskey and words. Accordingly, he squandered no syllables with Stedloe.

The Palouse warcamp was reported to be a bare twenty miles northeast. Why not send a reliable white observer up there to check the Indians' information? Naturally this was no job for an amateur. The colonel had better send his best man. Sergeant Bell took leave to suggest that his best man was Sergeant Bell.

Since the suggestion, as the big noncom had dearly meant

it to, coincided with the column commander's own major worry, Colonel Stedloe agreed at once.

Minutes later, with his staff hastily reassembled, he announced he was dispatching First Sergeant Bell and the Nez Perce, Timothy, on a scout to determine the true strength and location of the hostile forces and, if possible, the whereabouts and welfare of Miss Rainsford.

As a concession to Lieutenant Craig's quick suggestion, he also agreed to send Victor back to Kamiakin with his formal request for a council next day, terms of such talk to be the release of Miss Rainsford against the column commander's word to retire to the Snake. It was now 10:00 p.m. Sergeant Bell had estimated his return at about 2:00 a.m. Pending the information brought by his return, the final decision would be taken.

Leaving the stubborn staff still bickering over the makeshift arrangement, Bell withdrew. Padding silently behind him, half-trotting to match his giant strides, went his gargoyle-faced followers, Timothy and Jason and Lucas.

With the shadows of their departures scarcely passed, the powderly *cal-lump, cal-lump* of Victor's unshod pony echoed briefly over the hum of the aroused camp. The Coeur d'Alene chief's bulk hung suspended for a moment between the batcave black of the crouching hills, and the pale, anxious wink of the camp's watchfires. Then it was gone. Swallowed all at once and sucked completely up by the formless felt of the early moondark.

At his fire, Bell spent a frowning five minutes tugging at the bone of consolation Stedloe had tossed him over the heads of his obstinate staff. At the end of this time, having reached his own conclusion, he glanced up to where Timothy and his two Nez Perces waited beyond the jumping light of the flames. In response to his gesture, the Nez Perce chief came forward, obediently dogged by the frozen-faced Jason and the grinning Lucas.

Seeing the two following him, Timothy chopped his right hand back and down. *"Me'tx'uit!"* he barked in Chinook. "Stay were you are. Ametsun wants to talk to me."

"Let them come in," said Bell quickly. "We're all in this together."

"Just so, Ametsun," acknowledged the Nez Perce. "I only thought you didn't trust my brothers."

"You trust them, don't you?" Bell's sharp question was seconded by the sudden demand of his narrowed gaze.

"I trust them," responded the Nez Perce simply.

"*Lka'nax,*" growled the white man. "They are chiefs, then."

Saying it, he watched the Indians, seeing from their immediate little nods that he had made the right point. Jason and Lucas came forward to squat beside their chief, the left hands of both going silently to their foreheads toward the white soldier. Bell returned the gesture, fell at once to talking to Timothy.

"All right, now, Tamason. You heard the officers talking with the colonel. What do you think about this mess? First off, about our scouting the Palouse camp."

"There should be no trouble in that. We have scouted together before, you and I. Your skin is white, Ametsun, but your feet are red. They toe in like a Nez Perce's. We will make no noise."

"Good," Bell grunted. "Now then, what about our chances of seeing anything once we are there? Can we get any accurate idea of their strength?"

"Yes. There will be a big council fire when Victor returns. All will be at the fires, eager to hear what is said. And to sneer at it."

"How about the girl? Any chance of seeing her?"

"Very little."

"All right." The gaunt white man's lips flattened. "Tamason, you know I trust you?"

"Yes, Ametsun."

"And that when you said there were a thousand braves in that camp, I believed you?"

"Yes."

"Well then, why do you suppose I worked on Colonel Stedloe to let me go up there?"

"I don't suppose, Ametsun. I know."

"Well, am I right or not? What do you think, brother?"

"I think you're right, my brother."

"That white girl won't have much of a chance if those bucks decide to jump us tomorrow?"

"I believe that."

"And they are going to jump us?"

"Victor says so."

"How about you?"

"I, too."

"All right, then. Do you think we can do it?"

"No."

"Good. I don't like to see a man overconfident." For the first time in twenty-four hours Bell's scum-ice grin touched his mouth corners. "We'd best go right now then, eh? Before our friend Victor gets too far ahead?"

"Yes."

"Good." With the short acceptance, Bell turned to Timothy's two companions. "Jason. Lucas. Listen to me. Do you want to do something tonight that your people will be telling your great-grandchildren ten times removed?"

The two shrugged, palming their hands, Jason frowning, Lucas grinning wolfishly.

"If we do it, there will be extra pay? Perhaps some old blankets or a team of crippled mules? Many big smiles from the oak-leaf chief?" Jason, the elder and more sober of the two scouts, put the queries seriously.

"If we do it, my friend"—Bell added his slight grin to the Indian's studied scowl—"Colonel Stedloe will likely hang the lot of us from the front gate at Fort Wallowa."

"Oh well"—Jason palmed his hands again—"in that case let us be going. You said I was a chief. Would a chief be concerned with a small thing like the displeasure of one pony-soldier chief? Or a thousand Palouses?"

"Lucas?" Bell turned quickly to the other brave.

Jason's squat companion spread his loose-lipped smirk another six teeth. "This thing you intend doing? It will make Kamiakin very happy?"

"Very," Bell assured him. "If we are able to do it, his spirit

will be spitting on us from the Land of the Shadows for the
next ten thousand moons."

"I'll go," shrugged the Nez Perce. "A little matter of three
spotted mares and a prime young Yakima squaw he out-traded
me on last spring."

Even as the second Nez Perce was shoulder-hunching his
answer, Bell was on his feet. "All right, then. Let's get out of
here."

"He'nau'i," agreed Jason. "Indeed, let's do that."

The three red men followed Bell to their picketed mounts.
No grain-fed, corn-fat cavalry horses these, but the half-dozen,
wire-thin cayuse scrubs which made up the Nez Perces' little
string of favored scout ponies. Each was unshod, barebacked,
haltered only by a feather-light, horsehair hackamore. The
white sergeant looked them over, quickly nodded his satisfaction.

Where these potbellied little brutes were apt to be treading
before the night was many hours older would be the last place
in Washington Territory for the merry clink of a stirrup buckle
or the squeak of saddle leather.

Swinging up on a steel-blue roan, Bell took the lead ropes
of the two spare ponies and guided his tiny group quickly out
and away from the camp, keeping his clouded gray eyes sharp
for Stedloe or any of the junior officers. No time, this, to be
answering academic questions about the extra mounts or the
unauthorized use of Jason and Lucas.

Well out of the short, stabbing range of the fires, he halted
his mount to let the others come abreast of him in the gloom.

"Well, here we go," he muttered tersely. "From here on,
Timothy leads and nobody asks any questions. Is that clear?"

"It's clear, Ametsun." Timothy made the answer for his
fellows. "There will be no questions."

In the moment of silence pressing in on the soft heels of
the chief's statement, Lucas, the incorrigible, provided the demurrer. "Well, just one small question, cousin. Not much of a
question, really."

Bell, staring through the darkness, could read the leering
grin as clearly as he might have at broad noon. He elected,
nonetheless, to give the challenge to Timothy.

The Nez Perce chief didn't keep him waiting, his voice going short and sharp to his fellow tribesman. "Well, brother? If you had a mind, what would be in it?"

"Nothing," declared Lucas earnestly. "Really nothing. Just that I don't remember anyone saying what it is we are going to do."

Bell opened his mouth to set the limp-witted member of the expedition straight, found his words blocked by the velvet hand of Timothy's deep bass.

"Oh nothing, cousin." The Nez Perce chief's tones were in mastery mimicry of his vapid companion's. "Really nothing. Just that Ametsun has it in mind to lift that white girl out of Kamiakin's lodge while Victor is making his big peace oration at the council fires."

3

♦

East to the Ingosommen

For the first hour Timothy held the ponies at the rhythmic, mile-rolling lope which is the northwest cayuse's natural way of going when let out to move as he will. It is a gait which, looking slow, eats trail dirt at a pace that would choke a thoroughbred in the first forty furlongs.

Fortune and the Nez Perce chief's shrewd boldness also favored their progress. Stedloe's column had been advancing in its northeasterly course along the well-traveled track of the old Lapwai Trail, the historic and principal Indian road through the Bitter Root wilderness. This broad, relatively level path led on from the Palouse River toward the Ingosommen and the reported hostile camp. Timothy, demonstrating that notable and nerveless combination of gall and instinct which made of his kind the inveterate and dangerous gamblers they were, had chosen to guess the Palouses would have no scouts along the Lapwai at such an hour and date.

Fortunately for the long braids of his two cohorts, and for Bell's short stand of auburn stubble, he chose to guess right.

The uneasy sergeant had just gotten around to asking him if he meant to gallop them right on through Kamiakin's tipi flap, when the Nez Perce slid his gelding to a stop. Wasting not a Chinook guttural, he laid it out for them tether-short and tack-sharp.

"Stand a moment, my children." Timothy's lean arm, black against the lesser purple of the night, pointed the directions which now tumbled, staccato-quick, in the rolling belly tones of the dialect. Noting the infrequent use of the fluid Chinook, Bell tensed. When the mission-drilled Tamason so far forgot himself as to abandon his hardwon English for the belching vowels of his heathen forebears, it was high time for a lone white sergeant, fifteen miles into hostile Palouse-land, to bend an attentive ear.

"This clearing we talk in," the Nez Perce grunted, "is on the south bank of the Otayouse. The Lapwai Road crosses the stream here, and it is unwise to follow the main trail past this point on ponyback."

"Aii-eee!" interrupted the insubordinate Lucas. "It is unwise to follow any trail past this point on ponyback!"

"You are right, cousin." Timothy ignored the breach of discipline. "From where we stand, we go on by the soft moccasin and the big medicine. Or we do not go on at all."

"Xax na-i-ka," muttered Bell, uneasily. "I hear you. What else?"

"Jason will stay here in the clearing, holding the ponies in readiness. Lucas will accompany you and me. No," the dark chief replied, in answer to Bell's immediate question, "there is no need for concern over his addlepate. The squat one may talk like a fool but he fights like an idiot, and that is what is more likely to count before this night's shade is faded by the sun."

"Go on," Bell nodded grimly. "Our ears are uncovered."

"Just so, Ametsun. From here it is a scant mile and a half up the Otayouse to where it mouths into the Ingosommen. And from that place a man may conveniently spit into the middle of Kamiakin's main council fire. Even with a little breeze against him, he can do it. *A'kxamit,"* concluded the Nez Perce abruptly. "Do I have your attention, Ametsun? You understand?"

"We sneak this creek a mile and a half, hitting Kamiakin's camp where she joins the Ingosommen." Bell kept his recitation short, dropping harshly back into English. "After that we pull up our crotchcloths and turn it over to *Choosuklee*."

"Amen," echoed the reverent Nez Perce, thus at once following Bell back into English, and agreeing with the white soldier's use of the Chinook name for Jesus Christ. "After that it is in *His* pale hands."

"How about our guns?" asked Bell. "You reckon we ought to leave them here?"

"Aye, leave the guns. The knife has the best tongue for talking in the dark. Just bring the knives."

"*K'a'ya','*" differed Lucas with a grin. "Not me. I'll take the stone ax, cousin."

"You'll take what Timothy tells you!" Bell ordered sharply, beginning to be nettled by the slackwitted clown's airily perverse attitude.

"He can take the ax," said Timothy. "Every artist to his own brush. There's no sound to a good stone on a soft skull."

With the words, the Nez Perce chief turned away through the darkness, heading swiftly up the starlit track of the creek-bank sand. Bell fell in behind him, tailed by the bow-legged, gross lump of Lucas' shadow. Indian file, the three trotted forward through the tunnel-like gloom of the creek timber.

There was no more talking now.

Bellydown, Bell lay in a clump of scrub pine cresting the riverbluff overlooking Kamiakin's warcamp on the Ingosommen. The scene below was one of pagan wildness, holding even the irrepressible Lucas in unnatural silence.

The confluence of the Otayouse and the Ingosommen formed an amphitheater of mountain meadow a mile long by half as wide. Shouldering down to the edges of this grassland and probing its ragged fingers out into it, ran the black cloak of jackpine and spruce which formed the continuation of the cover in which Bell and the Nez Perces were hidden.

Close below the bluff upon which they lay, the Ingosommen cut the scythe-sharp swath of its course, while directly beneath their hiding place the precipitous gorge of the Otayouse knifed the rearing bluffs. Just beyond the noisy rush of the confluence, not two hundred yards from the bluff's base, sprawled the warcamp.

Roughly counting the smoke-dirtied apexes of the cowskin cones, Bell caught his breath in surprise.

Putting the slide rule of frontier calculation to the number of lodges in that meadow—two adult braves per smoke-hole—he came up with the nape-bristling figure of twelve hundred trail-age bucks! The sergeant let his held breath go softly free.

Emmett Bell was a man who liked his odds long and his whiskey strong. In a tight scrape, be it settlement saloon brawl or outpost Indian scout, the sergeant was rarely the one to run a close tally on the opposition before winding up and wading in. Nor did he mind, if that were the way the luck of the evening went, being knocked on his sinewy backside.

But four hundred to one! That was a pony of a different hue and far from Bell's idea of picking a daisy patch to fall in.

Pressing deeper still into the pine needles to blot up the sudden trickle of sweat coursing his chest, he bent his alarmed gaze on the milling scene about the sparking council fire.

In a crouching circle, their corded bellies gleaming copper-dull in the bouncing light of the flames, squatted Kamiakin's firstline faithful, the six-hundred-odd cobalt-and-vermilion-smeared flower of the Palouse tribe. Ranging behind these, stood the remaining five to six hundred warriors of the Yakima Federation, principally Spokanes and Yakimas, with a sprinkling of reservation-jumping Coeur d'Alenes, Klikatats, Pisquoses and Oche-chotes. Back of the outermost fringe of this crowding ring, the few squaws selected to accompany and service this restless group waited and watched their war-painted menfolk.

There were no oldsters, no children, no papooses.

In the center of the flamelit circle, a single Indian faced the sullen ranks of his fellows, gesturing and speaking dramatically.

Watching now, Bell was struck with the preternatural stillness of the listening braves. He had seen enough of treaty talks to know that an Indian crowd had one, constant peculiarity; given words they did not care to hear, they made no vocal sign whatever, squatting like so many dumb lumps of red clay, with not even the dust-shuffle of a moving moccasin to break the spell of their slant-eyed resentment.

The white man flicked his eyes away from the scene below, caught Timothy's answering glance as he looked around. Both men nodded, needing no words to convey the common thought. That was Victor speaking down there. And he was speaking to a silence as brittle as wind-carved lake ice.

"Good Lord, Tamason!" Bell's hoarse whisper broke excitedly. "I had no idea of the size of this camp. How in God's name are we going to get Miss Rainsford and her servant out of that swarm? There's six hundred lodges down there if there's three, and we don't even know for sure which one they might be in."

"I know which one," said Timothy unexpectedly. "Victor told me. Kamiakin is a great one for new squaws. He never heard the word of *Choosuklee.* It seems he took a fancy to the black woman. He keeps her constantly in his lodge, Victor says. And he keeps the white woman there to wait on her." Bell's laugh interrupted the Indian, who inquired with dignity, "What is it, Ametsun? Have I said something funny?"

"Only to a damn half-yankee who's spent most of his life in the South," Bell muttered caustically. "Go on, Timothy."

"That's all. She will be in Kamiakin's lodge."

"Yeah, that's all. Now all we have to do is guess which one of those six hundred is Kamiakin's lodge! And of course"—again the acid laugh—"that's a hair cinch. Any fool could do it!"

"Aye." Lucas broke his long silence with a typical drollery. "It's a good thing you have one with you."

"One what?" growled Bell.

"One fool," vouchsafed the whimsical Nez Perce. *"I* know which is Kamiakin's lodge."

"Which one, cousin?" Timothy's arrow-fast query shot in ahead of Bell's. "Quickly now!"

"Well, you see he stole this Yakima squaw from me. The one I was telling you about. The young one with the eyes like black stars and the breasts like sun-big melons. *Aii-eee!* Those plump—"

"Ho'ntcin!" snapped Timothy. "Be quiet, you fool! We

want only to know what the lodge looks like, not your Yakima sow's bulging paps!"

"I was just telling you," defended the injured Lucas. "I trailed Kamiakin down to the Bitter Roots when he took Tsikin. It was there I saw the lodge. Oh, I won't forget that lodge. It's that big red one down there to the left. Off by itself there, almost in the trees. You see it?"

"I see it," breathed Bell. "And by God there's our first break. Close to the river. On our side of the camp. And on this side of their horse herd. With good pine cover right up to its backpoles!"

"It's a miracle," announced Timothy soberly. "We might almost do it. *Choosuklee* has his gentle hands over you, Amet-sun."

"Let's hope he keeps them folded," grunted Bell. "Come on, let's get down there."

"One minute," advised the Nez Perce chief. "I want to hear the last of Victor's talk. He's finishing now."

"Hell, don't tell me you're a mind reader." Bell's jab was curdled with the vinegar of his impatience. "We can't hear him from here."

"A hand reader," replied the chief straight-faced. "An Indian talks with his hands, always. You know that, Ametsun. Even while he's talking with his mouth, too. There now." The Nez Perce pointed toward the distant figure. "He's finished. And I can tell you he has spoken the true words as he promised Colonel Stedloe."

"And you don't have to tell me what they think of them, either." Bell's rejoinder was burred with disgust. "Even a white man can read *that* silence, brother!"

"You're right, Ametsun. Kamiakin will talk now and there will be plenty of noise. All for fighting. All for killing the pony-soldiers. You'll hear it now, and it'll be the big noise. By it we will know the Palouses mean war."

"Yeah, and by it," said Bell dryly, "you and Lucas and I are going down there and crack that lodge."

"Aye," nodded the Nez Perce. "The noise will cover us like a blanket over signal smoke. There now! You hear it? That is Kamiakin coming forward down there. In the bright red three-point blanket. You see him? You hear that noise, brother?"

Bell's eyes followed the Indian's gesture to focus intently on the tall, strikingly garbed figure of the Palouse leader. And no more had they done so than his ears were bringing him the deep swell of the rolling, angry roar which greeted the hostile chief's appearance.

"*Staq! Staq! Staq!*—" The belly-rumbled cadence of the frenzied chant cannonaded up against the blufftop, unnerving Bell with its thousand-throated savagery, jumping his question at Timothy.

"*Staq?* That's the attack-word, isn't it, Tamason?"

"It's the war word," corrected the Nez Perce. "Not just any attack. The real word, Ametsun. Let's go now, and may *Choosuklee* go with us."

"Amen!" seconded Bell, fervently borrowing the Christian Nez Perce's trademark-rejoinder as he slipped over the blufftop to follow Timothy down the nearly vertical belly of the granite incline.

By the time the sergeant and his slant-eyed companions had dropped down the bluffside, waded the shallow Ingosommen and wormed through the pine timber to within fifty feet of the rear of Kamiakin's big lodge, the commotion at the council fire was in full cry. Evidently the hostile leader had made his pitch short and to the lance point, for his followers were already circling to the first drumbeats of the Staq Dance.

With the aid of the pine-filtered starlight, Bell could make out the contours of the lodge with little difficulty. In front of the entrance flap, her shadow squatting black against the blurred groundline, a lone Indian woman sat guard over Kamiakin's new black squaw and her highborn white servant-woman. The sergeant's warning went guardedly to Timothy.

"Damn it to hell, there's a squaw sitting out front there."

"It is nothing," breathed the Nez Perce. "But we will have to work fast. Others of the squaws may be leaving the dance soon. Lucas and I will take care of that one out there. We will go in now. You count twenty breaths and follow. Go in under the rear skins and don't look for us. We'll be out front, watching. Get your woman and go out fast."

Bell started his whispered reply, found himself talking to the pine trees. Timothy and Lucas were gone.

Feeling his belly pinch in small and hard as a green persimmon, Bell counted his twenty, tight-drawn breaths, went forward naval-flat, through the meadow grass. At the rear of the lodge he paused, listening for any least sound out front. There was only the rustle of the river breeze nodding the meadow hay. Slashing downward with the knife, he slit the taut lodge-skins and snaked his head and right shoulder inside.

"Who's there? Answer or I'll cry out."

The husky throatiness of the voice drove into the pit of Bell's stomach like an eight-pound war ax, reeling his memory backward across the years, freezing his poised tongue fast. Before he could free it a new, harsh voice joined its mistress's.

"Lawd, Lawd, we's done foh now! Oh, Missy, Ah jest cain't stand no moh. Ah's gwine ter yell, Missy—"

Bell writhed on through the slit skins, his whisper hissing ahead of him. "Shut her up, Miss Rainsford!" The fierce command knifing the tipi gloom brought a gasp of relieved astonishment from the captive girl.

"Glory be, a white man!" Calla's low cry, for all its surprise was held carefully down. Evidently she'd lost none of her Virginia ginger, was still in good control of herself.

"Sergeant Bell, ma'am. First Dragoons, with Colonel Stedloe." Tipi pitchblack or no, Bell took no chances with Calla's memories of the past, deliberately pitching his voice in the barking, guttural ranges of the Nez Perces to disguise it. "You all right to travel ma'am?"

"Lawd Gawd, Missy, dem Injuns'll kill us sho, now!"

"I'm all right, Sergeant. Be quiet, Maybelle! The soldiers have come to take us away."

"Ah ain't gwine ter go. Iffen dem Injuns ketches us sneakin' away, dey gwine ter scalp us sho, jest like dey warn us, Missy. Ah gwine ter start yellin' foh dat ol' Marse Kampiyackin right now—"

"Ma'am, either you keep her quiet or I'll kill her." Bell's voice fell harshly, the flat anger of apprehension in it.

"Maybelle!"

The white girl's warning was blotted out by a squat shadow looming in the starlight of the tipi opening. "Tamason says too much noise in here," grunted Lucas, stepping toward the moaning Negro. "He says the black one better rest, now." Bell winced at the sodden thump of the war ax. "So now she rests. Let's go, Ametsun."

"Goddam you, Lucas. Now we've got to carry—"

"No." The quiet denial came from Timothy, joining Lucas in the flap opening. "The black woman stays here. I can tell by the change in the drums up there that the dance is nearly done. We have only minutes, now, Ametsun."

"Seconds, maybe," Lucas agreed affably. "Let us disappear from this place."

"By God—" Bell began an angry refusal of the Nez Perce chief's cold-blooded order but Timothy's soft bass would not be denied.

"The black woman will stay here," he interrupted calmly. "That's the way she wanted it. I heard her. We cannot risk the delay to carry her against her will."

"Damn it, Tamason, we can't just leave her here. She's human, black or white."

"She is safe here," said the Indian, finality in his tones. "Kamiakin has taken her to squaw and he will treat her well. If you and your young woman are going with Lucas and me, Ametsun, you are going now. And without the black woman."

"Sergeant!" The white girl's suppressed cry leapt with indignation. "I won't leave Maybelle here with these savages. She's going if I do!"

Bell's tired mind caught desperately at the sudden shift of the situation. Damn it to hell! A man could squat there in that fish-stinking tipi of Kamiakin's all night worrying with his higher humanitarian impulses, and when first light hit those river bluffs over there he'd know just as clean as he knew it this minute that Timothy was right. Maybelle had to stay where she was!

And when a man got that far, he could peer through the lodge-dark at the faint bloom of that lovely white face, yonder, and know that he couldn't leave the Negro, no matter what.

"All right, ma'am." The low agreement went to the white girl. "Give me your hand, here. Lucas will take your woman."

Turning to the silent Timothy, his deep voice dropped lower still. He used the stiff formality of the Chinook phrase. "We two are brothers, you and I. That's the way I ask it of you."

"Ia!" responded the Nez Perce, "I reproach you for your foolishness."

"Tsk'es," murmured Bell, "I stoop before you."

Ignoring the white soldier's gratitude, the Nez Perce called quickly to his fellow tribesman. "Come take the black woman and carry her, Lucas. Leave ahead of us, now, through the front, there. Travel by the way of the Otayouse. We'll follow you."

With his usual grunted grin, the powerful brave shouldered the unconscious Maybelle and disappeared out through the entrance flap.

"Come on, now." Timothy nodded to Bell. "Bring your woman and let's go. Out the back slit. After me, here."

With the Nez Perce chief's command, Bell felt the reaching hand of the white girl brush his arm, slide in turn down its sinewed length to fall cool as a snowflake into the calloused bed of his palm.

"Let's go Sergeant." The murmured laugh was cool as the touch of the tiny hand. "I haven't a decent thing to wear, but I don't suppose we'll be meeting anyone really important."

"No, ma'am." Bell let a little of his admiration for the girl's nerve get into the slow smile of his answer. "Not unless it's Our Maker. And I reckon if we bump into *Him* the old boy'll nod quick enough, no matter how we're togged out."

Timothy led the way across the Ingosommen and into the yawning mouth of the Otayouse's gorge. Here he paused a moment to study the Indian village.

The Staq Dance was still in progress but from its whirling tempo even Bell could guess its end was not long distant now. They had maybe five minutes, no more.

"Choosuklee still has his hands above you," muttered Timothy, putting his words to the thought in Bell's mind. "They

haven't missed the woman yet. Let's go while Our Lord still shields us."

Bell started to answer in agreement but his words were forestalled by a sudden commotion among the cross-stream dancers. Even at that distance he could translate all he needed of the screaming squaw's outflung gestures.

"*Yakpa't,*" advised Timothy. "Let's depart from this place. That squaw comes from Kamiakin's lodge."

"*Yakpa't,* and then some!" said Bell grimly. "They'll be running our tracks harder than a hot-nose hound on a grounded possum!"

"Aye, but it's a good dark night. They'll have to follow our feet with their fingers."

"You reckon we've got a fair chance to make the horses, then?"

"Aye. Unless we stand here talking all night."

"I'm talked out," said Bell. "Let's drift." To the waiting girl he added, "Come on, ma'am. We're going to trot a spell. Do you still want my hand, or can you see now?"

"I can see, thank you. The sand seems very white."

Bell liked the way she said it, keeping her voice down and not blubbering like so many women would have. Well, he'd known Calla was tough. And ten parts tomboy. That had been the main reason he'd thought he could get away with the daft idea of snaking her out of Kamiakin's camp in the first place. Now, by damn, she'd made good her part of the half-crazy hunch. From here on it was up to him to do as much for his half of it!

"Squeeze on by me, here, and then follow the Indian. I'll be right behind you," Bell said. "Let's go, Tamason!"

"*Yakpa't,*" muttered the Nez Perce. "We are gone."

For the next half-hour there was no more talk, Timothy forcing the pace along the narrow banks of the Otayouse. But where the tongues of all three were stilled by the labors of the uncertain path, the mind of each was hard atop the panting pace.

Behind the trail-watching eyes of the Nez Perce chief, thoughts of the time and place were galloping at war-pony speed. *Tca!* Well enough! All had gone too easily thus far.

Back-trail there was no sound nor sign of pursuit. Lucas had apparently gotten as cleanly away as had they. Ahead now, just a little way, the horses waited. And beyond them, yet a little way again, huddled the doomed camp of the white pony-soldiers.

And then what? What awaited them there? What would the first sick light of the Ingosommen sun bring to Colonel Stedloe and his little band? To the good, brave Ametsun, and to his quiet young woman? To Jason and to Lucas and to Timothy, their chief?

The Nez Perce's mouth twisted viciously with the thought. All of them would be killed.

The slant eyes widened, flicking back through the ink dark to the laboring footfalls of his white followers. It would be so easy right now to get them to the horses, guide them nearly to the soldier camp, then melt away back into the safety of the hills with his brothers, Jason and Lucas. They had agreed to steal a woman, and they had stolen her. Their promised duty had been more than well done. Why should they, the Nez Perces, wait to share the Palouse hair-cutting with those pony-soldiers of Ametsun's?

As it was, though their hearts were good, Jason and Lucas would probably be thinking of these things now. They would not be riding with their chief and with Ametsun when the light of the soldier fires fell upon their return. They would be gone.

Well, they could not be blamed.

When his brothers looked upon the pony-soldiers they didn't see what Timothy saw. They had no eyes for that flag. It wasn't in their hearts and in their blood like it was in his. They saw only white skins and empty, pale faces, and always too many guns and too many ugly sneers.

Indeed, Timothy saw these things, too.

But he saw them behind that crimson and snow-striped banner. Behind the deep blue field of those bright little stars. And somehow they weren't so bad, those pony-soldiers, when you looked at them through those marching rows of stars, and through those long, clean stripes. Aye, that was a *real thing*, that flag. Beautiful. And exciting. A brave flag. Easy to remember, always. Hard to forget.

If you ever saw it and got it into your heart, then you followed it. That was all. Where it went, you went after it.

Behind the silent red man the mind of Calla Lee Rainsford, too, was pacing the past against the future and check-reining both against the present.

Following the wagon massacre on the Colville Road, Kamiakin's hostiles had treated her with patent concern, almost, she thought at times, with considerable respect. This had been after she had talked to a kindly, English-speaking chief named Victor, who had joined the savage cavalcade shortly after it came away from the gutted Colville caravan. This new-comer, a snow-haired oldster of apparent rank, had at once taken the facts concerning her identity and destination to the hostile leader. There had been an immediate halt followed by a bickering, sharp-gesturing caucus of the feathered horsemen. The ride had then resumed and the old chief had come back to tell her he had failed, but very narrowly, in attempting to get them to return her to Colville, unharmed. However, he had added, many of them were afraid at finding she was the woman of one of the soldier chiefs at Fort Wallowa, and there was yet hope they would decide to take her back to the white settle-ment. The question was still being hotly argued at the head of the column.

In its forepart, then, save for the stark murders of the Colville teamsters, the whole thing had all at once assumed the atmosphere of a gaudy, almost gay adventure; something lifted, whole-skein, from one of Mr. Buntline's yellow-backed penny dreadfuls. Something strikingly designed to spark the imagina-tion of a southern gentlewoman who had never been west of Memphis in her haughty, high-fenced life.

And small wonder.

Take a picked group of thirty Palouse warriors—seeded stock, carefully plucked from a riotous red bed of two thousand bronze-hard blooms, by a master gardener like Kamiakin—and you had yourself a copper-colored handful of prairie posies to look at that would squint the eyes of a Sergeant Bell or a Timo-thy. Let alone the wonder-wide gaze of a Calla Lee Rainsford.

The surface cream of the famous Palouse horse herd; but-ter-bright buckskins, blood bays, burnished blacks, glaring whites and blazing paints. The cascade and plunging foam of snow-tipped eagle-feather bonnets. The flash and sun-glitter of pennoned lance and horsehair-tasseled war ax. The lean, spare-muscled sway of the matchless northwest horsemanship. It was all there. With scarlet three-point blankets, garish cobalt, ochre and vermilion greasepaint and dye-stained warshields to spare. It was all there, and it held Calla breathlessly spellbound.

For the first, swift, hard-riding day.

The morning of the second day brought an abrupt change in the careless demeanor of her hosts. Indifference had over-night become sullen resentment and curious, bright-eyed stares had darkened to leering, loose-mouthed sneers. The squaws, who had joined their masters during the night and taken her and Maybelle in charge had, on Kamiakin's sudden order, sep-arated them. The women, who had not previously so much as touched her, had turned on Calla with the vilest curses, accom-panying them with vicious slashes from their short rawhide quirting thongs. In the afternoon Victor had brought her the explanation: more scouts had come in during the night, con-firming beyond all doubt that Colonel Stedloe and the Fort Wallowa column had turned off the Colville Road and were heading for Kamiakin's homeland.

The following days had been an equal purgatory of insults and squaw-spittings in the warcamp on the Ingosommen, re-lieved only by a single fillip of slave-holder's humor; the ludi-crous assignment of herself to Kamiakin's tipi as a white hand-maiden for the latter's new black squaw.

Then with nightfall of the present day and the deep tongues of the war drums, had come this so-far-unseen army sergeant and his two catfooted Indians. This sergeant who him-self talked with the deep-growling inflections of his savage henchmen, and yet in whose guttural voice rang the oddly soft tolling of some memory-bell which insisted on repeating the elusive chime of half-recognition.

And now this stumbling, blind flight through the black of the Washington wilderness. Toward what, really? Or whom?

Safety? Recapture? Colonel Stedloe and Wilcey Gaxton? Or Kamiakin and Malkapsi and the other evil-grinning Pa-louses, again?

Breath sobbing, unhardened limbs aching and cramping with the driving pace, Calla fought back the tears of nerve-break. She downed the impulse to cry out, to fall down and stay down.

The even white teeth ground into the petulant lower lip, the chiseled loveliness of the jawline quivering with the effort. Daughter of a regular-army general and service-bred by family clear back to the first Continental Army, Calla Lee Rainsford was damned if she were going to bawl out or break down in front of a clay-common enlisted man and a naked heathen Indian!

Back of the girl, First Sergeant Bell beat back the weariness of five days of forced marching. He choked down the whole, hopeless nightmare of the re-entrance of Calla Lee into his life and forced his mind away from the girl and himself. Away from the Sycamores and Lynchburg and the Academy. Away from lost commissions and honors and opportunities. He drove it back and repeatedly back to the only thing which could count now—the survival of forty-six white soldiers and one lone, Southern gentlewoman against the renegade Kamiakin and his twelve hundred war-trailing hostiles.

Anyway a man wanted to cut up that little carcass, the butchering was certain to give him plenty to do beyond worrying about what a high-flying southern belle was going to think when daylight and Stedloe's Palouse River camp let her find out what had become of her precious Second Lieutenant Emmett Devereaux Bellew!

The temporary relief of arriving at the horses to find Jason with all six mounts lined out and ready for the trail, was abruptly dispelled by the Nez Perce's disclosure that Lucas had not yet come in.

Timothy took Bell aside and expressed his fear that the squat buck had deserted, asking nonetheless that Lucas be given a few minutes of grace. Bell had no more than grudged the request than the broad-shouldered brave came shadowing into the creek clearing, giving the offhand excuse that he had heard them on the trail behind him and thought they might be the Palouses; had accordingly waited for them to go on past before following them in.

Bell turned at once to helping Calla onto the nervous, bareback pony which was to be her mount, and which was to follow Timothy's in the traveling order. With the girl safely up, he stepped back to permit Jason and the others to pass him and fall in behind Calla. Waiting irritably for the Indians and the Negro, he called out to the invisible Jason.

"*Ka'ok'o*, Jason! Didn't I tell you to mount that woman up and send her next?"

"Softly, Ametsun." The loose-lipping of the words let Bell know they came from Lucas. "She doesn't want to come. She says she is afraid of you."

"I'll make her afraid, damn her soul!" The sergeant moved back through the gloom until he could make out the figures of the two mounted Nez Percés, and that of Calla's servant standing motionless beside her pony.

"Here, you!" The command curled out like a bullwhip. "Get your stubborn black bottom up on that pony. What the hell's the matter with you, Jason?" The angry charge crowded atop the order to the waiting Maybelle. "You're not getting simple-minded too, are you? Help that girl onto that pony!"

"No!" The blunt refusal was edged with anger. "That girl doesn't need any help onto any pony!"

Before Bell could make anything of this rebellion, the woman bounded up onto the skittering cayuse in a leg-throwing, graceful way that not even the creek gloom could hide from the startled white man.

"*O'tx'uit*, stay where you are!" snarled Bell in Chinook. "Who is that woman?"

"Tsikin." Lucas' answer broke with ready pride from the screening darkness. "Little Chipmunk, my woman that Kamiakin stole from me."

"Where in God's name did you get her?" demanded the amazed Bell. "And where the hell is Miss Rainsford's black girl?"

"Oh, the black one she's back there in front of Kamiakin's lodge where I left her. I thought as long as I had to carry one of them I might as well take the one that belonged to me."

"It was Tsikin who was on guard in front of the tipi," defended Jason loyally. "Lucas thought that taking Tsikin would confuse Kamiakin more than taking the black woman. Make him think perhaps just some Nez Perces had done the job."

"In a pig's eye!" snapped Bell. "He meant to bring this squaw the whole damn time!"

"Can you blame him so much, Ametsun?" The elder Nez Perce's question dropped softly. "He went with you, unafraid. He loaned you his life when he didn't have to."

Furious as he was with the thistle-witted Lucas and cursing the luck which had put the Nez Perce idiot's squaw on guard this particular night, Bell was duly shamed by Jason's velvety reminder.

Ignoring Lucas, he addressed his apology to Jason. "It's true what you say, brother. The fool's heart is good. Let's say no more about it. I'll figure out what to do with 'Little Chipmunk' when we get back to camp."

"You won't have to, Ametsun." It was Jason who dropped the little shock into the stillness. "We're not going back to camp. Lucas and I think we'll do you a favor for calling us chiefs. We're going to stay out here in the hills and scout for you. Let you know when the Palouses come, and by what way. Goodbye, Ametsun. Look for us tomorrow."

"Goddam your treacherous red souls!" Bell's choking growl was answered only by the fading hoof-clumps of the Nez Perce ponies, and by the sodden spatter of the thick Washington dew disturbed by their ghostly passage. Wheeling his roan, the sergeant kicked the little beast viciously, sent him scrambling up the main trail after Calla and Timothy. Three minutes later, he pulled in behind the white girl's loping mount.

"Where are the others?" Timothy's call back came at once, his keen red ear counting out the hoof-sounds and coming up three ponies short.

"Oh, I sent them around by the other trail to split our track in case Kamiakin got to pushing us." Bell's too-loud rejoinder came in deliberately light English, was followed just as deliberately by an angry string of Chinook. "The bastard-curs have deserted us. That was Lucas's squaw who was guarding the lodge. He brought her along instead of the black woman.

They wouldn't come with me. Said they wanted to stay back and scout for me."

The silence rode in heavily ahead of Timothy's answer. "Perhaps they will at that, Ametsun," he said at last. "They are strange ones, you know. And it is a good idea for somebody to stay back."

"Kick up your pony," grunted the white man. "Your tongue's getting a kink in it, too, cousin. We've seen the last of those two, or a dead dog doesn't stink!"

Bell had told Stedloe they would be back by two. It was closer to four when they rode down on the smoking fires of the patrol's camp. Dawn pales early in that north country and though there would be another hour of thick semi-darkness, the first pallid fingers of the coming light were already feeling their uncertain way along the eastern crests of the Bitter Roots.

Looking toward the army encampment there was little to see save the tendrils of woodsmoke from the banked fires. The rest—men, animals and equipment—lay shrouded in the creeping sop of the river mists. But peering intently through the lessening dark, Bell's fatigued eyes saw something else.

It was one of those tricks of the tired mind wherein the inner thought is mirrored briefly over the outlines of fact. The thing which Bell's mind now projected above the eddying Palouse fog was just such a chimera—stark, grotesque, utterly absurd.

It was a granite block. A red granite block. Slablike, dull, darkly polished. In the brief moment it stood there, wet and cold in the drizzle of the Washington false-dawn, Bell noted the stone-cut symbol of the crossed cavalry sabres above the gothic lettering of its terse legend. Then his lips were moving soundlessly across the grim lines—

On this spot, Sunday the 16th day of May, 1858, Lt. Col. Edson Stedloe and his entire command of four company officers and 152 enlisted men of the First Dragoons and Ninth Infantry, were massacred by an overwhelming force of hostile Indians under the Palouse chief, Kamiakin. There were no white survivors.

Bell shook his head, cursing softly. When he looked again the mists were once more solid over the river's bend, and Timothy was at his elbow.

"You spoke, Ametsun? You saw something down there? What is it, brother?"

"Nothing, I hope," said the white man heavily. "We'd better sing out now. I've no mind to let one of the old man's Palouse-happy outposts do Kamiakin out of the privilege of drilling me."

"I was just going to suggest it," nodded the Nez Perce. "We're getting in too close, already."

Chucking his head to the Indian's advice, the sergeant reined in his roan, sent his hoarse challenge into the clotted fog. "Hello, the guard! Sergeant Bell out here. We're coming in."

"Halt where you are!"

The muffled counter-charge came with heartening promptness, followed by Harrigan's familiar thick form together with some further cogent advice. "All right, laddy buck. Let's have that hail again!"

"It's me, Bell, you goddam flannel-mouth baboon. Get your finger out of that trigger guard and call us into camp."

"Sarge! Ah, sarge, boy, it's you! God bless the ugly sound of yer heathen voice, lad. We thought you'd—"

"Quit thinking and take us on in, Mick. My time's shorter'n a grizzly's temper."

"Right you are, sargint!" His natural relief at having their redbearded brother-in-arms safely restored showed joyously in Harrigan's bellow to the invisible Williamson. "Hi you there, Bull! Sarge is back. Pass the word and trot along up here on the double, now."

Bell could hear the deadened passing of the alert. Then the gigantic form of Bull Williamson was hulking before them. The brutish noncom groped eagerly to the side of Bell's mount, his great arms reaching up to encircle it's rider's waist, the clumsy hands moving up to pat and stroke the sodden chevrons.

"Gosh Amighty, sarge. Don't you nevah run off on me agin. When I heahed you had gone up theah among them cussed Injuns, I neah had me the fantods!"

Bell disengaged himself from the bear-crush, reached out

to pat the thick shoulder. "Save the fantods, Bull," he nodded gently. "I'll see you and the boys as soon as I've talked to Stedloe. You look sharp now, boy, and hold this post. We might have some little friends following us in. Mick'll take us on up to Stedloe." Without waiting for the giant hillman's answer, he called to the Irishman. "All right, Mick. And watch your language. We've got a lady with us."

For the first time the two other sergeants swung their eyes away from Bell.

"Hail Mary full of grace!" breathed Harrigan. "It *is* a woman. You'll fergive me, ma'am. I truly didn't see you, now."

"A lady!" Bull's awed stammer unmeaningly corrected his companion. "A honest to Gawd, quality white lady!"

"It's Miss Calla Lee Rainsford, boys." Bell's dry reply braced the backs of the staring soldiers. "I reckon the old man wouldn't want you to keep *her* waiting."

"Glory to God," breathed Harrigan devoutly. "Miss Rainsford, God bless you, ma'am. I served with yer father, Miss Calla, down in Mexico. I'm sure that proud and happy you're safe and well, ma'am!"

"Thank you, Sergeant." Calla's voice, even after the grim hours just past, was level and steady. "But if we're going to bless anybody, it should be your friend Sergeant Bell, here."

"And if you don't get a move on, Harrigan"—Bell's voice edged sharply into the exchange—"I'll be blessing the back of your thick head with this carbine stock." The situation was getting a little too cozy for the uneasy sergeant. The light was growing and he thought he noted Calla beginning to peer at him a little too interestedly. Bell was tired, strung-up, nerve-shot. And he'd been away from his source of belly-wash supply too many tight hours. All a man wanted right now was to get rid of the girl and get back to his canteen.

Sensing the raw frazzle of fatigue in the big man's short words, the other sergeant nodded and moved off obediently. Bell wasn't a man to argue under the best of circumstances, and the present ones failed to qualify as such by a long-barreled rifle shot.

Following Harrigan through the graying dark, Bell was aware of the passing blobs of huddled soldiers, and of their suppressed, fog-thick comments. He was struck, as always, with the strange, psychic speed with which accurate information ran the ranks.

"Jeez, it's Sergeant Bell! He's got back!"

"Yeah, the Injun's with him, too."

"And a woman, too, by God."

"Must be that general's daughter. The one the Palouses grabbed. The Rainsford gal."

"Maybe now Bell's got the girl we won't have to fight them lousy Injuns. How the hell you reckon he done it, anyway?"

"Who the hell cares? He done it, didn't he?"

"Aw, sure, he knows all them stinkin' Injuns. I reckoned he'd bring her back right along."

"You reckoned no sech thing. You didn't have no more idee of what was goin' on than none of the rest of us!"

The voices faded with the anxious shadows of their makers, as the lamplit cone of Stedloe's tent bulked ahead of Bell. Touching Harrigan's shoulder, he murmured quickly. "You take the girl on in, Mick. The old man'll want to see her a minute. I'll hang back till they're done. Don't want to stir her up with anything I say about the hostiles. Which is going to be somewhat. Understand?"

As Harrigan nodded, Bell turned to Calla, raising his voice. "You go along with the sergeant, ma'am. That's Colonel Stedloe's tent, yonder."

Before the gruff direction was well out of his mouth, the girl was at his side. Her slim hand found his and the warm pressure of its grasp seemed to wrap itself more around his heart than his answering hand. "Aren't you coming, Sergeant? I'd like to thank you, you know. At least see what you look like. I haven't even *seen* you yet, soldier!"

Bell pulled back roughly, turning away from his questioner and from the pale light of the lamp now being turned up to new life before Stedloe's quarters. "Go along, ma'am. Have your say with the colonel and let me have mine. You're wasting time that'll mean men's lives."

He hadn't meant to put it so hard, wanting only to avoid being with her in the lamplight ahead, and to have her out of the way when he faced Stedloe. "You understand, ma'am—" he finished lamely.

"No, I don't!" She flashed the answer back at him, her words making far more sense than his. "There's no point to Colonel Stedloe fooling around with me while you've got your report to make. Come along, Sergeant." The voice softened with the pressing hand which slid swiftly up to his corded bicep. "I want to make my own report to the colonel after you've made yours. And mine won't be about Indians, soldier. It'll be about *you!*"

Bell broke away from her in real anger, now, but before he could put further words to his rising confusion, Stedloe's face, rumple-haired and sad-eyed, was swimming through the lamplight.

"What the devil? Is that you, Bell? Get in here, man. It's four o'clock. Where in God's name have you been?"

Bell's chronically short supply of patience was run-out by the C. O.'s irate greeting, and by the realization the growing lamplight had him trapped beyond retreat. His answer came snapping with loaded sarcasm.

"Escorting a guest of Lieutenant Gaxton's down from Colville, sir. By way of Kamiakin's private back road." Jaw set, he took the girl's arm and stepped forward into the full light. Hitting one of the dodo-rare, proper braces of his enlisted career, he announced belligerently, "First Sergeant Bell reporting. Miss Calla Lee Rainsford, Colonel, The Sycamores, Lynchburg."

"Calla Lee—" Stedloe's astonished recognition, fast as it started, ran a poor-shaded second to the girl's. But after all, hers had only to travel the three feet which separated her from the redbearded ragamuffin at her side.

"Emm! Oh Emm, it *is* you!" With the cry, Calla's eyes ignored the indignant colonel, riveted their unbelieving stare on the yellow-limned swartness of Bell's craggy face, her lithe figure hanging, shock-bound, in its first, quick turn of discovery.

Looking for the first time in five years on the charcoal-eyed beauty of the southern girl, Bell felt the rush of the blood to his temples, the wringing grip of the nerve-fist around the

core of his belly. His stumbling words came behind the awkward drop of the clouded gray eyes.

"Yeah, Cal, I guess it is."

When he had said it he looked up at her, his expression
half between faint hope and comic, hard despair; for all the
world like some gaunt hound who had just come home, mud-
covered and river-dripping, to be caught sneaking the sacred
confines of the mistress' sitting-room rug. He waited, now, with
the same animal mixture of defiance and dumb appeal, not
knowing whether to tuck his tail between his long legs and run
for it, or to jump up on her with his muddy feet and wag it off.

Then she was against him, her hands clutching the rough
lapels of his open shirt, her dark head pressing against the
bareness of his dirt-stained chest, the hot tears coursing their
scalding channels through the caked trail-grime. He stood an
instant, confused and vacant-eyed, then his long arms were
around her as the short red beard buried itself fiercely in the
perfume of her high-piled tumbling curls.

"Cal! Oh, Cal—"

Colonel Stedloe, having coughed three times without ap-
preciable effect save on his own larynx, indulged himself in one
of his infrequent, stiff-backed little flights of humor.

"Colonel Stedloe to Sergeant Bell. Begging your pardon,
sir. Did you have a report for me?"

The C. O. backed the stilted overture with a look of undis-
guised affection, but quickly covered the brief letting down of
his guard to the enlisted man, and the momentary twinkle in
his brown eyes clouded suddenly with the seriousness of patent
reality.

"Yes, sir. Excuse me, Colonel." Bell, sensing the return to
military status quo, released the girl and stepped back with a
perfunctory salute. "As soon as you say, sir."

Calla moved obediently away from him to meet Stedloe
and by the time the latter had delivered his paternal, clumsy
hug and formal, forehead kiss, his junior officers were beginning to appear out of the fog and crowd around the embarrassed girl.

What Kamiakin's sullen savages had left on Calla of her
original gentlewomanly attire, was something less than white

frontier propriety allowed. Stedloe, throwing his campaign coat hastily over the gleaming shoulders, gave his ogling staffers a few seconds to get rid of their first bursts of curiosity and compliment, then quietly asked the girl to retire to his tent and rest while he and his officers heard Sergeant Bell's report.

With a dazzling smile thrown to the tall noncom over the hungry eyes of the staff, Calla disappeared in compliance with the request, leaving the officers to fall tardily on Bell with their questions.

In the fifteen minutes of hushed discussion following Bell's report, the staff voted the only course it now had—to hold fast to the Palouse River campsite, waiting for Fanning to come up with the main column and gambling, meanwhile, to keep Kamiakin off with peace parleys. As an eleventh hour copper to his optionless decision, Timothy was dispatched with an express to Fanning.

Bell came away from the meeting with one satisfaction: Stedloe and his dashing command were at last aware of their true situation, and of Timothy's real character. But they had learned too late that the Nez Perce was one Indian who talked with a tongue as flat and straight as a Sharp's shot.

To the east, now, as far as fifteen miles or as near as five hundred yards, an overwhelming force of aroused hostiles crouched and waited for daylight and the lifting of the mist. Ready to jump the pitiful few pony-soldiers.

With but a lone hour of half-darkness remaining before broad daylight, Bell dismissed any thought of sleep.

It was still only minutes after four when he reached the tent to find its sole occupant, the sallow-faced, sleepy-eyed Demoix, just rolling out of his blankets. *"Bonjour,"* nodded Bell, in his bad French. *"Où avez-vous passé la matinée?"*

"Ah diable!" answered Demoix tartly, in his touchy Gallic way as glad to see Bell as had been the others. "You're a fine one to be asking *me* where *I've* been all morning. *Sacrébleu!* Where have you been all night?"

"Up the river," grunted Bell, throwing the answer over his shoulder as he rummaged through his bedroll. "Looking for trouble."

"Bah! Fi donc, mon ami! You have talked of nothing but trouble since leaving the fort."

"Quand on parle du loup, on en voit la queue!" quoted Bell acidly.

"Beaucoup, beaucoup!" Demoix flashed his white-toothed smile, the sudden breaking of the unexpected grin lighting his dark face. Bell's halting command of his mother tongue was one of the foreign sergeant's few small pleasures within the unpolished company of his American military equals. "My old grandmother used to say that to me many times when I was a boy. 'Talk of the devil and you will see his horns,' eh? *Ma foi!* And did you see them, *mon* sergeant? Those horns of his?"

It was the longest, most affable address the redbearded noncom had ever received from his swart fellow sergeant, but Bell was in no mood for belated affability. He was on his second trip through the rumpled folds of the bedroll without yet uncovering the flat metal container which had been his best companion and only trusted confidant for a sight longer than he'd known any of his brother noncoms. Not Demoix, Harrigan, or even the blundering Bull Williamson, could come between Sergeant Emmett Bell and his bourbon-corroded canteen.

Demoix quit smiling, his quick temper darkening the question. "I asked you if you saw his horns?" he repeated sharply.

"Horns, hell!" snapped Bell. "I saw *him.* Six feet tall. Red as raw copper. Naked except for a breechcloth, and wearing a forty-feather war bonnet!" With the angry words, he was turning to the Frenchman, shaking the empty expanse of his blankets. "But where the hell is my canteen?" He leaned over the smaller Demoix, his voice shaking as demandingly as the big hands which held the violated bedroll.

Again, unexpectedly, the little ex-hussar smiled. "Tut, tut, *mon sergeant.* Softly, softly. You have but to ask and *voila!* it appears!"

Demoix turned, reached swiftly into his own bedding and produced, with adequate flourish, the missing container. "While you were away, the colonel sent Lieutenant Gaxton to take all the whiskey. The men had begun to drink, *mon ami,* and without your capacity to hide the fact. You see?" With the question, Demoix relinquished the canteen to Bell, let his voice turn serious.

"It is the fear which does it. It was the same even in the Grand Army. A big battle. Bad odds. Darkness. Day coming soon, and with it, always, *le blessure mortelle.* You follow me, sergeant? With death coming, the bottle is the best friend. *A la fin,* we are all alike. In the end we all carry something in our bedroll."

Bell, the grateful fire of the bourbon still burning in the parched flue of his throat, lowered the canteen, let his indebtedness and curiosity come in the same breath. "Thanks, Frenchy, for services rendered. And what," he concluded acidly, "do you carry in your bedroll?"

Knowing the dark-tempered Frenchman never drank, Bell had put the question flippantly. He expected no hard-edged answer but got one all the same. In steel. And four feet long.

Reaching again into the meager roll of his blankets, Demoix slid the naked blade from its careful camouflage of oiled leather. Even in the uncertain tent-gloom the burnished Toledo gleamed wickedly, its nude shimmer accenting Bell's amazed grunt. "I'll be goddamned—your saber!"

"Naturellement. But of course. And why not?"

"But Stedloe specifically ordered no sabers on this junket, Frenchy. He'll scalp you."

"Eh bien." The little Frenchman nodded, his Gallic shoulder-hunch accompanying the upturned palms. "In that case our hair will hang together. He also ordered no whiskey."

"Touché," agreed Bell, returning the smaller man's gesture of inevitability. "I give up. And you better get out." He motioned to the tent flap. "It's after four."

"Bon soir," bowed Demoix, turning for the entrance. "Enjoy your sleep, *mon sergeant.* It'll be a short one, eh?"

"Short as a beagle's back legs," grunted Bell, the cryptic acknowledgment echoing the departing footfalls of First Sergeant Victor Pierre Demoix. Then, with the tent to himself, he put the liquor-lifted level of his mind to the more important concerns of the moment.

A man of considerable taste in such matters, the sergeant now felt his first duty at this historic hour was to wash his hair!

After all, it would never do for even an improper soldier to allow a lousy Palouse to catch him dusty-headed. If First Sergeant Bell's auburn topknot were scheduled to dangle from Kamiakin's scalp-belt ere sundown, he'd be damned if it dangled dirty!

And anyway, it was Sunday and there was a lady in camp.

At the stream he shucked out of his filthy shirt and leggings, soaped himself, lay gratefully back in the gentle-rinsing current of a pine-sheltered sandbar.

Ten minutes later, full stretched in the silence of his tent, the leaden flood of fatigue released by the cool wash of the river waters rose swiftly up and bore him under. When he awoke it was to the muted ringing of the instinctive alarm system frozen into him by his four winters in the Indian Northwest.

From the depths of exhausted slumber to full consciousness was only the matter of an eyewink to a man who'd been taught to sleep by Nez Perce experts.

"Who's that? Mick? Bull? What the hell time is it?"

Even as the questions rolled, Bell's nostrils were expanding to a scent never in the world born of a saddle-sweated first sergeant. And seconds later his vision, adjusting to the tent's darkness, was confirming the hasty diagnosis of his nose.

"Calla! What the devil!"

"Shhh!" The warning slid tensely in ahead of the throaty laugh. "Remember your regulations, Sergeant. A general's daughter in enlisted quarters!"

He looked at her a long moment, his eyes continuing to push back the dimness of the close-crowding canvas—and of the long-stretching years.

"I can remember a lot more than that, Cal." His answer, when it came, matched the low-voiced tension of hers.

"Like when you weren't a sergeant?" she asked quickly.

"Like when you were seventeen," he answered slowly. "And engaged to Emmett Bellew's best friend."

"Is that all you remember, Emm? About Wilcey, I mean. Can't you remember beyond that?"

"I can remember when I was a lieutenant," he muttered.

"And I can remember"—the murmur was subdued, husky, uncertain—"when I was in love with that lieutenant."

"We were kids then, Cal. And crazy, that's all." He said it with the monotone finality of something long gone and best forgotten.

"Are you sure that's all, Emm?"

"Yes, that's all," he echoed, the dull, precise tread of remembered heartache in his tones. "You were engaged to Cousin Wilse, and I was the damyankee ingrate making sneak love to his Sunday girl!" His anger was out in the open now, hammering viciously at him with all the force of his bad-lot temper, to hurt this girl. To tear apart this full-lipped, sloe-eyed nightmare which had come so unwanted out of his past to taunt him with its compounded failures.

"All right! I was in love with you," he snarled suddenly. "I did what I could about it. I got out. What more do you want of a man, Calla? To have him go crawling back to Old Colonel and all that 'army tradition' and 'honor of the name' hog slop? I made my jump"—the whiskey was burning its way in now, heating up the ashes of the old anger, fouling the habitual decency of the hard mouth—"and so help me I aim to land where it damn well takes me. On my own two lousy feet. Or flat on my worthless back!"

"Oh Emm, Emm! What's happened to you, boy?" The soft cry came from the heart of a woman, grown. Not from that of a girl suffering the familiar star-flush of a first love. More of a mother's cry, it was, than anything else—desperate, pleading, all-forgiving. Calling out in the empty night after the fading footsteps of a lost and only son. She ended it with a simple, level-eyed appeal, her quiet face backing the soft fall of the words.

"I want you to come home with me, Emm."

"Home!" The gaunt sergeant grimaced angrily, his bitterness flaring anew. "What home is left for me back there? What can I expect from my kin after what I've done to them?" But as though the bare mention of the word had broken the gallop of his thoughts, Bell's hoarse voice slowed.

"When I first met you that night after graduation at the Point, you were engaged to the boy whose father picked me out of a St. Louis gutter. A man who took me into his own home like I was a blood-son. And broke his old heart trying to make a gentleman of me.

"Cal, it wasn't anybody's fault that my mother was Old Colonel's only sister, and the low-flying family hussy she apparently was. Nor that all anyone ever knew of my father was that he was a Northern no-good who left my mother with nothing but me and his name and no marriage license.

"But it's nobody's fault but my very damn own that I've become the disreputable, dirty drunk I have.

"I'm a *bastard,* Cal, and I've spent the worst part of five years and fifty drums of rotgut whiskey proving it. I think I've done a ringtail job of it and I don't mean to see anybody else stand in the way of my finishing it. Now if you still want to play me that hominy and honeysuckle 'Old Folks At Home,' go ahead and strike up your tune."

"I don't think you heard me, Emm." The girl's clear eyes held his wild ones, steadily. "I said I wanted you to come home *with me.*"

"With you!" The unbelieving repetition of the girl's words labored through the compressed trap of the wide lips. "Cal, you can't mean that. Not for *me.*"

"I don't mean anything else, Emm Bellew!" The confirmation came chin-high and defiant. "I wish to glory you had half the sense about women your cousin Wilse has!" Calla's words tumbled, now, spelling out the relief and happiness of a victory considered already won. "Honest to goodness, Emm, you lead like a blind ox and drive like a blue mule! Wilcey and I broke our engagement as soon as you disappeared. Naturally, I had to tell him about you, right off. And of course I'd have told him, anyway!" A little of the lost defiance crept back into the excited voice. "But you, you stubborn donkey, you wouldn't give a girl five minutes to mend her back bridges. Oh, no! You had to go and—"

"What about Wilse?" Bell's interruption came without any shading of the released emotion apparent in Calla's eager words and the girl, quick-sensing the prematurity of her hopes, fell back at once to straighten her lines.

"He took it without a peep, being a real Gaxton, which is something you'd probably not understand! When he was assigned out here, he kept mum about having found you for a long time. Finally, last month, he wrote me you were here. Even then he didn't tell me your new name or anything else. Just told me he'd thought I'd want to know you were here, and asked me if I wanted to come out and see what I could do. Said he'd done all he could and drawn a postive blank. Said he'd been waiting all this time for you to, to—"

"To sober up and turn myself in as a deserter," Bell broke in bluntly. "Is that it, Cal?"

"Yes. Oh, Emm!"

"Save it, Cal. He'd have had a longer wait than Lot looking back at his wife."

"I got Dad and Colonel Gaxton to pull their rank," the girl was continuing, ignoring his grim retort, "and get me army transportation past Salt Lake. Once I knew where you were, I had to come.

"The others all want you back, Emm. But I just *want* you. They've had you before. I never have. And I do, Emm. *Now.*"

With the dropping murmur of the last word, Calla moved a step away from the tent entrance, partly raising her arms toward the soldier, pausing in midstride, her lips parted in that Mona Lisa smile that has invited men to madness since the Year One.

Bell, letting his head settle forward, put his eyes to drinking of the waiting girl like a tall horse that had been long without water.

Calla Lee Rainsford was twenty-two, tall, full figured, graceful as a willow wand in moving water. Her hair, tumbling in deep waves past her shoulders, was night-black, soft and summery as an August wind. An ivory-skinned woman, her face had about it the oddly pagan look of an Inca altar carving. Under the low forehead heavy lashes swept the long slant of the brilliant eyes. The nose was short and fine, the mouth full and wide, the chin, firm. Nowhere, unless it could be read into the moisture of the parted lips, was there a trace of low breeding in her features. Hers was a face to hit a man's heart with a jolt that would carry clean past his bent knees.

"Come away from that flap, Cal. Let go of it. Let it drop."

Bell didn't hear his own voice, the order falling harshly as his eyes kept drinking.

Her body, erect as a drummer boy's, seemed yet to consist of nothing but crouching lines. The coarse army coat, draping from the rounded shoulders, was fastened high at the throat, seeming to hide all, yet hiding nothing, for every sensuous line of the moving body beneath it was seized and sculptured by the rough cloth.

"Come on, girl. Move in here. To me."

"Emm, oh Emm!" Her voice was deep and wild as mountain water around mossy rocks. It put Bell's blood to pounding like Cheyenne drums.

He stepped back as she swept toward him, still not directing his actions, his clouded eyes following the sway of her body.

Moving to meet her, arms spread, his nostrils were all at once full of the heated, fresh smell of her. And then she was in his arms. Their locked bodies surged back, the force of him throwing her against the giving slope of the tent-wall. Her yielding body answered the demand of his cording arms, the arching movement thrusting the eager breasts upward across his bending chest.

"No, Emm! Not here. Not like this—!"

With the muffled cry she fought him furiously, twisting one arm across his straining face to hold him from her, the fierce motion breaking the blanket pin at the throat of the army coat, flaring the crude garment.

Bell, his slitted eyes widening, drove his close-cropped head forward and down, crushing his flushed face into the satin coolness.

In the tiny second of freedom thus allowed her arms, Calla wrenched back and away, the snakeswift blow of her flattened hand smashing across Bell's blood-dark cheek as she did so.

He stepped back to stand a moment swaying and growling like an angry grizzly, one hand moving in awkward, abstract motions across his distorted jaw. Then the livid white of the anger gave way to the deep rush of the shame, and the moving hand dropped away from his face to hang in motionless company with its dejected fellow, limp along the faded seams of his leggings.

"I'm sorry, Cal." The voice was think with control. "I'm not your boy any more. I'm like this now. Crazy bad. No good to you, nor anybody. Get out, Cal. Get out and don't come back. *Ever.*"

She was turning, now, clutching the torn coat tremblingly, reaching for the opening, her acknowledgement coming wrapped in a hurt-deep husk of broken humility.

"God help you, Emm—I can't."

Pulling back the flap, she stood framed for a moment in the growing grayness of the dawn, her black eyes once more sweeping across the tent. Only for an instant she let them linger on the fist-clenched, head-hung figure, her glance dropping hopelessly, nonetheless, even in the brief second of its stricken accusation. "And God help *me,*" she said. "I still love you."

She was gone, then, for all his belated, stumbling rush to the tent entrance and the intense, tongue-tied humbleness of his want to cry out after her. She was gone and in her place was only the grim light of the growing day, and the swiftly mounting stir of the wakening camp. The stir brought the harassed Bell back to hard reality of the day and its somber date—Sunday, May 16th, 1858.

It was the end of the Indian Trail for Lieutenant Colonel E. S. Stedloe and his dashing, forty-man command.

4

◆

Beyond the Gray Palouse

Moving like blue-gray ghosts, Bell and Lieutenant Craig shadowed forward under the patchy cover of the lifting river mists. At the outer picket post two hundred yards across the Palouse they found Harrigan and Williamson in comparatively high spirits. The two sergeants had shared the watch since 2:00 a.m., hadn't heard so much as a pony whicker or a bird whistle to indicate there was an unfriendly Indian within owlhoot distance of Stedloe's stalled patrol.

This bland assurance was no sooner uttered than the raucous, barking cry of a startled magpie shattered the morning stillness.

"So help me, Sarge"—Harrigan's grin went to Bell—"that's the first bloomin' thrush we've heard the whole of the bloody night!"

"Uh huh," grunted Bell. "The first human one, anyway."

"What is it, Emmett?" Craig's low query came as his eyes trailed Bell's to a quarter-mile-distant thicket of lodgepole pine. "Palouses?"

"Nez Perces," said the sergeant, following his growling answer with a staccato echo of the alarmed bird cry which had

102

his companions looking at him in head-shaking wonderment. There had, naturally, to be an end somewhere to this bad-tempered noncom's talents. But so far as any of the three had prospected, there was no lessening of the ore-streak of his ingenuity.

Before any of them could put words to their admiration, however, Bell's chattered answer was being picked up by the hidden songster up the trail. After another short-bursting magpie reply from the sergeant's side of the harsh exchange, the big man turned abruptly to Craig. "I don't know who it is over there, Lieutenant, but I've given him the all-clear to ride out. Keep your guns up. We'll see in a minute. It'll be a Nez Perce one way or another, though."

The seconds-later fulfillment of Bell's prophecy brought a grunt of surprise even from him. "I'll be damned, Lieutenant. It's Jason."

"Our Nez Perce?" asked Craig, quietly eyeing the Indian horseman's galloping approach.

"Our Nez Perce," nodded Bell. "Chalk me with another clean miss. I thought the red son was long gone by now."

Jason's iron-faced report removed whatever trace of starch might have been left among the members of the forward post. Kamiakin and his hostiles were slow-riding the Lapwai not half an hour behind the Nez Perce. They would be up to the river in a matter of minutes.

How was that? Were they painted? Oh yes, they were painted all right.

What colors? Charcoal and ochre, of course. What had Ametsun expected?

"Black and yellow," Bell asided grimly to Craig. "That's their war colors, Lieutenant. We'd best pull back across, pronto."

The brassy echoes of First Call were still bouncing back from the cross-river hills when Bell and his company commander hurried up to Stedloe to relay Jason's information. The command, already assembled at the colonel's tent, began at once to interrogate the returned Nez Perce. Their queries added nothing to what the Indian had told Bell and Craig until the former tacked a brusque demand onto the staff's questions.

What the infernal hell, the lean sergeant wanted to know, had become of Lucas?

Jason's reply, though failing to entertain the anxious staff, put the brief brush-stroke of a grin on Bell's wide mouth.

The feather-headed one, Jason said, had made a gall-bitter discovery shortly after they had parted company with Ametsun. Little Chipmunk, his bosom-blessed love, had not been wasting her talents in Kamiakin's tipi. Already she was seven moons gone with the Palouse chief's noble progeny. Profoundly moved by this delicate admission, Lucas had knocked the Yakima squaw off her pony with the haft of his ax, commended her to hell and the back-trail to Kamiakin's camp, and taken off with the spare mount in the general direction of the Snake, his imbecile's outlook suddenly overwhelmed with the idea of riding a relay back to the main column of pony-soldiers to acquaint Lieutenant Fanning with the fact that a thousand or so of his red-skinned relatives had his friend and fellow chief, Ametsun Bell, pretty well snowed under at the main crossing of the Palouse.

For the benefit of the nerve-tight staff, Bell put face value to this unexpected show of loyalty, estimating it might easily mean an unhoped-for early arrival of Fanning and the reserves. Perhaps, with luck, even as early as late forenoon of the present day. In any event the command could use the knowledge as a bargaining point when Kamiakin showed up across the river, providing no more time were squandered before deploying the forty Sharps carbines along the near side of that sluggish watercourse.

Unabashedly Stedloe consulted Bell as to the best disposition for the troops. The sergeant's short suggestions were at once put into effect.

This was a question of white man's bluff versus red man's bet with West Point rules deep in the discard. If a thousand hard-gambling hostiles were to be backed down, even for a few hours, it would only be by the quirky palaver of a tongue they heard and could answer in. And that tongue wasn't Army American or King's English but Five Tribes, bastard Chinook. And the colonel and Craig and Winston recognized that Bell alone could deal in that language.

Accordingly, the scowls of Gaxton and Baylor to the contrary, the white table was set to the sergeant's bobtailed orders.

On either side of Stedloe's tent, which was pitched in the center of the tiny, half-moon meadow fronting the crossing, the mounted troopers were stationed at regular ten-foot intervals. The short, dull-gleaming barrels of their carbines were unbooted and laid athwart their horses' withers. The four company officers and their sergeants, also mounted, were stationed slightly in advance of their respective commands.

In the center of this thin, resolute circle, ten feet in front of the dropped flaps of his tent, Stedloe took his nervous ease in the lonely isolation of his camp chair. Flanking him, right and left, stood Bell and Jason, their hackamored Nez Perce ponies drooping listlessly behind them.

Glancing quickly over the tight-jawed array, Bell knew he had done what little he could. Even a bad lot like Kamiakin would think three times before front-charging forty picked white rifles in broad daylight.

The land across the Palouse from the patrol camp lay in the form of a triangular, up-sloping valley, the broad base bordering the stream, the narrow apex buried in the pines of the rising hills six hundred yards from the river. Down the center of this tree-bare slope ran the main track of the Lapwai Trail, and smack down the middle of that old road now came riding the war chief of all the Palouses, a simple honor guard of two lone henchmen jogging his flanks twenty yards to the rear.

Bell nodded to himself. Trust an Indian to do it up brown from the suspense standpoint. The red sons had a natural instinct for dramatic staging; never overlooked the least opportunity to torture an enemy halfway to tears before ever they laid a coup stick on him. And in this case Kamiakin had fully lived up to his heritage of evil showmanship.

Bell could sense the hypnotic effect his bald effrontery was having upon the watching troops. Not a man nor a mount moved in the frozen line. All eyes, human and animal, were bent unblinkingly on the startling figure of the infamous Palouse.

Bell's mouth pulled down at the corners in a passing grimace of understanding. Startling was scarcely the word for that Indian.

Six-three if he were an inch, the hostile messiah towered over his two retainers. His shoulders were as wide as Bell's, his belly as flat. His head, high-held and hawk-lean as a Hunkpapa Sioux's, featured a mouth that appeared to hinge somewhere behind the small, flat ears; a tremendous, arching nose made unlovely by God to begin with and subsequently laid half over toward his left cheek by a deep lance slash; and an undershot jaw as long and sharp-hooked as a steelhead trout's. As for costume, save for a cartwheel warbonnet, elkskin breechclout and moccasins and the blood-red three-point blanket carelessly draping his Appaloosie stud's withers, he was as naked as the dark day which witnessed the grim accident of his birth.

His two companions were lesser men by far, and at the distance offered nothing of note in appearance.

"*Kenuokin! Kenuokin!*" Jason's excited whisper at his elbow turned Bell's eyes from the advancing hostiles. "That's *Kenuokin,* Ametsun!"

"I saw him last night, brother." With the curt phrase Bell acknowledged Jason's reference to Kamiakin by his Chinook name. "Thanks just the same!"

The sergeant stepped forward, his voice booming ahead of his upflung arm. "*O'txuit!* Stand where you are! How do you come, now? And don't lie. I can read the color of your paint."

"*Palau!*" responded Kamiakin, checking his gaudy stallion, his voice rolling heavy as summer thunder. "We come to talk!"

"Talk English then," advised Bell, straight-faced. "My chief doesn't hear Chinook."

"All right." Kamiakin complied with the requested tongue, "We're coming, now."

"*L'saqt,*" remonstrated Bell, cutting his hand sharply downward. "We'll meet you over there. On your side. And meantime look well on these guns we have." The tall sergeant pointed dramatically to the ready carbines of the troopers. "They're the new ones that look short and shoot long."

"I see them," answered the Palouse, his black eyes sweeping the line of ugly-snouted Sharps. "They look like fine guns."

Bell turned to the colonel. "Come on, sir. Here's where we face the red scuts down. Never drop your eyes while we're over there, and don't glance back at the troops at any time."

"I hope you know what you're doing, man!" Stedloe was taking his horse from Jason with the statement. "I don't like to put the river between us and our rifle line."

"The hell with what *I'm* doing, Colonel," grinned Bell frostily. "It's what *he's* doing that'll gut the beef for this barbecue!"

But when Kamiakin had said he'd come to talk, he'd been stating the literal fact. After half an hour of politely cautious pointing and counter-pointing with the Palouse chief, Bell had heard nothing but a wordy, boastful jumble of the latter's prowess in war, together with a routine rehash of all the wrongs any white man had ever done any Indian. At the end of this sterile time, the sergeant turned to the chief's totem-silent henchmen in a last effort to learn something tangible.

The first of these was an elderly, quiet-faced Spokane wearing the occupational accoutrements of a tribal *Tshequyseken,* or Indian priest. He was a pleasant-looking, sane-eyed sort of fellow and, to Bell's slight relief and professional interest, wore the cobalt and chalk-white paint of a man of peace. He replied to the sergeant's question as to what he was doing on this ground by addressing himself, quite properly, to Stedloe.

"My people," he said gravely, touching his left hand to his forehead in the white leader's direction, "have been told that your soldiers have come into their lands, here, to make war upon them. If this, indeed, is your purpose, we Spokanes are prepared to fight. What do you say, now? What is your true word?"

Stedloe answered carefully, his dignity and tact, along with his obvious frankness, backing his slow words with a weight that registered even on the indelicate scales of Bell's stiff-springed sensibilities; let alone on the hair-trigger shift of the touchy hostile balance pans.

"My true word," announced the C. O. quietly, "is that I have come into this country for the purpose of passing peacefully through it on my way to Colville. There, as you know, I have asked all of you to meet with me and to have talks. And I promise you these talks can end in a better rule of friendship for all of us, red and white."

The *Tshequyseken* smiled and nodded, raising his left hand again toward the colonel.

"That is good talk, and I hear it. I will tell my people. You may believe me."

Encouraged, Bell turned to the third Indian. Stedloe, well content to turn the floor over to the big noncom, reined his horse slightly aside to allow Bell's scrawny mount to move forward. But even as the sergeant kneed the little animal toward the remaining hostile, Jason was at his side, touching his elbow quickly.

"That's a real bad Indian, Ametsun," he growled. "Watch that one. Under that shirt his heart is black as a dead bear's liver. That's Malkapsi, brother!"

"The bad chief Lawyer said was with those Palouses at Red Wolf?"

"Rotten!" Jason snapped viciously. The word sounded more like a challenge to Malkapsi than an answer to Bell. "Rotten as a sun-stunk salmon!"

Bell took a second, longer look at the man.

Malkapsi was a Coeur d'Alene, a young, bone-thin warrior and by his trappings a chief of standing. Bell, given to running five-second assays on his opposition, needed no more than three for Malkapsi.

With a face narrow enough to pass for an ax blade on a cloudy night, eyes as puffy and oblique as an Eskimo's, lips thin and bloodless as a day-old knife-cut and a receding chin which exposed a set of yellow, hand-filed upper teeth which would have shut a dog wolf's mouth in mortal shame, the Coeur d'Alene chief was patently no less than Jason had named him— a real bad Indian.

Bad Indian or no, he was a good talker. The words flowed out of him thick and bitter.

What had the Indians done to the soldiers that the soldiers should come now to seek them? If the soldiers were going to Colville why did they not take the main road? If they had done so, not one of the Indians would then think of molesting them.

Why did they go to cross the Nez Perce, the river they called the Snake, so high up? Why direct themselves, then, upon the remote places where the Indians were only peaceably occupied in digging their winter roots? Was it the Indians who had been to seek the soldiers or the soldiers who had come to fall upon the Indians with their two big cannon?

"Let your chief answer those questions, tall man with the red hair!"

Bell didn't play to the rising passion in the Coeur d'Alene's charges. Wheeling his pony, he saluted Stedloe.

"I'm afraid that's it, Colonel. You can see what they've got in mind. I think we may as well go back."

"I agree, Bell. Tell them we shall talk again when the priest, there, has kept his promise to take my word to his people."

The sergeant conveyed Stedloe's directions to the Indians with careful gravity. The Spokane *Tshequyseken* nodded soberly. Kamiakin said nothing, only continuing to look stonily over the heads of Bell and his companions toward the cross-river line of rifles. Malkapsi at once began to curse and threaten.

Bell put his horse's shoulder into that of the Indian's cayuse, leaned in his saddle until his square jaw was a scant foot from the Coeur d'Alene's snaggled teeth. "Do you know me, Malkapsi? Ever hear talk of me from the Nez Perces? Ametsun Bell?"

The Indian shifted his glance, hawking after a sullen moment to spit disdainfully into the ground in front of Bell's mount. "I've heard you don't talk much. That's a bad joke. You wander on like a homesick squaw."

"Did you ever hear I don't lie?"

"Perhaps."

"Well, hear this then." The white soldier spread the dry cake of his statement with the thin icing of his grin. "And don't make the mistake of 'Perhapsing' it. I've heard you're a real bad Indian. That you carry lies to *Kenuokin* and the Palouses about the white soldiers. I've heard this, now. And see that you remember it when the *Tshequyseken* is speaking Colonel Stedloe's true words to the Spokanes."

"I hear you, Redbeard," sneered the Coeur d'Alene. "But what are you saying?"

Bell looked at him steadily, the opaque dullness of his eyes holding the nervous brightness of the Indian's. "I am saying that if fighting comes of our talk, here, I myself will kill you for it."

With the warning, Bell gave Kamiakin and Malkapsi his broad back to look at, while touching his forehead to the Spokane medicine man. "Goodbye, father. May your tongue be strong. There's no winner in a bad war."

The three Indians were still sitting their ponies, slant gazes tracking the white men and the Nez Perce in motionless quiet as Stedloe, Bell and Jason put their mounts to splashing back across the murky Palouse.

On their return to camp, Stedloe at once ordered the troops to dig in and prepare to stand where they were. With the men at work on a line of shallow rifle pits facing the river, Bell asked permission to take Jason and scout back along the line of approach Fanning must take. He hoped thus to determine the proximity of the relief column and to ascertain whether any considerable hostile bands had gotten between that force and the forward patrol.

Permission granted, the big sergeant and the owl-sober Nez Perce swung up on their cayuses and departed. The country to the rear being fairly open they made no attempt at concealment but put the ponies to a hard lope and held them there. Half an hour later they were sitting their lathered mounts atop a three-mile rise and gazing southwest at as fine a sight as ever regular sergeant and native scout laid longing eyes to.

A mile beyond their ridge, moving at a brisk canter, the climbing sun flashing off musket barrel and harness metal, the maroon-and-white guidon of the First Dragoons snapping, color-to-color with Old Glory in their lead, came Second Lieutenant Henry B. Fanning and the tight-ranked balance of Stedloe's Colville Column.

Dispatching Jason to bear the news to the river camp, Bell rode down and joined the column.

After giving the brief details of Stedloe's position to Fanning, he asked about the lieutenant's trip up from the Snake. The young officer, a quartermaster by experience and hence no very able informant, reported no signs of Indians, hostile or otherwise, along his route of march. His relatively advanced position at the moment was due to a warning a band of Lawyer's Nez Perces from Red Wolf Crossing had brought into his first night's camp beyond the Snake. They had reported that the whole country past the Palouse was aswarm with Kamiakin's hostiles.

"Thicker than nit lice on a Kathlamet camp cur!"

And the night just previous, about 4:00 a.m., the Nez Perce, Lucas, had found their camp with the news of the patrol's grave situation. Camp had been broken at once and the march resumed through the morning darkness. An hour later the other Indian, Timothy, had found them.

At this point the Nez Perce chief had taken over the guiding of the column from Lucas, and the latter had dashed off down the backtrail toward the Snake. Timothy had disappeared ahead of them with daylight, had been seen no more since.

"Frankly, Sergeant," the young officer concluded, "until the moment you rode up I was somewhat concerned. That Lucas is clearly a willful dog, if not a downright treacherous one."

"Yeah," grunted Bell, curtly. "I wish to God we had a hundred more just as willful and twice as treacherous."

"How's that, Sergeant?"

"Never mind." For his brevity and lack of deference, the bearded noncom might as well have been jumping a private for losing his way to the latrine. "You say Timothy and Lucas had a pow-wow as soon as Timothy showed up?"

"That's right."

"What'd they say?"

"God only knows." Fanning was belatedly beginning to pull the cloak of his commission a bit tighter about his answers. "I can't follow that damned dog-talk of theirs!"

"Chinook, eh?" For the least second the fact that his two Nez Perces, both mission-taught masters of simple English, had seen fit to fence off their talk from the ears of the white officer with their own native tongue, clouded Bell's mind. "Well, don't worry about it, Lieutenant. Then what? You say Lucas dusted his butt off in one direction and Timothy in the other?"

"Yes, yes, that's right—"

"And you haven't seen red hide nor black hair of either of them, since. That it, Lieutenant?"

"That's it, Sergeant." The young officer shortened the rein of his replies, yet further. "And my guess is, we won't, either!"

Bell flicked a side glance at the distraught youth, nodded understandingly to himself. A man could appreciate a boy like this bearing down a mite abruptly with his bridle-hand under the circumstances. Stedloe had thrown a hell of a hasty harness on him back there at Red Wolf Crossing. Then dashed off leaving him to buckle up all the stray straps and loose cinches of 112 half-green dragoons and mule-mounted infantry. And ride them, roughshod, over nearly a hundred miles of territory that would have broken the heart of a Coeur d'Alene cayuse.

The dirt-caked sergeant broke his glance away from the apprehensive Fanning long enough to shoot it on its regular, sixty-second tour of skyline inspection. It customarily took Bell no more than half a held breath to sweep the hill-ringed compass clean. In this case the breath wasn't even well taken before Bell broke it into a wide grin. The easy, outflung gesture of his long arm accompanied his nod to Fanning.

"You're a bad guesser, Lieutenant. Yonder comes my Indian, now."

Fanning stared into the distance and caught the brief flash of harness metal against a ridge. He made out, a moment later, the toy-small figure of the mounted man, smudge-dark against the haze of the morning sun.

"My God, Sergeant. The man's two miles off!"

"Closer to three."

"Don't tell me you can identify him!"

"I reckon." Bell was vain enough to be pleased with the other's look of incredulity. "First off, it's an Indian by the cut of the horse and the way he sets it. Next, it's my Indian by the way he flung up his arms when he spotted me."

"You mean he's singled you out, too? From that distance?"

"You watch him," grunted Bell, suddenly stretching both arms straight up above his head, then dropping them, elbows bent and palms out, before his face. Three times he repeated the dramatic gesture before pausing, slit-eyed, to await its reaction from the far-off hillside.

Young Fanning thought he saw the small blot of the tiny horseman shimmer the least fraction. He turned quickly to Bell for confirmation of the doubtful diagnosis.

Bell sat his wiry roan like a six-foot hawk claw-perched atop a motionless granite splinter. Every ounce of the suspended energy in his hulking frame seemed concentrated in the narrowed slate-grayness of his eyes.

One look at the self-assured sergeant and the youthful officer was ready to concede, his untrained eyesight notwithstanding, that the distant Timothy had indeed flashed his lean arms in a precise mirroring of the noncom's signal.

"With your leave, Lieutenant"—Bell was already swinging his pony—"I'll ride on out and hook up with him. If he has anything to say, I'll report back. Otherwise, we'll scout on ahead of you."

"All right, Sergeant." Two bars were under-ranking three stripes at this nervous moment. "Do I follow on along this trail?"

"Spang along it, sir." Bell paid the youngster his first little commission-courtesy. "And I'd kick it up to a lope. The colonel'll be center-pleased to see you. It's right lonesome over there on the Palouse, just now."

With the hand-waved advice he was away at a flat gallop and seconds later was pulling the roan sharp-up to return the rare grin of Timothy's greeting. At that, Bell wasn't quite sure it was a grin, never having previously seen one nicked into the narrow ax blade of Timothy's face. But giving the sober-sided red devil his due, he put it down for a try, anyway.

Beyond the exchange of what passed on both sides for pleased expressions, and a mutual short grunt of Chinook greeting, no further coin of inquiry was spent at the meeting point. The two men at once swung wide, and north, to outride the head of the relief column.

As they rode, Timothy talked and Bell listened—a not unusual and nearly always profitable arrangement for the outsize sergeant.

From the Nez Perce Bell learned that Lucas had been dispatched to gather a force of Timothy's Red Wolf Nez Perces, under Lawyer, and to guide them forward with all speed. As the lean chief phrased it in formal Chinook, "To aid the pony-soldiers and make liars of those who whispered the Nez Perces sought to destroy their white friends." He had also instructed Lucas to send three Nez Perce riders to Fort Wallowa with the news of Stedloe's peril.

Bell grunted softly when the chief had finished. *"Lsaxo'ita,* my brother. We shall do to ride together, you and I. You have done well."

The Nez Perce looked at him sharply, his slitted eyes flickering from Bell back to the head of the advancing cavalry column. "I follow the flag, Ametsun. That's all. Now it's in a very bad place, but I am still with it."

Riding a little way in silence, Bell turned to the Nez Perce chief. "I've never asked you, Tamason. Maybe now I won't have another chance. What do you see in that flag back there?" Bell paused, adding with a thoughtful spread of his hands, "Certainly you've spoken of it enough for me to know you see more in it than the other Indians. Just what is it, now, brother?"

The chief didn't answer immediately, letting his little pony pick its own way up the dusty track while his eyes peered ahead, looking neither at Bell nor the surrounding land, but up and away and far beyond the rolling ridges.

"Well, Ametsun, you can't blame my brothers. When they look on that gay banner of yours they truly don't see what I do. They have no eyes for that bright cloth on its rounded lance-haft." Unconsciously, the Nez Perce slipped into the fuller phrases of his mother Chinook. "They can't feel the blood and the snow of its stripes. They can't touch the deep blue of its sky nor reach the bright glitter of its stars. Well, *wuska!* Let that be the end of it. If they can't see the flag, how can they follow it?"

"But you, Tamason?" Bell sensed the emotion building behind the inscrutable red face, prompted with soft care. "You can see it, eh brother?"

"Aye." The answer came as the Nez Perce let still more distance into the mile-reaching farness of his gaze. "I can see it.

I have always seen it. From the day the old chief, Menitoose, my father, who walked with Lewis and Clark these fifty-two winters gone, drew its design and color upon my first boyhood shield, I have seen it.

"The old man bade me take the emblem of its blood and snow and to walk behind it with its image in my eyes for all the days of my life. I have done that bidding. Where that flag goes, Tamason will follow it."

The white man, embarrassed by the Indian's simple faith and by the childish statement of its context, tried to make his hard grin lighten the sudden, strange sense of inferiority he felt to this half-naked savage.

"You're a good Christian, Tamason—"

"Aye, *Choosuklee* is my Lord."

"Well"—Bell's grin widened—"you're going to have to follow that blessed bunting of yours farther than your Lord might like."

"And where is that, Ametsun?"

"To hell, brother!" answered the tall soldier tartly. "Because that's where it's going to lead you. And before another sun sets on it, too!"

"Amen," nodded the Nez Perce, kicking up his pony. "*Choosuklee* will show me the way."

An hour later, with the command rejoined at the Palouse Crossing, a decision was hurriedly reached to attempt to push on to a more defensible position before Kamiakin could argue his way past the peace efforts of the old Spokane priest. In this regard the objective was a small lake described by Timothy as being five miles up the main road of the Lapwai, and a mile west of that broad trail. Beyond that point, the Lapwai entered a rocky defile of some length, offering a perfect trap for a hostile ambush.

The column of march was hence resumed, the first slow hour bringing the nervous troops within sight of the defile named by Timothy as the point of turning toward the lake.

It brought them within sight of something else, too. Something that put the saddle-sweat to streaming down every horse-clamping leg in the command.

Bell, leading the column with Timothy and Jason, caught the warning metal-flashings and feather-sproutings only a breath behind his two red companions. His abrupt backwave was picked up by Stedloe and relayed to the close-following column. With the troops halted the colonel and his staff rode forward to Bell's position.

"What is it, Sergeant?" Stedloe's voice was edgy. "I do wish the red devils would show themselves soon. This waiting is intolerable."

"Keep your eyes peeled, Colonel." The sergeant's dry admonition accompanied his nod toward the shouldering walls of the defile. "You'll get your wish quick enough. They're clotted up in those rocks thicker'n tickbirds on a bull's bottom."

"Damn it, Bell! I can't see a blessed thing."

"You will." The lanky noncom shrugged. "Timothy had them pegged in the right hole, all along. If we'd gone into that slot, yonder, they'd have been over us like squaws on an issue beef. They'll pour out of there in a minute, you watch."

At Bell's blunt words the staff closed in a tight nervous knot. Congress's five gentlemen seemed moved by a mutual and impelling urge to seek the comforting shade of Sergeant Bell's broad back.

The big noncom's minute came and went and still no sight nor sound of movement in the sun-glaring rocks ahead. Behind the motionless officers, the men and animals of the Colville column appeared to be oil-painted against the drab canvas of the Washington hills, suspended death-still in the morning sunlight.

"By the Lord, Bell"—Stedloe's control cracked first—"maybe you're wrong. Maybe—"

"Not a chance, Colonel." The sergeant's contradiction came, sidemouthed, the steady angle of his slate-gray glance never leaving the mute rocks of the defile's ragged throat. "We've marched ourselves right into the pit of a big red belly-ache and it's going to be all over us before you can bat your eyes again."

The bearded noncom had no more than diagnosed the hostile colic than it erupted in a thunder of war screams and startled pony neighs.

"Tell the troops to hold their fire!" Bell's low call went to Stedloe. "This is a bluff charge. Nerve stuff. They always pull at least one. Tell the men to hold off till they're under a hundred yards. If they pass that, give them everything at once."

"Relay that order, Baylor!" Stedloe's command jumped unquestioningly. "You go with him, Wilcey. Craig and Winston stay with us."

By the time the two officers had reached the troops with the bellowed warning, the rocks around the defile's mouth had spewed forth no less than five hundred howling warriors, the van of which was now not over two hundred yards from Bell and his advance group. It looked for the moment as though Stedloe and his command would be swallowed down in one vast, gulping bite.

But Bell had gauged the Indian appetite for soldier meat almost to the foot.

One hundred twenty-five yards from the waiting white troops, fifty from the advanced Stedloe, the front line of charging hostiles pulled their galloping cayuses to a rock-showering halt, the following hundreds piling up behind them like an angry red wave dashing headlong against the thin dike of feathered rocks in front of them. Behind these, moving their ponies out from the screen of the higher hillside brush, sitting them in full and soundless view, another seven or eight hundred savages were now visible.

"Let them stew a minute," advised Bell tersely. "They're not set to fight just yet or the others wouldn't have clung back there on the hill. They still want to palaver."

Implementing the sergeant's claim, a dozen gorgeously painted chiefs rode forward to within thirty yards of Stedloe and his group. "Spokanes," Bell said. "Now we'll hear how loud that old priest talked."

The ensuing parley followed the precise pattern of the earlier meeting with Kamiakin. And Stedloe replied to the same questions regarding his presence here with the exact straightforward answers he had given before.

The Spokanes, either satisfied or feigning satisfaction, advised the commander that while his words were reassuring they could not at the same time allow his soldiers to proceed to the boundary of their tribal lands, the Spokane River some few miles beyond the Ingosommen. Stedloe patiently replied he had no such intention, was only moving to better water for his many pack animals and would turn back the next morning.

The Indians again seemed content. They began waving back the results of their parley to the waiting hundreds on the hillside. The pony-soldiers were turning back. They sought only friendship and a council, not a fight. They had come into this land only because they had lost their true way to Colville. It was even as the *Tshequyseken* had said. The white chief's words had a good sound. What had Kamiakin to say?

Apparently Kamiakin had more than a little.

No sooner had the hopeful trend of the talk been hand-signed to them, than the Palouse chief and his Coeur d'Alene lieutenant, Malkapsi, began to gallop the front of the restless warrior line, haranguing the painted braves to cover their ears and not to listen. In response to their barking exhortations the packed ranks of their followers began the chant which had blossomed Bell's spine with perspiration the night before.

"Staq! Staq! Staq! Staq!"

"Good Lord! What a beastly sound. What is it they're yelling about now, Bell?"

"War, Colonel. They're going to fight, sir. *Staq* is the last word on the subject according to Timothy. We're wasting our time and risking our ragged butts up here as from right now!"

Stedloe nodded, turning to the Spokane chiefs. "You talk of peace while your brothers shout for war." The colonel's ordinarily mild eyes were snapping. "Go back and tell them we'll fight. But tell them we still want peace. Tell them they'll fire the first shot."

The white truce party returned at once to the waiting troops and Stedloe solemnly instructed his command that they would have to fight. Since the ground they were on was badly suited for a stand, every effort would now be made to reach and take a strong position on Timothy's lake. Not a man was to return the hostile fire until given orders to do so.

The troops turned at once to the left and west, pushing up the rising, broken ground between them and the water.

During this tedious and exposed advance, the whole, boiling mass of the hostiles foamed along the right flank a scant hundred yards out, taking the opportunity to dazzle the white soldiers with their superb horsemanship and to acquaint them with the fact that they had ammunition to burn and first-class rifles to burn it through.

No fire was directed into the troops during this time, all the considerable volume of the hostile fusillade being thrown over the command's line of march, along with the bitter torrent of Indian invective and insult which Bell knew was always part of the red man's mental build up to the climactic charge. And sneer as he might, personally, at such heathen yelling and screaming, the sergeant had only to look about him to see the effect it was having on Stedloe's column.

Having done most of his life's reading from the open books of men's faces, Bell didn't need glasses to translate chapter and verse from the chalk-white pages hurrying past him as he outrode the flank of the retreating force. General Panic wasn't in command here, yet. But he was taking a man a minute away from Lieutenant Colonel E. S. Stedloe, even before Assistant Surgeon Randall had swabbed his fuming nitric acid into the first bullet furrow.

Notwithstanding the growing fear of the men, the lake was reached without further incident. Stedloe at once arranged his companies in defensive order with their backs to the water, the entire command remaining mounted, arms ready. The two howitzers were wheeled into position and stripped, the pack and ammunition mules, now crazed with the Indian pony-smell, being herded close and hard-picketed behind the outer line of nostril-flaring dragoon horses.

At this point, the crowded, solid ring of the Indian lines parted to let through the familiar, hatchet-headed form of Malkapsi.

The renegade Coeur d'Alene wanted to inform the white chief that his lies had failed. The Spokanes had lost their case. None of the others believed the soldiers came in peace with the two big guns and so far off the Colville Road. Furthermore, far from being satisfied with the column turning back short of the Spokane River, large hostile forces were even now racing to cut it off from the Nez Perce River. The white soldiers were penned up like pigs, and they were going to die that way. Slashed through their pale, hairy throats with bright Indian steel!

As the Coeur d'Alene's flamboyant diatribe rose to its full pitch and flower of phrase another figure rode up to join it from the hostile ranks.

Bell, sitting his mount alongside Timothy, muttered to the Nez Perce. "That's the *Tshequyseken* who talked peace with us earlier. I thought he talked straight then."

"He probably did," said Timothy. "That's *Qoe'lqoel*, The Owl. A good Indian, Ametsun. But what's one owl among a thousand fishhawks?"

"A dead duck," grunted Bell. "Damn it to hell, Tamason"—the sergeant's deep voice rose irritably—"what do you suppose is keeping them off of us? They could have cut us to pieces two hours ago!"

"Who can say? Perhaps it's the day."

"Where does the day figure in it?"

"You've forgotten the day, Ametsun?"

"It's the sixteenth. What's that got to do with the price of pony-soldier scalps?"

"Sunday." The Nez Perce nodded soberly. "The Lord's Day, Ametsun."

"Thank God!" murmured the sergeant with fervent irony. "I'd plumb forgotten. So help me, Timothy, I think you're getting limpwitted in your old age."

"Don't thank our Lord like that, Ametsun. He's still riding with us. You'll see."

Bell, readying another impious blast at his red comrade's literal concept of old Marc Whitman's prayer-book tonic, had the earth cut out from under his heathen feet before he could open his mouth.

The cutting was being done in the cracked voice of Malkapsi's newly arrived fellow, the Spokane *Tshequyseken*.

"Hear me, my brothers!" The old man's words carried clearly in the sudden hush. "A few among us have done what we can. I name Victor and Vincent of the Coeur d'Alenes among these. And Jacques and Zachary. We have failed but this one thing we have done."

The white-haired priest broke his words to fling his

withered arms skyward with the measured roll of his conclusion. "Today there will be no fighting. Tomorrow they will give you battle. But they promised not to defile this day by fighting. We could do no more. But this is Sunday—"

For the remaining five hours of afternoon daylight the command sat their saddles, muskets and carbines loaded and unbooted, expecting each minute of the entire time to produce the constantly threatened Indian charge. The dragoon horses, pushed unmercifully for five days and without a decent feed or water in three, were rapidly becoming unmanageable under the ceaseless screaming and firing of the galloping hostile horsemen. The pack mules, always more susceptible to the alien odor of both Indians and cayuses, were requiring the attention of the complete Ninth Infantry company to keep them on picket and under their various loads.

With the whole column, mule, horse and man, close to the breaking point of ordered array, sunset brought an unexpected delay of execution. With the first shade of evening the hostiles began pulling back into the hills and within ten minutes there was neither sight nor sound of an enemy horseman within five miles of the tiny lake.

After waiting another half hour in the saddle, Stedloe ordered camp made and disposed his command for the night. Every mount, pack and cavalry, was picketed under load and saddle, and each trooper billeted with his charged carbine or musket for a blanket. Double sentry lines were run around the entire perimeter of the huddled camp, the men not on guard duty sleeping in company groups within hand's reach of their ready horses.

Back of this thin bulwark Colonel Stedloe and his staff sat the night away planning the retreat to the Snake. In this course there were now no demurrers. The low supply of ammunition, the overwhelming forces opposed to them, the absolute proof of their own eyes that the Spokanes and Coeur d'Alenes, tribes hitherto without a spot of white blood on their hands, had joined Kamiakin's rebellion, held the discussion strictly to ways and means of extricating the command from its present trap.

In this regard it was proposed to send an express to Wal-

Iowa by Jason and Timothy asking for reinforcements. The Nez Perce chief bluntly refused the mission, stating he had already sent a good man in the same direction and that furthermore that man had a twelve-hour start. The country behind them would be swarming with hostiles by this time and there was no sense in either he or Jason getting killed to prove it. If Lucas could not get through, Jason and Timothy would have no chance whatever of doing so.

This flat rebellion brought a fitful reflaring of the hotspur section of the command's original doubt as to the Nez Perce brand of loyalty. Captain Baylor at once pointed out that the officers had no assurance beyond Timothy's own that Lucas had been instructed to carry such a message. And that, granted he had been, there was no solid hope that the already discredited Lucas could or would discharge a trust of this vital and risky character.

Baylor was uneasily joined in these warmed-over suspicions by Gaxton and even, brow-furrowed and earnestly, by the plodding Harry Winston. Young Craig, alone, defended the Nez Perce chief's blank-faced logic. Stedloe, as was his unvarying habit, withheld his own opinion until those of his juniors had been entirely tabled.

Listening to the belated resurgence of this one and two-bar bickering, Bell found himself sudden-sick of Colonel Edson Stedloe's staff—with that whole frontier white, regular-army, anti-anything-with-red-skin attitude which it so self-righteously epitomized.

The thought that such a misfit management held a twelve-hour option on the lives of 152 sheep-huddled men and a white-faced southern girl of Calla's quiet bravery, was enough to sicken a man's guts.

The picture of Calla's wan face, thus called up against the morbid dark of his thoughts, sent Bell's mind stumbling along the backtrail of the hours which had stretched since the tent-flap had closed behind her in the camp on the banks of the Palouse.

In the pile and drive of those hours—covering Kamiakin's dramatic appearance across that gray and sluggish stream, the searching out and finding of Fanning's main column and the ill-considered decision to advance to Timothy's lake—Bell had not had sixty seconds to call his own. No chance even to smile at the girl, let alone seek her out to tell her all the thousand-and-one thoughts of misery and heart-longing which had hammered at him from the moment she had turned, dress-torn and wide-eyed, to throw him that last look.

And even now, stealing seconds to think of her during Stedloe's staff meeting, he was being denied the slim comfort of the mental vision by the chiding encroachment of the colonel's worn voice.

"Bell—wake up, man! We've gotten around to you again."

There was that in the resigned, almost appealing way Stedloe said it which let Bell know the colonel's thoughts were silently adding a grateful "as usual," to the short address. He saluted wearily, shaking his head to clear it of the cloying fog of fatigue, and forced his desperately tired mind to follow the words of the column commander, make his own answers come clean and hard and quick.

Stedloe, after his brief discussion with Bell, announced his readiness to stand with Timothy and his statements, adding that the sergeant and the two Nez Perces constituted the column's sole remaining scout and hostile-contact force and, hence, could not at any cost be spared.

Under this agreement the final marching orders were arranged with the departure scheduled for early, predawn darkness of the following morning. The troops were to be in saddle and moving off at four, each of the officers being charged with seeing that every man and animal in his command was present and accounted for, and above all, that each individual trooper was precisely aware of the exact order of the march and his place in it. Meanwhile, under Bell's and his Nez Perces' assurances that Kamiakin's crazy henchmen were still well back in the hills and would stay there until daylight, the main thing was to let the exhausted men get what sleep they could, and to encourage them wherever possible against the grim prospects of the coming retreat. Finally, though Stedloe assumed he had destroyed the main source of it at Palouse Crossing, a sharp eye was to be kept out for any drinking in the ranks. The mild-eyed C. O. had been too long a regular army officer not to know that where a will as strong as a frightened soldier's was present, a way would somehow be found to soften it with spiritus frumenti.

With the colonel's solemn reference to Bell's sole source of spiritual and fleshly sustenance watering the dust-dried spittle of his mouth corners, the big sergeant made his way through the seemingly endless clutter of ground-sleeping troopers. Presently, through no conscious direction of his own, his course veered to bring up against a small pyramid of darkness, blacker than the dense shade of the Palouse night which backed it.

Stedloe's tent. Now, what the hell was the matter with him? His own horse and company were forty yards to the left, out there on the fringe of the picket line. He must be losing his Nez Perce touch. Couldn't cat-see the dark anymore. Well, goddamit, a man—

With the half-started excuse, Bell quit talking to himself. Left off horsing his mind about what was really in it. And what was in that night-black tent, yonder.

Two long steps took him to the rear of the silent canvas, another sliding three, to the hanging entrance flaps. A moment then, he hesitated, his mind trying to frame the way he would say it to her, his wide lips moving soundlessly in their awkward, uncertain rehearsal.

Somehow the words would not rise above the flood of fatigue now bearing him under in earnest, would not surface themselves against the warm crest of the night air bearing her remembered fragrance from within the tent. Then, even as he knew he couldn't do it, her voice was breaking softly through the darkness.

"Who is it? Who's there, please? Just a moment—"

Followed then the soft quick movement within, succeeded by the appearance of the parted flaps of the faintness of a white face. But the sounds went unheard, and the face unseen. Outside the tent there was nothing but dust and dark, and the muffled snuffling of the wakeful cavalry mounts.

Sergeant Bell had long since joined the crowding blackness of the night which, moving noiselessly in on the heels of his departure, now gave the only answer to Calla's husky query.

"Emm? Oh, Emm, is it you?"

* * *

Locating H Company's bed section, Bell's narrowed eyes made out the back-humped smudge that was his short-picketed Nez Perce roan. At the little mount's slat-ribbed side, he felt along the stirrup leathers for the treasured rawhide thong. Seconds later the familiar silhouette of the battered canteen was topping the pony's hip-shot rump, and the first of the corn of old Kentucky in twenty-four hours was running the corroded gamut of Bell's gullet.

After a long peg, the big man stood for a moment by the drooping pony's side, letting the whiskey's fire burn into his bloodstream. As always with the first, deep-drinking pull, he felt the welcome release of the body tensions. The momentary, magical lightening of the backpack of fatigue. The swift, clean-steel sharpening of the senses.

Then suddenly, without apparent cause, he found himself listening. At first there was nothing. Only the grave-quiet of the waiting night. And the vapored hush of the rising lake mists. Damn! A man hated to let himself get to jumping like that. Thinking he'd heard something where there was nothing to hear. Feeling his belly pinching in dry and tight, when it was only just opening up to the swell of the bourbon. He'd not heard a damn thing, really. Not a horse snuffle. Not a buckle clink. Nothing.

And yet. . . .

In the unnatural stillness Bell became all at once shiveringly aware of a sound he'd never heard before. A crawling, shadowy sound without substance or definition. A slow-pulsing, evil sound. Lisping, sibilant, loathsome.

The gaunt sergeant wasn't listening with whiskey ears now as he tensed to the rolling, formless hush of the eerie disturbance. As he crouched, head-cocked, the nameless sound rose suddenly in pitch to fill a momentary vacuum in the passing of the night wind.

It was then he had it. Had it in a flash and beyond all question.

There were 152 frightened men out there in that dark. Closer to him than he could toss a rock underhanded. Half asleep and half awake, nodding, drowsing, starting up, settling back. Staring-eyed and silent-lidded, but not moving and not talking and not making a sound nor a shadow of a sound.

Bell was listening to *fear.* . . .

The motionless figure by the little Nez Perce pony straightened slowly, hesitated, lifted the canteen once again. For a space of three, even breaths, the rusted container remained uptilted, then the long and grateful sigh saluting its lowering echoed lingeringly.

With religious care the big noncom returned the canteen to its saddlehorn lacings. With equal deliberation he stepped away from the jug-headed pony to cock a professional eye eastward at the low set of the stars over the ragged spine of the Bitter Roots.

It was almost 2:00 a.m., Monday, May 17th.

"Damn the whole lousy mess to hell," grunted First Sergeant Emmett D. Bell, reposing his gaunt length on the ground. "We're all dead and we might as well lie down and admit it."

5

◆

Tohotonimme Creek

The column was formed moving toward the Palouse by 4:10 a.m. On Timothy's advice a route was taken diagonally through the hills and bearing across blind country in a crowline for the river crossing, this to avoid the probability of Kamiakin having ambushed their previous day's line of march up the main trail of the Lapwai.

Bell concurred in detail with the chief's suggestion, his own respectable experience with the northwestern red man's military mind having shown him that more than any other horseback, Plains Indian, the thinking of the Washington Territory hostile ran to *Le'gtsen,* The Box Trap.

Nevertheless, the choice of routes was a frying-pan-and-fire one. Where the chance of an ambush along the Lapwai was almost a tactical certainty, there, at least, within and along the widely cleared, dirt-bare course of its broad road, troops could be strongly formed and expertly maneuvered. In the frowning country ahead of them, now, existed no track or path worthy of the name.

Nonetheless, despite lack of a recognizable trail, the gamble was made and taken. Of the options open to the Colville column, it was the least of the devil's dirty choices. 4:30 a.m. and the first hint of coming gray to the east found the straggling troops a bare mile from their lakeside starting point and already bogging down in the highland swamp of choking brush, crowding timber and countless gully-cuts which blocked and trapped the cross-country route.

Since this issue, militarily, had been definitely joined the previous night, there remained little use for scouting the present day's advance. Bell, accordingly, was enjoying a comparatively rare experience, riding his regular place in line with Lieutenant Craig at the head of H Company. Jogging the sergeant's right flank, came his omnipresent red shadows, Jason and Timothy. The rest of the marching order, too, was straight out of the regular field-command handbook, having been determined by Stedloe and his staff in final disregard of the pleadings of Bell and his Nez Perces for a closer grouping.

Looking back along the column's tenuous, broken length, the bearded noncom groaned audibly. Timothy, his quick glance tracing Bell's, spoke guardedly, keeping his words too low for Craig's ears.

"It's about time for you to spit again, Ametsun. That's a bad way to march back there."

Bell grinned, shifted his cud of longleaf, prepared to comply with the Indian's straight-faced suggestion. As long as he'd known this red rascal he hadn't been able to figure him for certain sure. Either he was what he appeared to be, stick-straight and dull-serious, or the deadest-pan Indian cynic in the business. In either event, he seldom missed his point. And he hadn't missed it now.

Bell spat and spat hard.

"Plumb bad, Tamason. Look it over and get a prayer-book express off to old *Choosuklee!*"

The Indian nodded, saying nothing, both men twisting anew in their saddles to regard the object of their dissatisfaction. Bell's cloud-gray eyes lowered threateningly as they traveled the long line.

His own H Company Dragoons under Lieutenant Davis Craig held the advance as usual. Then came Captain Oliver

Baylor and his C Company Dragoons. Following these came the twenty-five men of Captain Harry Winston's Company E, Ninth Infantry, with the two mountain howitzers. Next the pack and ammunition train and finally, Lieutenant Wilcey Gaxton's E Company Dragoons.

And then came the part to shift your cud and spit about. The dragoon companies were carefully holding an ordered separation of over a *thousand* yards!

Blessing Stedloe's faultless West Point form with another acid benediction of burley, Bell swung back around in his saddle, his humorless grin going to Timothy.

"You in touch with your Lord yet, brother?"

"My hand is always in his." The Nez Perce chief's response walked the little silence in quiet dignity. Bell's quick nod checked its sober course.

"Well, squeeze it then," counseled the gaunt sergeant. "There's room enough between those companies to hold a county fair, with a half-mile horse race on the side!"

As soon as full daylight allowed, about forty-five minutes from Timothy's lake, the harassed column was aware that its sneak departure had been a little too noisy. The distant hills lining both sides of the march were covered with thin stringers of moving Indian horsemen, and shortly after these were sighted Sergeant Williamson rode up from Gaxton's rearguard company to report a heavy hostile concentration off both flanks of the column's rear.

Stedloe, taking Bell and the Nez Perces, at once rode back to check the giant Kentuckian's report. Arrived at the rear, neither Bell nor Timothy could make sense of what they saw.

Bull Williamson's hostile concentration was heavy enough, all right, but it was acting as queer as a Palouse goose. Not a rifle shot nor a war cry disturbed its rapidly growing ranks. The excitement among the hostiles was evident. But it was almost certainly not of the grade of full *Staq*. It was far more as though Kamiakin had gathered his brightly clad hundreds to wave and bid the pony-soldiers an extravagant and demonstrative farewell.

"I give up, Colonel. I've never seen the likes of it. Maybe Timothy can make something of it."

The column commander's questioning gaze joined Bell's with the latter's statement, both men waiting for Timothy to speak. The Nez Perce shrugged.

"I can only say this—something has happened. The Indian is not like you. He makes a plan and then if something unthought of occurs, he is defeated. He has to stop and make a new plan. They're defeated over there, right now. They'll have to get a new plan. *Choosuklee* has given us a little more time."

"We can use it," said Stedloe, breaking out one of his rare, stiff little smiles.

"Heads up!" growled Bell suddenly. "Yonder comes your 'something,' Tamason. And by the flap of that black crepe hassock it looks like Sergeant Bell owes your Lord another apology!"

"God in Heaven!" breathed Stedloe fervently. "It's Father Joset!"

"*Choosuklee's* right-hand man," added Bell acidly. "That is, if Timothy will settle for Marc Whitman being his left-hand one."

"Amen!" echoed the Nez Perce. "The Black Robe is on the right today."

The Coeur d'Alene mission priest slid his slobbered pony into the rear of Gaxton's company to come down off the wind-broken little beast in a legover stepdown that would have done credit to the slickest Indian rider in the Northwest Federation. In the following delivery of information the Jesuit padre exhibited a brevity and modesty that added up to everything of solid honor and Indian-sense Bell had heard of the man.

"By the Lord, Joset." Stedloe opened the interchange with commendable calm and a thoroughly Baptist ignoring of the priest's religious title. "We're glad to see you, sir."

"*Vraiment!*" smiled the famed Jesuit. "And I, you!" Holding his odd little grin, the Catholic missionary let it grow a bit as he added quickly, "Alive, that is!"

Hearing him say it, and noting the puckish smile which went with it. Bell knew, for all the black frock and backwards collar, that he was looking at a frontiersman.

Pierre Joset, if you measured in inches from the ground

up, was a little man. By any other rule he was something else again.

His head was big, jut-jawed, eagle-beaked—wide across the broad bones of it, narrow as a ferret's where the tiny, sun-slitted blue eyes bored out at you from either side of the craggy nose. His mouth was as wide as Bell's but unlike that of the grim sergeant seemed set in a perpetual, quizzical grin. He carried his big cranium continually thrust forward on a neck as long and heavy as a chunk of stovewood. The narrow slope of the shoulders fell loosely away into a pair of arms that brushed his kneecaps. His hands and feet were literally enormous. The whole effect of the man, shrouded in the calf-length, ludicrously oversized cloak of his calling, was that of a great domed, squatly powerful bird of prey.

Father Pierre Joset was certainly the toughest-looking dove of peace Bell had ever cast his eye upon.

And he talked as tough as he looked.

As his and Stedloe's hands fell apart, the Jesuit put it to him without benefit of any further amenities. "Colonel, I've ridden all night to ask you one question. What, in the name of our Lord Jesus, are you doing up here in this Palouse wilderness?"

The column commander, taken aback by the priest's bluntness, stammered through a halting résumé of his by now well learned litany of excuses. Halfway into the limping peroration his official dignity caught up with his faltering tongue and he broke his explanation, sharp-off, to demand one of his gimlet-eyed guest. "Uh, by the way, Joset. You've asked me what *I'm* doing up here. I might ask the same of you!"

"Allons donc," replied the little Jesuit, shrinking his smile and palming his huge hands with the agreement. "Indeed you might, Colonel. Though it's to be hoped I have a better story than yours."

"I'd like to be the judge of that, sir!" Stedloe let the injured condition of his ego show in the lameness of the rejoinder. "May I hear it, now? And be pleased to keep it brief, sir. I don't like my column being held up here in the open."

In the slight pause that covered the Coeur d'Alene missionary's understanding nod, Bell edged his blue pony even with Stedloe's mount, that he might not miss a syllable of the priest's answer. It was plain to him, from his knowledge of the entire federation's half-fearful half-loving regard for the little Jesuit, that Father Joset's arrival among the hostiles was all that was holding Kamiakin's horde off the exposed column. The details of that arrival were being crisply put down even as Bell brought his pony forward.

"At three a.m. yesterday," the priest began, "my Coeur d'Alenes brought to me one of my old friends, Vincent. Vincent, an old man like myself, had ridden twelve hours on two horses to tell me of *Kenuokin's* warcamp over there on the Ingosommen."

As the priest paused, Bell nodded to himself at the use of Kamiakin's Chinook name. A little thing like that was all a man needed to tell him the little Jesuit not only knew Indians, but "thought" them as well.

"I rode back with Vincent," Father Joset continued, "to see what I might do to stave off the threatened attack on your forces. I now have to tell you, Colonel Stedloe, that my night-long efforts among them have been unsuccessful."

Bell quickly thought the gnomelike missionary might also have told Stedloe what an undertaking a ninety-mile night-ride was for a sixty-year-old white man. And what mammoth guts it took for a single white, black robe or no, to walk into the middle of Kamiakin's *Staq* Dance. Or to contemplate, as was his patent intention in this case, riding back into the milling Palouse mob, once he had come safely away from it. But the sergeant's blunt thoughts remained unimplemented in the little priest's following words.

"And so, Colonel, all I can do is warn you an attack on your force is imminently certain. *J'en suis fâché.* I am sorry for it, but there it is."

In the swiftly succeeding course of conversation, since it was his first meeting with Stedloe, the bony-faced Jesuit earnestly inquired if the officer had had the report that he, Joset, was arming the hostiles. Upon Stedloe's admission of the fact that he had, the priest indignantly denied the allegation, adding that from his own information he was certain the rumor of a Nez Perce plot to involve the white troops with the tribes of

Kamiakin's Yakima Federation, was true. "In this very regard," he concluded soberly, "I started early last month to ride to Wallowa and personally warn you. At the last minute, however, my own Coeur d'Alenes reported a Nez Perce plot to ambush my party, using that as their excuse to get this tribal war going. Under the circumstances I did what I could. You received my various letters, no?"

"Yes Father, I did." Stedloe's first use of Joset's title perked Bell's ears. Good. The little priest's obvious honesty and valor were beginning to soak into the colonel's issue-thick hide. "And I want to express my gratitude for them, and for this amazing ride you've just made in our behalf. But frankly, sir, I cannot believe these Indians mean to attack openly. They've been demonstrating for twenty-four hours now without closing the issue."

"Well, Colonel, they mean to close it now."

"Is there no way we can stop them, man?" Stedloe's deadly serious mien caught Father Joset's eye as quickly as it did Bell's. "I shall do absolutely anything within my powers to placate them. We're not up here to fight, Father. I've tried to convince them of that. Is there nothing further I can do?"

"There's one outside chance"—the priest nodded thoughtfully, his words weighing the sudden change in the army man's attitude—"providing you'll take it."

"Well for God's sake what is it, man?"

"Another parley." The priest punched the emphasis with the balled fist of one huge hand into the open flat of the other. "Right here and now. Halted where you are."

Glancing along the waiting line of the halted column, Bell grimaced bitterly. There wasn't a snowball's chance in hell's back furnace of holding the command up where they were. Stopped not over five minutes, the crazed pack mules were already beginning to break line, the excited, nerve-shot dragoon horses being of little or no use in curbing them. The sergeant's thoughts were quickly repeated in Stedloe's unhappy refusal.

"By the Lord, I'm sorry, sir. But you can see for yourself it will be impossible for me to hold these pack animals. My column has got to move and move at once."

Father Joset, the steadiest man Bell had ever watched,

nodded abruptly. "It can still be arranged, Colonel Stedloe. I might even suggest it *has* to be. There's yet a chance. Many of the older, less inflamed chiefs seem to feel you broke off yesterday's talk with undue roughness. I believe I can get them to come over and talk with you, *in motion.*"

"If they'll talk with the column moving, I'm entirely agreeable. But one way or another, sir"—Stedloe's military apprehension, re-keyed by a sudden increase of activity among the waiting hillside hundreds of Kamiakin's faithful, was taking abrupt precedence over his newly found respect for the homely Jesuit—"the column is moving. And right now, sir!"

Father Joset was legging-up on his walleyed Coeur d'Alene cayuse before the column commander's agreement was well out from behind his drooping mustaches. And his ragged pony was racing for the hostile lines in the same breath Stedloe took to bellow at Bell to get to the column's head with the order to move on, double time!

As the troops moved up the narrow-floored valley, the hostile van paced them along the flanks of the shouldering hills, a vastly disturbing quiet replacing the harsh whooping and shouting of their earlier appearance.

At the end of a day-long half-hour, Bell's roving glance picked up the distant figure of three riders detaching themselves from the screening hill cover. There was no mistaking the squat, Ichabod Crane horsemanship of the leading rider and Bell at once drifted his roan back along the laboring column. Behind him floated his obedient scout force, Timothy and Jason.

The sergeant was in time to see Father Joset ride up to Stedloe, and to identify one of the two lone chiefs accompanying him as the Coeur d'Alene, Victor. The other, Timothy noddingly informed him, was the priest's courier, Vincent.

The Jesuit was clearly upset at his failure to find more than the two old Coeur d'Alenes willing to ride back with him. He admitted glumly that the conference was thus robbed of much of its value, adding that such as they were, however, their hopes would now have to be pinned to the two elder chiefs.

With the dignified Coeur d'Alene headmen nodding in sober understanding of his careful address, Stedloe patiently repeated the promises of the previous talks, adding the further, very strong guarantee, that the whole idea of the Colville council would be dropped until such a time as the Indians themselves were convinced of its benefits. At this moment and for the first time in the entire series of cloudy parleys, Bell felt a last, half-chance truce hanging in the delicate balance of the Coeur d'Alene's agreeing gestures.

He had no sooner responded to this fleeting hope when even its slight string was brutally snapped.

It was one of those weird, unreasonable byplays which no one not deeply familiar with the real thinness of the mission veneer smeared over the basic uncertainty of the Indian character by the various Christian proselyters on the Washington frontier, could understand. And even Bell, an Indian veneer-peeler of five years' good standing, got hit by the flying chips of frontier varnish now exploding off the unpredictable Jason.

The Nez Perce subchief shoved his pony forward the moment Vincent's handsome old face broke in a genuine smile of understanding toward the perspiring Stedloe. The next instant, before the dumbfounded whites could intervene, the army scout had laid his heavy, four-foot quirt squarely across the Coeur d'Alene's mouth. The force of the unwarned blow nearly unhorsed the visiting chief but Bell, spurring forward, caught him and held him on his sidling pony. As he did, Jason's angry accusation was snarling its way into the stricken Indian's bleeding face.

"You talk with a forked tongue! I've struck you, now, proud man! Why don't you fire, then?"

Victor, moving his pony forward to come between the enraged Nez Perce and his fellow Coeur d'Alene, found himself included in the shouted charges. "And you, too, you Pend d'Oreille dog! I saw you lift your rifle just now to fire on the oak-leaf chief!"

By this time, Bell and Timothy had the raging Jason's pony pinned between their shouldering mounts and Stedloe was addressing his white-faced apologies to the visitors. But where for once the colonel moved with commendable speed, he still ran a bad second to Father Joset. While Stedloe was searching for words, the priest was finding them. Softly and furiously and bitterly. With no hint of the cloth in them.

And in heathen, bastard Chinook!

"L!L k!amonak! Here are a hundred bitternesses, my children. Forgive them, forgive them. *Q!atxal!* They are full of badness. Pray for them. These are mean men, but you are proud. Show them your pride. Show them you can still take the word of peace back to your brothers!"

Bell, fascinated by the Jesuit's oratory, watched the clouding faces of the Coeur d'Alenes lift under its spell. Saw them make the peace sign to the priest, then the respect sign to the breath-held Stedloe. *Wuska!* They would return now with the soldier chief's final peace word to Kamiakin.

But where the hearts of the two old Coeur d'Alenes were good, they were no better than the eyes of the watching hostile hundreds. The Palouses had seen the Nez Perce scout attack their emissary, translated the action literally. Even as Vincent and Victor were touching their foreheads to Stedloe, a young Coeur d'Alene warrior, no more than a boy really, broke from the waiting hostile ranks and whipped his pony forward. His black eyes snapping, the youth hauled his mount to a stiff-legged halt, shouting his warning to his kinsman, Vincent.

"Depart, Uncle! Come away, now! The Palouses are all through waiting. Kamiakin has said for them to fire!"

With his brave word delivered, the boy angled his pony away from the little group in a grass-top gallop. The flying dirt-clips thrown up by the wiry mount's getaway were still in the air when, without warning, Father Joset spun his own cayuse toward the hostiles.

"Joset! Damn it, man! Where are you going? Come back, man! Come back!"

Stedloe's alarmed demand was answered only by an unintelligible shout and a wild wave of one of the long arms. What it was the priest called back was lost to thought in the colonel's excitement over his patent direction—straight toward the howling mass of Kamiakin's hostiles!

"Good Lord, Bell! You don't suppose he's throwing in with the Palouses? Dashing off like that the minute the boy spoke—"

"Don't be a fool." The sergeant's flat recommendation was unsirred and uncoloneled. "Even you know better than that."

"Bell!"

"Skip it, Colonel. There goes the bravest little man you'll ever see. Crossed or uncrossed. Take a good look at what you can see of him. He's heading for heaven as sure as he's spent his life keeping the rest of us out of hell."

Any attention Stedloe may have given Bell's rank outburst of insubordination was immediately claimed by the delayed departures of Victor and Vincent. With the two chiefs turning their ponies to follow Father Joset and the Coeur d'Alene boy, Victor was handsigning a last farewell to the Colville column's commander, his deep voice rolling sonorously over the rising bedlam of war howls and vile invective from the hillside Palouses.

"We are sorry, my brother. But we don't want to die here in the middle, and it is too late, now."

"It's never too late to die, brother!" Bell held his soft curse underbreath as he watched the dust of the departing ponies. "And right here is where I and a hundred and fifty other enlisted heroes drop dead to prove it!"

The first, long-range shots from Kamiakin's hostiles were splattering the rocks around Gaxton's rear company before the dust clouds of Vincent's and Victor's ponies were halfway back to the Indians' hillside lines.

With typical methodicalness, Colonel Stedloe ignored the opening fire to pull his fat, brass stemwinder from inside his campaign jacket. Twelve hundred hostiles or no, it was of primary importance that the hour of the onset of the Battle of Tohotonimme Creek be duly noted for future and precise inclusion in his field report to headquarters. Of course Bell might be wrong about what he'd call the battle, though the name of the little creek they were on would serve as well as anything, but of one thing he was sure. Stedloe would get it started on time.

"Eight-three, Sergeant." The watch was being carefully restored to its pocket. "Please ride up the column to your company and tell Lieutenant Craig to resume march and hold all fire. Pass that order to Baylor and Winston on your way up. I'll get to Gaxton. Remember, Bell. Not a shot in return of this fire until the order is changed."

"Yes, sir." Bell wheeled his little roan. "Anything else, sir?"

"No. I'll be up directly. I want to watch this a bit back here."

Saluting, Bell sent his mount galloping up the left flank of the slowing column, shouting Stedloe's orders to Captains Baylor and Winston. "Colonel Stedloe's orders, sir. Resume full march. Hold all fire."

The two captains flicked their yellow gauntlets in understanding, relaying the shouted command in quick turn to their sergeants, Demoix and Harrigan. Looking back, Bell could see the unflustered noncoms wheeling down the flanks of their companies, could hear their belligerent yells bouncing back and forth across the narrow gully-track of the column's present course. "Close up! Close up! Column speed! Hold your horses down! Hold your fire! Repeat. Hold your fire!"

Bell nodded to himself. If a man had 152 Harrigans and Demoixs, and could turn the bunch of them over to Lieutenant Craig, he could damn well turn around and kick hell out of Kamiakin right here and now. As it was, with just the two of them, even with Sergeant Bell and Bull Williamson thrown in, it wasn't quite enough. Especially when you considered you were still having your orders issued by Stedloe, and executed by Baylor and Gaxton.

No, by God. The way the lousy wind stood this Monday morning of May 17th, it sure wasn't Palouse pants that were about to get the hell booted out of them. . . .

By 8:30, the hostile fire had built to a continuous snarl, the entire weight of it directed into Wilcey Gaxton's rear company. Glancing back from the occasional rises in the flat of the gully's floor, Bell could see the Indians crazy-galloping their ponies back and forth from hillside to hillside across the lieutenant's rear, their range of three and four hundred yards still too long to result in anything save accidental casualties. The ugly grimace this maneuver brought to the sergeant's bearded face was translated with hard words to Lieutenant Craig at his side.

"The colonel's making a hell of a mistake holding his fire,

Lieutenant. Those red devils will think we're bluffed clean down to our bootsocks. In five minutes they'll be seeping up our flanks and in ten they'll have us headed."

"I'm right with you, Sergeant." The youthful officer receipted the grimace, along with the sentiment. "And I don't like the looks of that big hill ahead. If they pass up and get on that, we're trapped. We can't go anyplace but right under it."

"Yeah." Bell's growling retort dropped all tone of rank. "And if they try it, guess who'll get the fun of running them for it!"

"Company H, for sure," nodded Craig.

"Company H for Hell," grinned the big sergeant. "Take a look back there, Lieutenant. Yonder they come."

As Bell spoke, the main force of Indians to the column's rear closed up and launched a full-scale charge into Gaxton's company. At the same time, two lesser forces split off and came bombarding up the flanks of the column. The distinctive, hollow booming of the issue muskets began immediately, letting the forward elements know Stedloe had released Gaxton's company to fire. Seconds later, Bell could make out the colonel's thin figure galloping up from the rear.

Stedloe brought the news that Gaxton had had his horse shot from under him and taken a rifle ball through the arm. He was now remounted and his company in good order, though taking additional casualties by the minute. Baylor's and Winston's troops had as yet taken no casualties but the Indians were massing on their companies. Accordingly, orders had been given for C and F Companies to commence short countercharges out of the column's line-of-march to keep the foe off balance, and to attempt to prevent the hostiles from gaining any elevation along the route—their now obvious intent and purpose.

Further orders had been issued to close up the company gaps, for there still remained several hundred yards between each of the units. It was to be hoped that Baylor's and Winston's side charges would keep the hostiles from heading the column in any force. The no-fire order had been altered to fire-permitted only on the counter charging necessary to clear the Indians from the column's flanks.

Even as the relay of the order, and the sorry hope therein contained, was released from the colonel's compressed lips, Bell knew both were futile. In the next two, brutal miles through the trackless brush, his knowledge was bloodily borne out.

Encouraged by the light fire from the troops, the hostiles were constantly charging, using their favored, prairie-wolf tactics—whirling in to pointblank range to draw a counter charge, fleeing before the charge until they had pulled it way out of line, then turning on it with savage fury to drive it back in.

The engagement was now general along the entire line, with Captain Baylor's and Lieutenant Gaxton's companies having sustained five murderous charges, and with Captain Winston's group of mounted infantry, howitzers and pack string included, beginning rapidly to lose all semblance of an ordered command.

During all this wild time, Bell had had occasional glimpses of Calla in a borrowed corporal's uniform. She had hastily donned it that morning at Timothy's suggestion that it would serve to give her anonymity among the crowded troops. Now she was being moved up as the pressure of the attacks advanced, from Gaxton's to Winston's to Baylor's company in swift succession. In a brief lull as Stedloe and Craig studied a larger force gathering off the left flank, Bell looked anxiously around for the southern girl.

Sharp as his hurried glance was, it swept over Calla twice before flicking back to spot her on the third pass. Well, by God, that was good, anyway. Bouncing along back there as the "ninth man" in H Company's third squad, she was about as safe as she could be in this insane hour and place. If he could miss her at fifty yards, it was a fair bet the hostiles could do likewise at two hundred.

At that moment, she caught his eye on her and waved, following the wave with a mock salute and a summer-lightning flash of a smile that would have lifted the powder smoke of any man's Indian battle. But before Bell could wave back, her horse was rearing in terror at the sudden lash of Indian lead which announced the attack from the new force off H Company's left, and in the hot work of repulsing the hostile slash, he lost sight of her.

That he ever saw her again was more a tribute to the guts and gallantry of Lieutenant Davis Craig than to any military right Company H had to survive the following Palouse maneuver: a maneuver which, ironically enough, the young lieutenant had himself predicted an hour and a half before.

In seconds, now, it became apparent the charge of the left-flank group of Palouses had been a feint, for no sooner had it broken than a much larger group of hostiles had bucketed out of the hills to the right, wheeled sharply south and raced for the high hill at the column's head which Craig had earlier marked for Bell.

Stedloe, measuring full up to the sergeant's unaltered estimation of his basic coolness, turned quietly to Craig.

"Lieutenant, you will go forward with H Company and beat those Indians to that hill." Then, as Craig wheeled to implement the order, he added calmly. "And Lieutenant—"

"Yes, sir?" Young Craig held his excited mount with difficulty.

"If you don't beat them *to* it, beat them *off* of it."

Bell, picking up the order from Craig, threw it down the ranks as he slammed his spurs into the roan and drove him after the jumping flag of the lieutenant's mare. His eyes swept the right-hand hills as he went. And opened wide with the tail end of that sweep!

Aii-eee, brother! Trust Kamiakin not to send a boy on a buck's errand.

That six-foot brave in the lead of the racing hostile warriors, cartwheel warbonnet, three-point blanket and all, was nobody but *Kenuokin* himself!

The headlong dash for the hill, though closer than a straight-razor shave, was won by the dragoons—a victory which proved as short-lived as Gaxton's first horse. Kamiakin, abandoning the race the moment it was apparent he'd lost it, swept on around the base of the hill and disappeared beyond its far side. Topping the elevation a few moments later, Bell cursed at length and wickedly.

No wonder the red son hadn't held up to bicker about the hill *they* were on!

Facing them, now, for the first time revealed by their new

elevation, stood a second and higher hill, its brushy crest not over 150 yards from their own, uncovered position.

And the van of Kamiakin's whooping henchmen were already piling off their scrambling ponies to dive into the rocks and scrub of its commanding top.

Craig, realizing he must take this new position without delay, left Bell and one squad to hold the present ridge and with the remaining three squads deployed in open skirmish line, at once went after Kamiakin. The assault, probably due to its quickness, was successful.

With lethal reservations.

The hostiles, no longer fearful of the dragoon charges, fell back only from the hill's apex, setting up their new lines just below and completely ringing Craig's hilltop troops. Bell, watching helplessly from his own hill, shifted his jaw-clamped cud of burley to spit viciously. Damn that Kamiakin, anyway. There was one cute redskin for you. He had the lieutenant and his men as flat-pinned as so many blue-and-gold butterflies in that granite and scrub-brush exhibition case, over there. And the pure hell of it was a man could only sit and curse about it.

With H Company split and isolated, the savages turned the full fury of their attentions on the remainder of the column. Winston, to whose company Stedloe had personally escorted Calla when Craig went forward, was the nearest to the young lieutenant's beleaguered troops—about eight hundred yards north and still trapped on the gully's floor. The chain of command being thus completely unlinked, the fighting became broken and independent. Now the inevitable, deadly, end result, was clear to all concerned. If the several sections of the command could not be speedily reunited the Battle of Tohotonimme Creek would go into the history books as lost on May 17, 1858.

Into this next-to-last extremity of the Colville column, as indeed he had since the first fateful camp at the main Snake Crossing, now stepped the reed-slender, mahogany-dark figure of the Red Wolf Nez Perce, Timothy.

Shortly after eleven o'clock, the first slight break in the deadly situation occurred, setting the stage for Timothy's remarkable ride. Captain Winston and Colonel Stedloe succeeded at that time in fighting their way with the howitzers and packs to Craig's hilltop position.

The howitzers were at once stripped and brought into action.

Their effect, contrary to Bell's earlier cynicism and supporting the colonel's laughed-at-pride in them, was little short of salvational. While even Stedloe would have admitted, perhaps, that not a solitary Indian was scratched by the noisy bursts, the fear and confusion temporarily occasioned by the cannon among the packed ranks of Kamiakin's hostiles was obvious and instant.

It remained for the slow-spoken Winston to see the true nature of the diversion.

"Colonel, those devils breaking and running like that mustn't fool us. Both Kamiakin and that rascal Malkapsi were present at Wallowa last summer when you held your demonstration."

At the mention of his "demonstration" the colonel's face reddened, and with ample cause. The previous summer he had called every tribe in western Washington Territory into the fort to deliver them an object lesson on the deadliness of the "big guns which spoke twice." The marksmanship of the fort gunners not being up to the colonel's bragging promise, not one shell had fallen on the targets. The red men's main profits from the fiasco had been a good laugh, the knowledge that the big guns were a bluff, and the thieving of the errant cannon balls from the target area for the later manufacture of their own rifle slugs.

For the moment, however, Stedloe's embarrassment was being quickly covered by Captain Winston's concluding warning. "Accordingly, sir, I'm afraid they'll rally their people quickly enough, once the first fright's worn away."

"Yes, sir." Craig's earnest voice joined his brother officer's. "Harry's right, Colonel. The reservation bucks in that bunch will have them back on us in ten minutes. It's the 'wild Indians' that've broken. I don't mean to sell your cannon short, sir, but we're up against it."

While this conversation was going forward among the officers atop Craig's hill, Bell, who had brought his squad over from the other hill when the howitzers first opened the way for the maneuver, was lying off to one side of the anxious group, belly-flopped among a jumble of granite boulders. By his side, the ever-present Timothy was letting his slant gaze join the sergeant's in scanning the still-broken ranks of the hostiles below. Suddenly Bell's gray eyes narrowed. Another moment of careful searching and his words were snapping at the Nez Perce chief.

"Tamason, do you see what I see, down there?"

"Aye. The field is almost clear between us and Captain Baylor. And Lieutenant Gaxton has fought nearly up to the captain. It's too bad they can't see it from down where they are. Is that what you mean, Ametsun?"

"You're damn right that's what I mean. Go get Stedloe, brother. And jump it!"

Seconds later the Colonel, along with Winston and Lieutenant Craig, had joined Bell in his rocky lookout. The big sergeant's rapped-out greeting at once widened the eyes of all three.

"Look down there, sir! Your howitzers have opened them up clean down to Captain Baylor's boys. And Wilse is near up to the captain!"

"We were just discussing it, Bell." Stedloe's voice was held down with its customary calm. "But Captain Winston and Lieutenant Craig feel they'll close up again within a few minutes. I'm afraid we haven't any reason for a celebration yet, Sergeant. Perhaps if Baylor could see the opening—"

"That's the devil of it," interrupted Craig. "They can't see a thing for the base of this damn hill we're on."

"That's just what I mean, Lieutenant!" Excitement was as rare in Bell's voice as a blizzard in Biloxi, and young Craig sharpened his attention accordingly. "If they can't see, neither can the Indians that're pinning them down. We've got a thousand yard slot right up this hill, as open as the devil's front door. If the colonel can keep his howitzers blasting another ten minutes, we can get a rider through to Captain Baylor!"

"By God, sir, Bell's right!" Craig was on his feet, blue eyes blazing into Stedloe's puzzled brown ones. "They've got a chance to get up here if we can get word to them there's a way open to do it."

"I'm sorry, gentlemen"—the senior officer's refusal fell softly—"there isn't a man in the command who'd have one chance in a million of getting down this hill alive."

"Not a white man, maybe—" Bell dropped the statement with deliberate harshness, his clouded eyes holding Stedloe's.

"What the devil do you mean, Bell?"

"He means *me*, Colonel Stedloe." The deep bass of the Nez Perce's voice came from behind them, pivoting their combined glances in time to see the scout swinging up on his piebald gelding. "I see the flag down there and I'm going to it."

"Get off that horse, you fool Indian!" Stedloe's angry command trailed the wheeling pony. "That's an order, Timothy. Dammit, Bell! Stop the idiot!"

The colonel's order and entreaty were lost alike in the shower of rotten granite chips churned up by the plunging descent of the Nez Perce's scrambling pony, and in Sergeant Bell's soft-muttered benediction.

"There's nothing in all hell will stop that Indian, Colonel. Nothing short of half a pound of Palouse lead, anyway. God help him, I wish I had his guts."

Stedloe broke his eyes from the lunging slide of Timothy's gelding, turned their earnest brownness with sudden warmth on Bell. With the look, his thin hand found the big sergeant's shoulder. "Yours will do until they issue a better set of intestines, Sergeant," he said softly.

While the anxious eyes of Craig's and Winston's hilltop commands watched helplessly, Timothy completed his suicidal dash to Baylor's company, apparently without a scratch. An instant later the watchers on the hill saw another tiny figure dart across the four hundred yards still separating Baylor's and Gaxton's companies. Even at that distance Bell could make out the rider wasn't Timothy. He knew, nonetheless, from his side-swinging, crazy way of hanging to a horse that it was an Indian, and concluded with a wry grin that Timothy had dispatched Jason to do his bit for the Nez Perce chief's precious "flag."

Following the contacts of the Nez Perce riders with the separated companies, Baylor and Gaxton began to drive at once for the base of Craig's hill, their lines of attack approaching one another diagonally. The Indian pressure on their flanks was unrelenting but Kamiakin saw too late the purpose of the pincers. He was able to rally about two hundred braves and throw them onto the base of the hill just as the two companies, in full dragoon charge, arrived at the same point. Caught between the desperate tongs, the hostiles took their first considerable casualties of the day; a round dozen killed and two score wounded: among the former, disastrously, Jacques, Zachery and old Victor, three of the five "friendlies" among the chiefs of the hostile command.

Baylor and Gaxton, scarcely breaking the momentum of their conjunction, turned their troops up the hill and, assisted by a counter charge down the slope by Lieutenant Craig and H Company, succeeded in reaching the top. With this achievement the several sections of the command were unified for the first time since leaving the lakeside camp seven and a half hours earlier. For the first time, also, a pause was gained to look to the medical needs of the wounded and to check total casualties and issue rations.

The time was 11:25 a.m.

The hurried labors of Assistant Surgeon Randall along with the accompanying casualty survey, revealed unexpected good news: thirteen troopers slightly wounded, four moderately, none seriously, one missing and presumed killed. Listening to Major Randall toll off the damages for Stedloe, Bell's big mouth twisted ironically at the use of the euphemism, "presumed killed." Presumed, indeed! If one of the boys were missing, Bell could tell them they needn't waste report paper tacking on any "presumed" to that "killed." If a man got knocked off his horse and left behind, he was done for. Even if he lit with no more than a bruise and a bullet scratch. If he found his feet faster than a dropped cat, he'd still have to hurry to find time to think he was all right.

After that, and probably before it, his skull would be laid open like a sun-split melon, with his hairpiece bleeding down some Palouses' buck-skins before his bare head felt the breeze.

Nevertheless, Surgeon Randall's encouraging report provided a momentary lift—just momentary enough for Supply Quartermaster, Lieutenant Fanning, to get up to Stedloe with his cheering news: the last of the water had just been issued to the wounded.

On top of this, Captain Winston turned in his figures on the pack string: twenty-four animals and their packs lost, half of the remaining forty head suffering bullet and arrow wounds, and near out of service.

Disturbing as were each of the successive intelligences, all facts waited silently before Fanning's fateful revelation. Without water the command was as dead as though its scalps were already cut and dried.

It was quickly brought out that the only hope in this dire direction must be placed on Timothy's information that the main Ingosommen, of which the earlier Tohotonimme Creek had been a tributary, lay only three miles to the south and west in its looping course down from Kamiakin's warcamp to the north. With utterly no alternative, Stedloe ordered his command regrouped and the advance toward the Ingosommen begun.

The start down the far flank of the hill was made at 11:55, Baylor and Gaxton holding the flanks as before, Stedloe leading with Craig's H Company, Winston with the precious packs and howitzers in between. Bell had just time to note, before taking H Company over the lip of the decline to begin the advance, that included in Winston's section was a floppily bundled bit of Lynchburg baggage he'd had no chance to check during the layover on Craig's hill—the half-forgotten, white-faced figure of "Corporal" Calla Lee Rainsford.

But time to note was all he had.

Immediately with the lining out of the descent, the course of the past morning's struggle assumed, by comparison, the harmlessness of a Sunday School picnic. Where Bell thought he and his comrades had been bucking the heat of hell's front yard in the earlier advance, he was now made to realize they'd hardly been up to the devil's mailbox.

With Kamiakin and Malkapsi screaming them on and with the holding counsel of the old Coeur d'Alene chiefs dead and gone, the hostiles swarmed in on the white soldiers like bottle flies at a bull-gutting.

At five minutes of twelve, E Company was sliced clean away from the rear of the column and minutes later Lieutenant Wilcey Gaxton was vomiting his life out with three Palouse slugholes gaping where his beltbuckle should have been.

Inflamed by the death of a "Soldier Chief," the hostiles tore into the leaderless company.

After eight hours of absorbing the main enemy pressure, Company E broke wide open. The bulk of its men succeeded in reaching Winston's section but as an organized command, E Company Dragoons was off the books. And more, in meeting the wild charge which had driven its survivors into his rear, Winston lost twenty-five of his remaining forty pack animals.

Captain Baylor's troop, which had been sheared off by the same onslaught which broke E Company, was now in equally desperate straits in trying to regain the main column as an integral unit. As had been Wilcey Gaxton before him, Captain Oliver Baylor, for all his rash temper and dramatic flare, was a fighting officer of the first water. He proved it now by taking his company straight through no less than five hundred enraged hostiles to once again make contact with Winston's forces.

And he proved it, too, by taking a .50-caliber, smooth-bore ball through the base of his throat sixty seconds before his inspired riding had brought his men through.

The column was now dead-halted in open, undefendable terrain, still two and a half miles from water. One company was broken and two leaderless. Lieutenant Wilcey Gaxton was dead, Captain Oliver Baylor, dying. At least thirty-five troopers were wounded, several mortally beyond doubt. The packs and ninety percent of the rations were strewn over the crimsoned granite talus of Craig's abandoned hillside and the ammunition count was down to six rounds a man.

It was time for Sergeant Bell to spit again.

6

◆

Stedloe Butte

With the perverse military logic which had saved many a white command before them, the hostiles, their disorganized foe surrounded, waterless, nearly out of ammunition and literally shot to pieces, now broke off the engagement and pulled away from Stedloe's bleeding column.

Watching them go, Bell was as nonplussed as the greenest dogface in the company, but Timothy, his lean form as usual shadowing that of the big sergeant, had his customary grasp of the glass-simple Indian mind wrapped firmly around the peculiar antics of his fellow red men.

"It's the packs, Ametsun," he shrugged eloquently. "Pretty soon you'll see them, now. Fightin among themselves back there on that hillside."

Even as the Nez Perce spoke, Bell could see the first of the racing red warriors putting their lathered mounts up the broad incline down which the white column had just fought its incarnadined way, and along the grassy slopes of which were scattered the bulk of Captain Winston's cut-off pack animals with their precious loads of equipment and supply.

149

And in Bell's mind the thought was forming just as Timothy was putting his soft words to it.

"If the colonel will move quickly now, we may be able to reach that last big hill, there." Timothy gave a slight shoulder hunch ahead of the low-voiced conclusion. "And up there we can at least prepare to die like men."

Almost before the echo of the Nez Perce's final phrase was lost among the groans of the wounded and the ceaseless neighings of the terrified cavalry mounts, Bell was saluting Stedloe with the terse hope of the Indian scout's discovery.

"Begging your pardon, Colonel, but Timothy says if we hurry we might just make it up that butte, yonder, while the Palouses are scrapping over our packs. You see them clotting up on that hill we just left? That's why they pulled off of us. To divvy up Captain Winston's supplies. We've got maybe twenty minutes, sir."

Stedloe, who, with his remaining officers had just reached a decision to abandon the drive for water and move the command to an adjacent small hill for its final stand, at once grasped at Timothy's straw.

"Craig, you were with Mullins and his map-survey in here last fall. Do you recall that butte? It's big enough to be on the charts."

"I believe that's Pyramid Peak, Colonel. I can't be sure but if it is, there's half an acre of level ground on top with a fifteen-foot vertical drop-off of basalt and granite around the north and east perimeters." The young officer paused, his blue eyes squinting with the task of remembering as well as with fighting the noon-high sun. His conclusion came with typical clear candor. "The south slope is fairly steep as you can see from here, but you could drive a wagon up that long west ridge. I really can't say it's Pyramid though, sir. All these damn buttes look alike to me, now."

"Beg the colonel's pardon," Bell broke in abruptly. "But Timothy will know all that and he's already said we might make it if we jump fast and long."

"Bell's right." Winston's ordinarily quiet voice barked harshly. "We've no time to review the Mullins Survey. And we'd best stick with our Indian, now. He's led us straight so far."

"Agreed, Davis?" Stedloe turned the low question, with its infrequent use of the Christian name, to H Company's young commander.

"Agreed."

"Fanning?" Even a lowly supply officer rated his equal vote under the colonel's calm thoroughness.

"Yes, sir. As fast as I can, sir." The white-faced youth managed a pale smile. "Faster, if it can be arranged!"

"John?" The final question went to the Assistant Surgeon, Major J. K. Randall. John Randall was a southerner, a regular army man, Point classmate and close personal friend of Stedloe's. He was a dark, bold-faced officer, jet-haired and mustached, with a striking, silvery gray Vandyke. He was entirely competent, completely taciturn. By contrast with the major, Bell had often thought, he himself would have been considered a confirmed loose-mouth.

Randall's reply was as astringent as it was incisive. "I'll need room to lay them out," was all he said, yet none of his sweat-caked listeners felt any need for expansion or detailing of the grim nod. As usual, Assistant Surgeon Randall had said a mouthful.

"That's it, then!" Stedloe's brown eyes swept the little command. "Let's go, gentlemen. H Company, first. Fanning and Baylor's C Company, next. Major Randall and the wounded, along with Miss Rainsford, will accompany me with what's left of Wilcey's troop. Winston and the Ninth, last. Are you all clear?"

The "all clears" came hurriedly and within five minutes the ragged column was galloping for the base of the long western approach to Pyramid Peak. In another, lungbursting fifteen minutes the last of the column's panting horses were pushing onto the desolate, table-smooth top of the lonely butte. Taken off their greedy guard by the surprise dash, Kamiakin's warwhooping Palouses went screaming after it minutes too late. The command reached its barren objective without further casualties.

But Kamiakin and Malkapsi were still very much in busi-

ness. They proceeded now to prove it by the enthusiastic reck-
lessness with which they invested their considerable resources
around all four side approaches to Stedloe's waterless table-
land.

Kamiakin had lead to burn and was out to paint Pyramid
Peak bright red with fresh, white blood.

The 3,600-foot cone of Stedloe's butte lay hot and naked
athwart the slanting rays of the five-o'clock sun, its treeless,
deep-grassed shoulders thrusting twelve hundred feet above the
crowding neighborhood of lesser hills which hemmed it on every side. On its hard won summit the surviving troops of the
Colville column lay on their gnawing bellies among the rank
grasses ringing the perimeter of the tiny mesa, their red and
fearful eyes straining to catch the first signs of Kamiakin's third
assault against their granite bastion.

Twice now, once at two p.m. and once at four, the hostiles
had come swarming up at them on foot, each time being driven
back with heavy losses. But each time throwing the flood tide of
their attacking wave higher up the basalt walls of the command's barren reef. The third attempt, now clearly readying
below, might well mark the last white shots.

The ammunition ration, by Fanning's last careful count
made at three-thirty, stood at four rounds per man and Bell,
peering through his weedy cover at the red force massing on
the south slope, grimly concluded the young supply officer had
made his last inventory—for that or any other day. Nor was
the tall sergeant's optimism fattened any by the fact that he and
fifteen H Company troopers were stationed along the exact
quadrant of the mesa which must bear the brunt of any new
hostile assault up the south slope.

Thirty seconds more and Kamiakin was attacking. The
red lines seemed to grow out of the sloping rocks by a literal
magic that had even Timothy blinking his slant eyes. Where
dozens had been visible seconds before, hundreds now sprang
war-whooping up the sun-bathed incline. This time Kamiakin
and Malkapsi were leading the assault with a picked group of a
hundred mounted warriors, the first employment of horsemen
in the past several hours.

"There's their first error," Bell grunted to Timothy, indicating the advanced group of galloping ponies. "If we can down a dozen of those cayuses right at the top of that rock slide—" He pointed out the steep pitch of the spot, fifty yards below them. The Nez Perce nodded. "Aye, Ametsun, that's the place. Tell the men."

"Hold your fire, boys!" The sergeant's shout caught the nervous troopers shouldering their Sharps' carbines. "Wait'll those lead bucks hit the top of that slide right below us. Then give it to them in the horses' guts. Don't sight on a man. Hold low and let drive square into the ponies. And let drive when I holler. All of you." Bell's drumfire orders fell off while his eyes drove along the tense line ahead of his final nod. "If I hear so much as one hammer-click before I yell, I'll drill the son that clicked it!"

The other sections of the white line were already lobbing long musket fire down into the mass of the charging Indians, wasting powder and lead as though they had a fortful of both to burn, completely ignoring the pleading curses of their officers and noncoms to hold down and pick their shots. But Bell's men, steadied with the picture of the burly sergeant and his slim Nez Perce companion, waited. Kneeling fully exposed now on the mesa's rim and cradling their carbines as casually as though they were waiting for a trapmaster to release tame pigeons, they clamped their gritting teeth and held their fire.

"You take Kamiakin." Bell grinned at the slit-eyed Timothy. "I'm shooting Coeur d'Alenes this afternoon."

"Malkapsi?" asked the Nez Perce, raising his gun.

"I made him a little promise back at the Palouse," grunted Bell, his gaunt cheek sliding into the stock.

"May your word be as good as usual," murmured the Indian. "Now, Ametsun?"

"Now," snapped Bell. "Let 'em have it, boys! Low down and reload lively!"

Kamiakin and Malkapsi with perhaps thirty of their wildest riders were just heel-hammering their foam-flecked ponies across the top of the rock slide when H Company's long-delayed volley cut into them. The effects were gratifying.

At least fourteen horses dropped in the first murderous

blast, those of both Kamiakin and Malkapsi among the number. But the dropping was the least of it. As they went down, kicking and screaming, the loose surface of the incline beneath them sent them hoof-thrashing down among the close-packed line of following horsemen, knocking down some twenty or more additional mounts and adding the tumbling figures of their own and their riders' bodies to the cascading melée of Bell's beautifully timed barrage.

The spectacular breaking off of their spearhead of ponies slowed the following dismounted braves enough to allow the second, timed-fire shots of H Company's reloaded carbines to begin to arrive among them. And aimed fire with a Sharps at sixty yards, nervous troopers or no, is convincing. Additionally, some of the backing musket fire from the other companies was getting home at the pistol-blank range. Shortly, about eight or nine belly-drilled braves later, Kamiakin's faithful decided, with notable lack of formal conference, to call it an afternoon.

Twenty minutes more and there wasn't a painted face within Sharps' shot of Colonel Stedloe's arid retreat, and the only Indians to be seen were those whose bones would bleach the bare cone of Pyramid Peak.

The main body of Indians was shortly afterwards noted to be reassembling along the banks of the main Tohotonimme, the Ingosommen, south and west of the butte, where it was soon evident a major council was in progress. A considerable number of the hostiles, however, remained stationed among the scrub of the lower slopes and continued to lob a long and steady fire onto the mesa top. With dusk, a number of mounted riders were seen to leave the creek camp and go among the braves still on the firing line. The loud calls and barking signal cries of these presently informed the anxious white command, via the running translations of Timothy, that the fighting was to cease for the night and to be saved for a better day.

No man among the watching whites had the least doubt as to when that better day was due.

It would be tomorrow.

On Stedloe's butte the unnatural hush of the early darkness was broken only by the groans of the severely wounded and the low-pitched commands of the officers and noncoms.

Here and there little clots of frightened, huddled troopers squatted together and whispered in the fireless dark. Sergeant Bell, his own wounded accounted and cared for, found himself with his first spare time since snaking Calla out of Kamiakin's gaudy red lodge. His thoughts, naturally, turned to the Southern girl and to the weird warp of circumstance which had brought her to this empty Washington mountain top three thousand miles from her genteel Virginia home.

She was presently assisting Surgeon Randall with the wounded, he knew, as indeed she had been since the bloody descent of Craig's Hill. Knowing all too well what the sight and sound and touch of a beautiful woman meant to these lonely men, even in the bloom of health, Bell understood that Calla Lee Rainsford had repaid her debt to the officers and men of the Colville column many times over in the past hours.

Hers had been the soft lap and gentle hand which had cradled the mortally wounded Oliver Baylor's head as sunset had brought the last, ugly rattle up into his torn throat. Hers, the slow touch and lingering smile to ease the wrenching pain of Demoix's lungshot strangle. And of Bull Williamson's gaping belly wound. And the picture of her lovely face, clear and high-colored in the afternoon sun, or white and faint in the gathering night-gloom, had been the last vision to close the tortured eyes of more than one agonized enlisted man on that bare and stony butte.

"Timothy—"

"Aye, Ametsun." The Nez Perce's answer came out of the darkness at Bell's side.

"Go tell the girl I want to see her when she's done over there. I'll be here."

"Aye, Ametsun. I'll bring her back."

"Just tell her where I am. She'll find me. I want to see her alone."

"I knew that, brother—" The soft reproach of the Indian's answer faded with his departing shadow, leaving Bell to face the further loneliness of his darkening thoughts.

Five troopers were dead. Two more, dying. Bull Williamson and Frenchy Demoix, hopelessly wounded. Thirteen other troopers helpless with bad bullet holes. Another two dozen cut up with flesh wounds and not to be counted on for effective action. Wilcey Gaxton and Captain Baylor, whose rash courage had held the column together all morning, were gone. The men had been without food for sixteen hours, without water for eight. Company E Dragoons were leaderless. Company C, little better off under the beardless, battle-shy Fanning. Two first sergeants, a brave but green dragoon lieutenant, a slow thinking infantry captain and a barracks-bred, overly cautious artillery colonel were all that remained of leadership to the nerve-broken men huddled in the crawling darkness of Stedloe's butte.

Bell hunched his shoulders, the shiver of raw fatigue shaking him with its sudden chill. It was a hot night, but a man's fingers and feet felt like they'd been half frozen. Funny about that cold. Bell had seen his share of men shake to it, before now, but damned if he'd ever expected to live to see Emmett Bell frostbitten by it. That was fear-cold, and it would freeze a man to death quicker than a snowdrift.

Bell came up off his haunches, his eyes swinging through the gloom to the half-sound which had startled him. "Who's there? That you, Cal?"

"It's me, Emm. Oh, Emm—"

She was up close to him then, her tears coming with her breaking voice, hard against his sweated shirt.

"All right, Cal baby. It's all right. Don't cry, honey. Don't let down now, girl."

His voice, thick and deep with the huskiness of his own emotions, stroked the sobbing girl like a great, awkward hand. "It's over for tonight, honey. All over, now. You're going to stay right here with me till daybreak."

"Emm, just hold onto me. Hard. I can't stay with it. Emm. Not any more. I just can't—"

He took her in his arms, gingerly and over-careful as he might a month-old child, carrying her as easily as a feather pillow.

"Here's my pack, Cal. And blankets." With the words he placed her gently down, his old grin going through the darkness. "Not much of a boudoir for the prettiest girl in Lynchburg, but there's plenty of fresh air and it's awful quiet!"

She didn't answer and he sank down beside her, easing his

aching neck against the support of the pack, letting his long body go limp with the first relaxation in forty-eight hours. As he did, he felt the slim nakedness of the reaching arm slide over him and trembled foolishly to the soft, sighing nestle of the dark head as it sought and found the eager hollow of his shoulder.

"Let's don't talk, Emm." The whisper came to his ear just ahead of the searching lips. "We've said it all before. That first night on the Plain at the Point. A million years ago—"

"We've said it, Cal." His face was turning with the promise. "All of it. Let's both remember it, girl. From here, out."

"From here out, Emm. From here—"

The clinging moistness of the full lips came into the iron fury of the wide, hard ones, crushing off the sigh and its vow. He rolled his body to meet the sudden reach of hers, letting her softness come up against him like a curling wave of warm, drowsy water. Then the heavy clamp of the muscular arms was tightening the relentless bar of its demand across the surrendering curve of her arching back.

Not brutally and passionately, this time, like the man who has seized tonight and means to have fulfillment now, but reverently and protectively and finally, like the man who has grasped tomorrow, and means never to let it go.

Bell had not meant to sleep but his next memory was of Harrigan's broad paw on his arm.

"Psst, Sarge!" The Irishman's whisper was held down so as not to awaken the sleeping girl. "Where the hell have you bin? I've crawled twicet around this blastid mountain feelin' fer you."

"What's up, Mick?" Bell was disengaging himself from Calla's soft arm. "I must've dozed. What the hell time is it?"

"Eight o'clock," came the grim reply, "but all ain't well, Emmett boy."

"How's that?"

"Hell's to pay, lad. And the divil holdin' all the duebills." By this time Bell had folded the blanket carefully around Calla and was moving away with his fellow noncom. "First off, right after yer Injun come to git the gal fer you, we caught the other red scut hollerin' down to them slimy Palouses."

"You mean Jason? What the hell was he hollering about?"

"I don't mean Kamiakin, boy. We didn't think nothin' of this redbird's yellin' until yer Injun comes up and hears him. He was jabberin' in that heathen Chinook and we wasn't payin' him no mind, of course."

"For Christ's sake, Mick, get on with it!"

"Take it easy, Sarge." Harrigan was pushing Bell's fierce grip from his arm. "You're gettin' jumpier than a pet coon. I'm tellin' you, just listen. Yer Indian grabs this Jason the minute he hears him. Throws him around and hands him a cut acrost the kisser with his backhand, then tells us the bastard's bin eggin' the enemy on. Hollerin' *'Courage, brothers. You've already killed two chiefs and seven Pony Soldiers!'* and a lot more slop like that."

"The hell!"

"Precisely." Harrigan's thick voice rose in pitch. "And when yer Injun braced him, he jest shrugs What the hell? The white men up here are all dead come tomorrow, anyway, and he's just tryin' to build up a little social goodwill with Kamiakin's lads so's maybe they'll remember he's a fellow countryman come tommyhawk time tomorrow!"

"Oh, hell. That doesn't mean anything." Bell shrugged his relief. "Sounds pure Indian to me. Typical of them, Mick. What'd you do with him? Truss him up?"

"That we did. And stuffed his yap, good. Timothy's idea."

"Well then, that's that. Nothing more to it. What the hell did you roust me out for?"

"That ain't quite all of it, Sarge—"

Bell sensed the tightening of Harrigan's speech and clipped his own to match it.

"So?"

"Yeah, so. When we git this Jason bird laced up and stuffed, low and behold the other one's clean flown."

"God Amighty, not Timothy?"

"Gone as a goslin' down a fox's gullet."

"I don't believe it!"

"Believe it or else, lad. It's why Lootenant Craig sent me

to locate you. He's up to Surgeon Randall's section with Captain Winston. Wants you over there right away. They were powwowin' about some idee the lootenant's got on how to git off'n this bloody mountain, when this Injun trouble broke."

"Well, come on, Mick. Lead the way. How's Bull and Frenchy?"

Moving through the dark of the mesa top, Harrigan gave his answer with a softness to echo that of his footfalls. "Both spittin' blood. Frenchy kin still move but Bull's sittin' agin a rock grabbin' his belly and holdin' his breath. Surgeon says if he lets go to scratch his head, he's dead."

"You talked to him?"

"Yeah. You'd best see him. He's got some crazy notion you was killed. It'd break an Orangeman's heart to see the big ox squattin' there grievin' about it. Not a sound, mind you. Just sittin' there mutterin' 'Old Sarge, Old Sarge,' and the tears runnin' off his jaw like water—"

"All right, Mick." Bell's lips cinched in around the words. "Let's get done with Craig, first. Bull'll wait, I reckon."

"He will for you," nodded Harrigan. "There's Randall and them, just ahead. I'll be tellin' Bull you'll be along."

"Yeah, you tell him." The redbearded sergeant was turning away. "And you tell him he can do the words to 'Old Smokey' all the way through." Harrigan, already melted into the blackness, didn't answer and Bell, after a moment which found his big fingers unconsciously searching for the reedy spine of the harmonica in his shirt pocket, added softly and to himself, "Happen he can hold his poor dumb belly that long!"

A dozen, cautiously feeling steps brought him the subdued voices of Lieutenant Craig and Captain Winston. And another three, bent-kneed paces found his own deep bass undertoning the nervous converse of the officers. "Sergeant Bell reporting, sir. Harrigan said you wanted me."

"Damn!" For once the imperturbable Harry Winston was taken off-balance. "Why don't you cough or something, Bell!"

"An Indian wouldn't," was all Bell said. But the way he said it, quick and dirty, like the twist of a gutting-knife, brought the meeting to harsh order. Young Craig was on top of his answer in a flash, turning it abruptly to his own ends.

"Exactly! An Indian wouldn't, and those Palouses won't!"

"How's that, Lieutenant?" Bell jumped the query sharply, thinking he knew what Craig meant and agreeing with him even before he'd heard him say it.

"I've got a hunch they'll come up after us, Bell. Tonight."

"I've got a hunch you're right," said the big sergeant. "What about it?"

"What would *you* do about it, Sergeant?" Captain Winston put the counter question.

"You mean about sitting up here in the dark and waiting, sir?"

"That's precisely what we mean, Bell." Craig's crisp agreement backed the older officer's slow query.

"Get the hell out," grunted Bell. "Wouldn't you?"

"Aye." The lone word stalked in out of the darkness from a new quarter of the conversation's compass, and Bell, knowing Surgeon Randall had made another of his dead-center diagnoses, felt, accordingly, called upon to return the little compliment.

"Why, thank you, Major, sir. Since we're all in agreement, what's keeping us?"

Randall had made his speech for the evening, and ignored the sergeant's flippant acknowledgement. But Lieutenant Craig, again, was quickly atop it.

"Stedloe, of course."

"Of course," nodded Bell, grimacing. "What'd he say, Lieutenant?"

Craig wasted no further bitterness bringing his hard-bitten noncom up to date.

He and Winston and Randall had been to see the column commander earlier in the evening, all three pushing Craig's proposal to leave the butte under cover of the Ingosommen fog now seeping up the lower flanks of the bald pyramid. The colonel had refused, outright. As he saw it, any descent, even though initially successful, would bring an immediately following pursuit and running fight with the hostiles. And in this resolution their ammunition supply, now just over two rounds per man, would be utterly squandered. To further argument he had proved adamant, insisting the command would stand on the butte. Here at least it could make its last shots effective, and even might possibly arrange some sort of "surrender truce" with Kamiakin's besiegers.

Returning from this refusal, the three officers had run headlong into Jason's treachery and Timothy's apparent disaffection. They now wanted Sergeant Bell to evaluate the latter Indian's disappearance and to furnish his opinion, based on his admitted knowledge of the red men, as to the possibility of getting off the butte and out through the Indian lines. And they intended returning to Stedloe with that evaluation and opinion for a final try at convincing him of the soundness of Craig's projected retreat.

It was acknowledged, naturally, albeit a bit wry-facedly, that First Sergeant Bell had more influence with Colonel Stedloe than any commissioned man on his staff.

When the lieutenant had done with his disclosures, Bell kept his replies straight and short, his respect for the young officer's frankness and confidence, notwithstanding.

"Thanks, Lieutenant. I can give you my ideas ABC simple."

"Sound your 'A'," said H Company's commander, quietly. "We're all ears."

Bell sent the young gamecock a night-hidden grin, put his heavy voice at once to the required note. " 'A'," he grunted, unmusically. "I've still got complete faith in Timothy. There's only one place he could have gone and that's down to scout Kamiakin's lines."

"All right, all right—" Harry Winston was beginning to show increasing evidence he possessed, after all, a nervous system.

" 'D'," continued Bell, ignoring the infantryman's break-in. "Our troops can expect no quarter from those Indians down there. They're like circus cats. Shy as so many barn-born kittens till they've seen and smelt blood. Then you can't hold them off with six chairs and a bullwhip."

"So?" Winston, again treading the heels of Bell's remarks, stepped hurriedly on the last one.

"So," grunted the big noncom, "any hope of the Old Man's for a truce with those babies is built on bull chips.

They've uncorked our claret and they mean to have the whole jug of it."

"Any more music in your soul, Sergeant?" The flat-toned probe came from Lieutenant Craig, the dullness of its touch keying Bell's final note on Kamiakin's harsh scale.

"Yeah, 'C.' Your idea of a forced night sneak is the shortest shot we've got. And that's about five hundred to one, long."

Three minutes after his original lecture on the subject, Bell was repeating his Palouse ABC's to Colonel Stedloe, while Craig and the other officers waited in hard-lipped silence for the last-chance lesson to sink in.

Unexpectedly, Stedloe broke down.

Fanning had just come in to report that men had broken into Major Randall's liquor commissary half an hour ago, had already gulped enough of the surgeon's medicinal spirits to be well on their way out of hand. In view of this deterioration, some activity seemed imperative. If Sergeant Bell would go at once with Lieutenant Fanning to commandeer the illegal liquor supply and completely destroy it, Stedloe and the remaining officers would begin at once to map plans for the descent.

Bell, quite naturally, was to return immediately to lend his scouting experience to the mapping.

The next twenty minutes of heavy-handed and hard-voiced groping around the murk of the mesa-top convinced the boyish Fanning that the fear-ridden enlistments obviously admitted one concern greater than that for Kamiakin—and that was for First Sergeant Emmett Bell. They surrendered their bottled bravery without a fight or any suggestion of one.

With the liquor gathered up and cached, the frightened men temporarily buoyed with the orders to ready for departure, and a hasty visit to the dying Sergeant Williamson under his drawn-up belt, Bell returned to the command council.

Under his belt, also, was something else. Something which at once attracted the refined nostrils of the teetotalling Stedloe.

"Sergeant Bell!"

"Yes sir. Mission accomplished, sir."

"Bell, I told you to destroy that whiskey, not surround it!"

"It's destroyed, Colonel. Leastways hidden, sir. Uh—what's left of it."

"Bell, you're not drunk?" The colonel's soft question speared the sergeant's grin in mid-spread. "I want your word on it. I'm depending on you in this. We all are. You'll not fail me now, man?"

"No, Colonel—on both counts," said Bell, setting his long jaw on the denial before letting a shade of the grin return. "I must've spilled some of the nasty stuff on me in pouring it out. I'm ready as a ripe banana, sir. What're the orders?"

Stedloe shook his good, grave head hopelessly. This boy was one for the books—but not the Academy books. Half-inebriated all the time, all-inebriated half the time, and rebelliously insubordinate, drunk or sober, he was a shame and a disgrace to his uniform.

And if a column commander only had a hundred like him right now, he could walk down and spit in Kamiakin's Palouse face!

"Craig will give you the details, Sergeant. You can go along with him, now. But before you leave there's a little something I want you to hear. And you other gentlemen, as well." With the words, Stedloe was turning to his staff, the three officers watching him closely as he concluded.

"This is the order of the retreat. Remember it.

"C Company to take the advance, with Lieutenant Fanning. Ninth Infantry next, with Captain Winston. Then H Company, with Lieutenant Craig."

Stedloe broke his orders to swing his quiet brown eyes on Bell, his three staffers following the look and the suspended statement with puzzlement.

Catching Bell's frowning glance, the colonel held it for a long three seconds.

"Then E Company," he said at last. "With Lieutenant Bellew—"

With Bell's tall shadow dogging his hurried movements, Lieutenant Craig made his way from one company to the next, calling each outfit together and repeating the general orders.

The column was moving out. No equipment was to be taken save musket or carbine and ammunition. All metal harness was to be wrapped with torn cloth and all loose, metal-

buckled tack; canteens, scabbards, trenching shovels, axes, anything which might possibly make a noise in traveling was to be
left behind. Right down to spurs and spur-chains! Every
trooper was to ride with his right hand on his mount's nose and
the horses bearing the wounded were to be muzzle-wrapped.

Thus briefed, the squad corporals began at once to check
their men and mounts and to fall them into rough company
order. Craig and Bell, with a picked squad of regulars chosen
by the latter, went on about the grim business of the main issue
—faking the camp to "look normal" after their departure.

This project was one upon which the dour sergeant had
insisted as the minimum guarantee of a successful getaway, and
Craig gave him no question on it. As a matter of fact neither
the young officer nor any of the rest of the staff had called the
obvious question on Stedloe's peculiar reference to Bell as
"Lieutenant Bellew," all accepting the sergeant's new rank and
name along with his running fire of "suggested orders" without
a murmur.

Thirty-three of the command's horses had been killed and
it was now necessary to Bell's strategy to eliminate another
dozen. These were all the gray and other light-colored animals
which would stand out well even in the Ingosommen gloom.
These were quickly cut out and picketed around the perimeter
of the mesa where prying Palouse eyes might note them with
deep-grunting satisfaction.

While Craig and the sergeant went about their labors,
other work squads were busy with equally grim chores: the
knocking down and caching of the howitzers, the collecting and
burying in a shallow common trench of the trooper dead, the
tight lashing of the severely wounded on the few remaining
pack mules, and the hurried moving of strings of led-horses
over the burial sites of the colonel's beloved artillery and of his
honored dead.

When a similar treatment was proposed for the considerable pile of packs and supplies being abandoned, Bell objected
at once. The idea was to stack these as bulkily and obviously as
possible. Not forgotten by the gaunt sergeant, even in these
tightly strung minutes, the well known red cupidity. The Indi-

ans fighting over the tribal sharings of these spoils might easily mean an hour of vital delay in pursuit.

Shortly before nine o'clock, Craig and Bell returned to Stedloe to report the column in readiness. Winston and Fanning, already there, nodded their silent agreement. Surgeon Randall announced the wounded ready to move, with the exception of First Sergeant Williamson.

Questioned at once on his exception, Stedloe's orders had been explicit—no wounded left behind, the surgeon explained the noncom was all but cut in two with four hopeless abdominal wounds and that to move him a foot would be to kill him. "I won't give that order, Edson. The man can't live an hour, and he wants to stay. I'm sorry."

"Gentlemen?" Stedloe turned the question to his juniors.

"Let the poor devil alone," said Craig slowly. "Major Randall knows best. A dead man can't help us down that mountain."

"I talked to him just now," Bell's deep voice added. "He wants to help by staying here. I'd let him, Colonel. He's cold clear up to his kidneys."

"How about Demoix?" Stedloe turned again to Major Randall.

"Demoix might make it. I've got him ready in any event."

"All right." There was no hesitation now in the commander's agreement. "Let's get on with it. Do you still want to scout that western slope before we start, Bell?"

"We've got to. That west slope looks *too* good to me. The easiest way down and the only damn one they haven't got watchfires burning behind. I think it's a trap. Kamiakin was born a lot of yesterdays ago, Colonel."

"All right, Bell, get to it. The rest of you look to your men and ease the wounded as well as you can while we're waiting."

Bell left at once, declining any company. He was gone ten minutes. Then fifteen. And finally twenty. The only sounds from below were those of the night winds in the serviceberry bushes, the occasional sleepy twitter of a ground bird, and the distant mutter of the drums from the river camp of the Palouses, pitched along the big Tohotonimme at the south base of the butte.

On the mesa top 147 hopeless whites cocked their straining ears and waited. Waited for the first triumphant war whoop which would announce their scout had found his trap. Found it and stepped squarely on its trigger-light Indian-set baitpan. Stepped on it and snapped its ringing jaws hard shut on their last, thin chance of escape.

Twenty minutes stretched endlessly to thirty. And then to forty-five.

To the nerve-torn watchers on the hill, Bell's soundless reappearance minutes before ten o'clock, came as a distinct jolt. A jolt occasioned by a most unnatural phenomenon.

Tall white men very seldom throw thin red shadows on foggy nights. But Bell was throwing one, now. A reed-slender, wordless shadow which stepped quickly past him to touch its sober forehead toward the dumbfounded Stedloe and his staff.

"Timothy, God bless my soul!" gasped the colonel, his simple candor riding ahead of the dark suspicion due to follow the first surprise.

"Never mind *your* soul, Colonel." Bell's cynical reminder spiked the little pause. "You'd better bless this Indian's!"

"And never mind your insubordinate tongue!" snapped Craig, his temper breaking under the temporary lieutenant's acid coolness. "Where the hell did you get this Indian and why in God's name did you let him follow you back here?"

"And you, Lieutenant Craig—" Bell's hard advice broke in a perfect imitation of the young officer's outburst—"never mind your little silver bars. I'm talking to Colonel Stedloe."

"Go ahead, Bell. Answer Craig's question." Stedloe's voice showed a touch of West Point spine. "After all, Timothy's been gone two hours and the Lord alone knows what doing!"

"*Me* and the Lord," amended the big sergeant, softly. "As for Craig's questions, Tamason speaks better English than I do, Colonel. I'll let him talk."

And the Nez Perce chief talked. Low. Deep. Child-simple. The throaty gutturals of his mission-school English fell swift and short, their soft delivery wickedly lifting the nape-hairs of Stedloe's dry-mouthed staff.

At the bottom of that long west slope down which the colonel intended taking his troops, the red scout began, he,

Timothy, had encountered Ametsun Bell, advising him to go
no further, providing he still held his short, auburn scalp in
some esteem. Beyond the base of that slope the Palouses had
driven their horse herd, hiding at least eight hundred of the
uncertain little mounts among the scrub pine bordering the
Tohotonimme at that point. And beyond the horse herd, waiting to respond to its first alarm of inquiring neighs, Kamiakin
and Malkapsi lay with a big force of picked warriors. *Any* of the
white officers, the Nez Perce stressed quietly, could thus see
what their advance down *that* slope would have brought them
into.

Now. Beyond that. Would the officers look carefully at the
way in which the enemy had his signal fires burning?

Apparently the officers would, for without so much as a
loud breath Stedloe and his juniors were following the fog-
shrouded point of the lean, red arm. Bell, no whit less tongue-
bound than the others, hung his scowling gaze over the moving
mark of Timothy's forefinger.

You see there now, the Indian continued. To the north,
just a few. To the east, just a few. Look out for those places
where no fires were burning. They looked thin, and were
swarming with warriors. Then see that darkness to the west.
No fires there, at all. And as Ametsun Bell had warned them,
that was the worst spot of all. And as for Ametsun, too, when
he said something let them all listen. For had not Timothy,
himself, trained him?

So. Where were the fires brightest? Where were the drums
beating? Where was the last place the pony-soldiers would
think of going down? To the south, naturally. Down there
where the lodges lay. Down there where even Ametsun Bell
would never have looked.

And what was down there?

Nothing.

Nothing save a dozen squaws feeding the big fires, and a
few old chiefs pounding the buffalo hides. . . .

At the end of the Nez Perce's disclosures, Stedloe and his
staff occupied themselves with the most pressing necessity of
the moment—letting their held breaths go in sibilant unison.

Before any of them could gulp a fresh lungful, Sergeant

Bell was putting his brief valedictory to the suspected scout's address.

"I'll save you all the time of hashing over Tamason's chewed-up loyalty. This Indian's been wading in ambushed hostiles up to his crotch-cloth for two hours. Nobody asked him to and he knew full well nobody'd believe he'd done it. Not even *me.*" Bell paused, letting the silence fatten a little before concluding.

"So he took me on two little trips down there. One just across the creek, due west. One a half-mile down it, straight south. Gentlemen, I can smell horse sweat and manure when it's blown to me eight-hundred strong. And I can see an empty village when I'm looking at one in bright firelight.

"Any questions?"

7

◆

Snake River Retreat

At ten p.m., Colonel Stedloe with Fanning's company of dragoons and Winston's Ninth Infantry moved in orderly silence over the rim of the mesa. There was a muffled shifting of loose rock as their mounts struck the steep slide where Bell's carbines had broken the back of Kamiakin's last charge, and then pin-drop stillness.

The first companies were successfully away.

Lieutenant Craig, collecting the last of his outposts and enjoining Bell to follow him in unbroken order, went next. When the settling of the rock trickle below told the sergeant H Company was safely past the slide, he turned abruptly to the lean trooper at his side.

"Get going, Clay. Take the lead and hang your horse's nose on H Company's cruppers."

"Hold on, Sarge!" The bearded soldier pulled his mount back. "I thought you was supposed to lead this here quadrille? Harrigan told us the Old Man'd breveted you to take over Company E. Cuss it, I won't—"

"I said get going, *Corporal*," Bell's command leapt

169

through the gloom with ugly shortness. "Never mind that brevet business, you hear me?"

"Yes, sir."

"I'm aiming to be the last man off this goddam hill. Got that?"

"Yes, sir."

"All right. Move out!"

Corporal Sam Clay was a Carolina man and a six-year regular. Four of those six years had been sweated out as a buck private under the tender tutelage of First Sergeant Emmett D. Bell.

He moved out.

And after him went the sixteen survivors of Wilcey Gaxton's Company E Dragoons. Bell counted them carefully over the rim and gave each mount a slap on the haunch and each anxious rider a terse reminder to, "Watch the horse in front of you, soldier. Don't let your own horse hang back, and keep your hand on his nose when you go by that village down there."

With the last man and mount over the edge, Bell waited a tense two minutes until the final, faint movement of the granite below told him Corporal Clay had gotten E Company past the slide. Then he turned noiselessly away from the rim. As he went, a less dark night would have limned the slight, frosty grin which turned with him . . .

Below the slide, Corporal Clay picked up the gait of his troop, soon overhauling the ghostly rumps of Craig's H Company. Another five minutes of slow-walking progress along the sharply falling face of the south slope and the column was unaccountably halted. Word was at once relayed back from the head of the line that Colonel Stedloe wanted Sergeant Bell up front. The hostile village lay just ahead and the colonel felt the need of the hawk-eyed noncom alongside the guiding Timothy when the passage was made.

The message, passed back along the muffled line of E Company, was shortly returned with an ugly postscript. Sergeant Bell was not among those present and accounted for.

This intelligence had no more than been passed back up to

Stedloe when a shifting night breeze brought the answer to the question already framing the commander's compressed lips.

From the north that breeze came. From the north and across the abandoned mesa top. Dropping softly down the darkened south slope. And bearing on its mountain-scented breath a sound known to every last member of the Colville column. And to not a few of the reservation-bred, hangers-on among Kamiakin's swart-skinned followers.

The soulful and ardent, if not artistic, harmonica playing of First Sergeant Bell.

"Faith and be Jazus!" The muttered expletive broke from Sergeant Harrigan who had ridden forward with Captain Winston to check the reason for the delay. "The crazy, blessed idiot has stayed up there with old Bull. And listen to that bloody tyune he's playin', will you, Colonel? That'll be Sarge's idea of somethin' funny."

"Rock of Ages—" Stedloe murmured the words like a man talking in his sleep and not hearing his own voice.

"The drunken devil." The clipped phrase fell in Captain Winston's flat monotone. Was followed with the softly qualifying afterthought. "Good God. What a bellyful of guts."

"Not drunk, Harry. Not this time." The thought came, surprisingly enough, in Stedloe's patient voice. "I know that man. He's playing to cover our withdrawal. And to make up for his own memories. There's a story there. I'll tell it to you if we get out of this."

"Emm. Oh my God, it's Emm!" The muffled delay of the cry burst from the stunned Calla. Riding with Fanning and Stedloe she had been the first to leave the butte, had not seen Bell since he left her sleeping at eight o'clock, had only realized the muted discussion concerned him.

"Don't worry, Miss Rainsford"—the gallant lie came from young Fanning—"he'll make out. He's got more lives than a three-toed cat."

"He'll need them," grunted the unimaginative Winston. "We can't wait for him."

"I'm going back!" The suppressed cry sprang from Calla. "It's just a little way, Uncle Edson. I'm going!"

"*No, miss.*" It was Timothy's iron hand which found the

distraught girl's bridle with the low-voiced denial. "Ametsun Bell planned it this way. I was to tell you when we were past the village. He knew we had no chance unless the Palouses were made to think all was well on the hilltop. Many of those Indians waiting back there know Ametsun Bell. They know his music on that mouth-reed. They will hear it and nod. And go on waiting. It was what Ametsun wanted."

"Oh, Emm!"

"Timothy's right, Calla." Stedloe's white hand found her arm with the gentle insistence. "We'll go along, now."

"And quickly," added the Nez Perce before the girl could answer. "While Kamiakin and Malkapsi are still grinning about that music up there."

"Column resume march," nodded Stedloe to the waiting officers. "On the double once we're past the village. Single file and slow walk until we are. Right, Timothy?"

"Aye," said the Nez Perce, turning his piebald pony. *"Ke-la'i, Ametsun!"* The low farewell, with the quick touch of the red hand to the forehead went to the now brooding silence of Stedloe's butte. "We shall meet again along that other trail!"

Bell laid aside the mouth harp, reached again in the dark for the canteen. "How do you feel, now, Bull? Easier, boy?"

"I couldn't pin no grizzly, Sarge." The huge man's words brought a groan of pain, deep and soft like a wounded animal's. "But I allow thet last drink helped summat."

"Want another?"

"Yeah, maybe. Hold mah cussed head for me. I cain't seem to get it off'n this rock no more."

Bell passed his arm behind the massive head, held the canteen steadily.

"That's enough, you dumb ox. You'll have it pouring out that hole in your belly. This isn't issue rotgut, you know."

"Mah Gawd, I know thet! Thet's sourmash bourbon, Sarge—Kentucky whiskey!" The brutish noncom's voice seemed to gain from the fiery draft, and from the pride in its native origin. "Wheah'd we get it?"

"Major Randall's best. That's officer liquor, boy. Can't you feel it in your dumb belly?"

"Sarge—" There was fear in the heavy voice, now. The unreasoning, nameless fear of a four-year-old, alone and lost in the dark. Childish. Pathetic. Turning Bell's stomach with its perfect faith. "I can't feel nothin' in mah belly no more. I'm cold clean up to mah elbows. Lemme feel yer hand again, Sarge. Jest this onct more—"

Silently Bell felt forward, bringing his hand to rest in that of the burly sergeant. Feeling the clammy weakness of the great, groping fingers, he shuddered.

"You cold, too, Sarge?"

"Naw, just nerves."

"Not you, Sarge. You jest ain't had yer quart today."

"Nor yesterday," said Bell aimlessly. "I'm about caught up though, I reckon."

"How many left, Sarge?"

"A couple."

"I'll split you."

"You're split, boy—"

Bell held his head again, tipping the canteen. Feeling the liquor splash his steadying hand, he pulled the container away from the slack mouth, eased the giant head back on the boulder. "You never could hold your whiskey, you big dummy. That's all for you."

Draining the canteen with steady gulps, he shied the empty container toward the nearest of the picketed horses. At its muffled bounce, the animals nickered curiously. "And that's for *Kenuokin*," he grunted. "Just to remind the red bastard he's got a bunch of ragged dragoons cornered up here."

"Sarge—"

"Yeah, Bull?"

"How long the boys bin gone?"

"Couple hours. You been dozing off and on."

"Yeah?"

"Yeah. Aren't you sleepy again?"

"Naw. Jest cold—"

Bell slid his hand out of the Kentuckian's rigid fingers, moved it up to the huge shoulder, recoiled quickly at the marble coldness. "I'll rummage you another blanket, boy."

"Naw, listen Sarge. You got to go. You was only goin' to stay a few minutes. You promised it."

Bell nodded without replying. He'd said that, all right. Hours ago. When he'd thought the big ox couldn't last ten minutes. Now it was crowding midnight, the column clean away and long gone. And still the tremendous brute hung on.

"Yeah, Bull. I'll be going pretty sudden."

Bull was dead. Maybe another five minutes. Maybe another five hours. But dead, anyway. Just as dead as though God had already reached down and gathered him up. Time was wasting for both Bell and Bull Williamson.

"Sarge—"

"Yeah."

"What you doin'? Thet's yer Remin'ton, ain't it? Why you wrappin' it up?"

Bell looked down at the heavy dragoon pistol. Folded the torn blanketing on over it. "It's my Remington, Bull. I'm fixing to leave it behind with you, boy."

"The old 'last shot' huh, Sarge?"

"The old last shot, Bull."

"I ain't goin' to need it."

"I reckon not."

"Sarge, boy, play us a tune 'fore you go."

"Sure, Bull. What'll it be?" The left hand was feeling in the linted shirt pocket. The right, easing the wrapped pistol into the cross-legged lap.

"Aw, you know."

"Yeah, boy. I know."

"And slow, Sarge"—there was that old touch of child-bright eagerness in the sudden plea, wrenching Bell's chest, hardening his wide mouth—"so's I can do the words of it—"

"Sure, Bull." The left hand was placing the harmonica to the dry lips. The right dropping to the motionless lap. "Second chorus, boy."

"Yeah, Sarge. Second chorus—"

The reedy thinness of the opening bars echoed with eerie lonesomeness across the deserted dust of the mesa top, startling the drooping horses. On the second, mournful chorus, the big Kentuckian began to sing.

"On top of Old Smokey, all covered with snow
 I lost my true lover from a'courtin' too slow

Now come all young ladies and listen to me
Don't hang your affections on a green willow tree

For the leaves they will wither
And the roots they will die
And leave you————"

The blanket-muffled shot reverberated dully, its flat tones not even disturbing the horses. Pulling the smoking weapon from its folded cover, Bell placed it gently near the slack hand alongside the granite boulder. "Like you said, Bull"—he nodded silently—"you won't be needing it."

With the raw powder burns of the shrouded shot still blistering his pistol hand, Bell set himself one last duty before leaving the mesa.

In this direction he was guided by his knowledge of Indian psychology and not, as some detractors were later to claim, by his sardonic sense of humor nor by his well-known agnosticism. His self-imposed labor cost him twenty priceless minutes. And Sergeant Bell was not the one to squander time like that for a laugh, or to prove his doubts of a living deity.

With an abandoned shovel, two canteen straps and an unearthed pair of oaken howitzer shafts, he worked in driving silence, pausing frequently to cock a dust-caked ear to the stillness of the slopes below. There was a limit to the illusion a dozen cast off dragoon horses and a harmonica-playing first sergeant could create. Sooner or later, Kamiakin was going to start wondering about the natural good behavior of 140 frightened men and six score nervous horses on that mesa top!

When he had done, stepping back to drop the shovel and survey his handiwork, he had a reasonable facsimile of what he wanted—a crude mission cross, planted squarely in the middle of Stedloe's deserted butte.

Grunting his satisfaction, Bell turned away. If he knew the kid-simple Indian mind, that cross would do its work. The fear reserved for the Christian symbol of the crucifixion by the northwest savage, was complete.

There would be no scalping among the stark bodies of the colonel's abandoned dead.

At the western mesa rim, the sergeant pulled his gelding up, stood forward in the stirrups, ears tuned to the night sounds from along the slope. A moment later he was sliding off the little roan, flopping, belly-down, in the welcome cover of the rank, rim grasses.

There *were* no nightsounds coming from along that slope!

At any rate, not the right ones.

His stomach drawing in like drying rawhide, Bell peered through the parted grasses, gray eyes scanning the unnatural quiet of the long western decline.

Then of a sudden, pupils expanding under the severity of the lower darknesses, he was seeing it. Seeing it and understanding the stillness of the ground hawks and of the serviceberry birds. Seeing it lapping slowly up the west slope and, turning quickly, along the south as well. There was no mistaking the ragged, extended lines of that creeping shadow.

The red night crawlers were out, and moving. *Kamiakin was coming up!*

Rolling back from the rim, Bell bent double and raced for his pack. There it was but the work of a moment to shuck out of his heavy dragoon boots and bulky service shirt. Another moment and his fingers were easing the trim tightness of Nez Perce moccasins around the outsized bareness of his feet. After that it took only seconds to belt on the skinning knife, sling the Sharps' carbine over his shoulder, slip across the mesa top and over the precipitous drop of the north wall.

Ten minutes of leaping, brush-torn descent and he was standing eight hundred feet below the mesa rim on the deserted north side of the butte. And seconds after that, he was hearing the war whoops and belly screams which announced the Palouse assault over the west and south rims.

With the disappointed howls and barking signal cries from above telling him Kamiakin's faithful had discovered their empty trap, he reslung his carbine and set off around the north slope—*heading west!*

He traveled, now, at a swinging dogtrot, finding the open grasslands of the lower inclines fairly level and free of gully washes. Shortly, he sighted the dark line of scrub pine marking the course of the Big Tohotonimme ahead. Slowing his pace, he speeded his mind, the wild gamble forming in it beginning to fall into hurried place as his crouching figure entered the screening gloom of the trees.

Just ahead, its position marked by the drowsy tinkling of the bell mare's musical neckpiece, lay the main hostile horse herd. Eight or nine hundred half-wild, white-hating Indian cayuses. There were your odds, brother, and they were long enough to satisfy even First Sergeant Bell. But still, maybe, not too long. If a man could get to that bell mare—That was a little daisy that would take some dareful picking. And a big piece of luck.

He ran into his needed chunk of fortune almost as its necessity was forming in his mind. And it was a bigger chunk than he could have asked for.

As he melted into the fringe of the pines, a low voice hailed him in Chinook. Turning, he was in time to see the silhouetted cartwheel of a Coeur d'Alene warbonnet following him down off the hill.

"Hold up, brother!" The guttural order foreran the chief's gliding approach. "Name your name and follow along with me. The white dogs have gotten away and Kamiakin has sent me to gather up those down here!"

"Omatchen!" hissed Bell, picking a known Coeur d'Alene's name out of the thin night air. "Who calls me?"

"Malkapsi, you fool. And say, didn't I just leave you on top up there? Why have you come down?" With the questions, the Coeur d'Alene was up to Bell, his ugly, ax-blade jaw poking forward through the dark.

"To run off the horse herd. Naturally, you fool!" Bell threw the growling retort into the renegade's hand-filed teeth a shaving of a second ahead of the clubbed steel butt of the carbine. Malkapsi's tiny eyes had time to jump wide open, and that was all. The next instant the Sharp's stock was splintering his gaping jaw and the spreading eyes were glazing closed.

Bell caught the swaying figure, easing it to the ground. A

hasty ear pressed to the hostile's deerskin shirt, picked up no discernible heartbeat. By all signs possible in such a hasty diagnosis, Ametsun Bell had kept his promise to Malkapsi, the Coeur d'Alene.

The sergeant now had what he needed to safely approach the Indian horse herd—deerskin and eagle feathers reeking of the familiar and friendly Coeur d'Alene body odor. Seconds after downing Malkapsi, he had donned the chief's shirt and bonnet, was rapidly circling the closely packed herd, south toward the tinkling of the bell mare's luring ornament.

The shirt and bonnet were a plenty tight squeeze for the towering Bell but with them and Kamiakin's bell mare, that horse herd could be scattered till hell wouldn't have it.

Not hell, nor the pursuing Palouses, either.

Those bell-broke hostile ponies would follow that lead mare wherever Bell might choose to boot her. And where Bell was going to boot her, was far away from Kamiakin's Tohotonimme war camp!

With the fog-sopping dawn of the 18th Stedloe halted his fleeing column safely across its fateful, former fording of the Palouse. There had been no pursuit, and no sign of pursuit to that gray hour.

However, there was as yet only a scant handful of miles between the fatigue drunken troopers and their hollow-flanked horses, and the windswept emptiness of Stedloe's rearing butte. No time could be taken to graze the wind-broken mounts, and very little to water them. Nonetheless, their first drink in twenty-four hours had a heartening effect on both man and mount, alike.

While the last of the lathered horses were still standing hock-deep in the shallows of the stream, Timothy rode in to report a high dust cloud rolling down the Lapwai Trail from the Tohotonimme. He didn't like to arouse false hopes in his fellow soldiers, said the Nez Perce, but he would think from the size of that cloud that no more than two or three hundred could be riding under it!

At the same time he could not be sure. It was a damp morning and many ponies might make only the dust of a few. It was no time to be squatting on the exposed banks of the Palouse, waiting to find out.

As if to put the lie to the Nez Perce's cautiously hopeful report, and the truth to his stern warning to move on, a veritable rash of smoke signals began to top the bare hills to the north and east. This hostile hint was more than enough for the haggard survivors of the Colville column.

It was still sixty-eight miles to the Snake.

To the hoarse calls of the officers and the dispirited echoes of their noncoms, the straggling column was reformed, and for the next four hours the failing mounts were forced to a laboring gallop down the brush-girt track of the Lapwai Trail. With the advance of midday, the climbing sun drove into the backs of the fleeing men with the deadening power of a Vulcan's hammer, sapping their little remaining strength and pulling the Palouse water out of them like so many saddle-jolting sponges. By eleven a.m. and the branching of the Lapwai toward the distant Snake, men and horses had reached their outer limits. In the spotty shelter of a jackpine-fringed creek, crossing in from the east, Stedloe called the halt.

And it was in this haven of sweltering shade and sluggish branchwater that the disorganized column got its first uplift in forty-eight hours of hell.

Shortly after the halt Timothy spurred his pony down from a neighboring ridge to announce a lone Coeur d'Alene chief galloping the Lapwai some miles to the north. The distance was too long for positive identification, but the solitary rider was astride a white pony and there was something familiar to the Nez Perce in his swinging, upright seat. Timothy would not care to guess who the hard-riding stranger was. It was not in his heart to speak the hope that was in his mind. He could say, however, that whoever he was, he, Timothy, would know him well when he rode in!

Lieutenant Craig at once took a squad of skirmishers out to cut off the newcomer's approach. This party was scarcely gone five minutes from sight over the first ridge, than it reappeared, the tall Coeur d'Alene cantering in its jubilant midst. As the returning riders broke into view of the mile-distant rise, the watching Timothy's stolid face split wide in an expression never before noted thereon by any of Stedloe's command—a flashing, lightning-bright and purely dazzling smile!

"Ametsun! *Ho-hoho!* It's Ametsun Bell!"

And Bell indeed it was. Cartwheel warbonnet, Coeur d'Alene deerskins, Palouse bell mare and all.

No Caesar returned triumphantly from Gaul, ever received a superior salute. Private, squad corporal, company officer and column commander, all joined in the rousing cheer which greeted the dour noncom's return from "the dead."

Alone among the company failing to aid the vocal reception, Calla sat her artillery mule in silence, letting the tears cascading her dirty cheeks splash their own grateful word of welcome. Looking over the heads of Harrigan and the rest of the intervening backslappers, Bell waved his understanding to the girl, sending the bright rareness of his quick smile to receipt the unspoken message in her tear-stained grimace. A man could understand, at a moment like this, that it's pretty hard to talk through a soft mouth full of salt water.

But Bell had brought other news than good. And long as his arms might to be around that slim waist, they'd have to ache a spell yet.

Keeping his eyes on Calla, he shot the stark words of his report at Stedloe.

Staying to the ravines paralleling the main trail, he had been able to avoid the hostiles while at the same time scouting their advance. About an hour ago, the Indian force had swung west to angle toward the Snake. Their present course would bring them back into the Lapwai eight miles short of Red Wolf Crossing. And right into the rocks of the Smokle Creek headlands. As pretty a spot for an ambush as ever a fagged-out scout would care to think about.

There were some 350 warriors in the pursuit party, all Palouses and personally led by Kamiakin. Further, it was the sergeant's sorry need to report that the red hell-hound Malkapsi, whom he thought he'd killed in his getaway from the butte, had somehow survived a Sharps' skull fracture and was now back at the Palouse chief's raging side.

As to the absence of Kamiakin's Yakima Federation allies, it was Bell's guess that *Kenuokin's* Coeur d'Alene, Yakima,

Spokane and Klikitat cohorts had suffered a temporary loss of appetite for white soldier meat following Stedloe's astonishing escape from the mesa trap. Together with a prolonged attack of "spoils fever" brought on by the neatly stacked column material abandoned on the bare-clean mesa top. Also contributing, it might modestly be added, was the delay occasioned by Sergeant Bell's run-off of their horse herd!

Under the terms of the sergeant's blunt report, no option remained save to race the hostiles for the Smokle Creek headlands. If the troops could beat the Palouses to that dangerous point, the day would be long spent and the precious safety of the Snake River but an hour's short ride. If not—

It was a long, long chance. And the battered column took it at a floundering gallop.

With four o'clock and the hulking landmarks of the Tahto-uah Hills behind them, the troops were slowed to a stumbling, rank-breaking trot. But the headlands of the Smokle were in sight! Another eight miles and they would know. Hope, that cat-lived spur which was as much a part of the dragoons equipment as his clumsy boots, began once more to straighten the seats of the sagging soldiers.

And then, rolling ominously up from the unexpected quarter of the low hills to the south, came a moving dust cloud which could denote no less than a hundred, fast-traveling riders.

Timothy and Bell, pushing their mounts to the nearest hilltop, were back in ten minutes with the news. Whoever those riders were, they were Indians. And their line-of-gallop was going to cut them into the Lapwai a good way short of the Smokle Creek headlands.

Again, there was no course save to push on. To retreat was unthinkable. To leave the marked trail, northward or southward, was now out of the question. It was by this time quite clear the wily Kamiakin had split his forces, sending half of them, no doubt under Malkapsi, to the south, holding the other half in his own huge hand to the north. Aiming, obviously, to bring the two jaws of his running trap hard together somewhere short of the Smokle rocks. And aiming to have the last of the desperate pony-soldiers between those jaws when they closed.

White-faced and shot raw with fatigue, Colonel Stedloe put his hoarse orders to his hollow-eyed officers: column resume march, double-time forward. Dull-gazing, ponderously slow, patently under final shock, the troopers fell raggedly in, stumbled aimlessly onward.

Ten minutes and two miles later, they pulled their foam-caked mounts to a halt and prepared to deploy for the firing of the remaining two rounds per man. The upcoming Indian attackers to the south, had shifted their course to bear directly on the stalled column. The Colville force had come a long way from Stedloe's dreary butte. Had almost come all the way. But this would be as far as they were going.

This would be the end of it.

The next instant, with the flat-galloping Indian ponies nearing four hundred yards and extreme range, Timothy gave a great shout and dashed his rat-tailed paint straight for the on-rushing cloud of grease-streaked braves. And the next second Bell was standing in his stirrups and yelling like a schoolboy at his first stake race. The swinging gestures of his wildly pointing arm, along with the bass bellowing of his cracked voice, were being aimed at a memorably squat and ugly figure quirting a lunging Nez Perce cayuse out of the foremost line of warriors and down upon Timothy.

"God Amighty, Colonel, that's Lucas!" Bell's mad shout went to Stedloe. "God bless the grinning idiot, he's done it. Those are *our* Nez Perces, sir!"

"Good Lord. There must be two hundred of them!" Craig's exultant cry joined Bell's, stopped the least bit short of hysteria. "Would you look at them, sir! I never thought I'd be so goddam glad to see *Indians* in my life!"

"Yes, thank God," muttered the colonel, his voice dead flat, the reins falling loosely from his dropping hands with the words. "Thank God—and our Nez Perces."

With the appearance of Timothy's Red Wolf Nez Perces under the grave-faced leadership of the stately Lawyer, the issue of the passage of the Smokle Creek headlands was as dead as last year's dog salmon. Kamiakin would never risk openly engaging a forewarned enemy of nearly equal numbers.

What matter, now, that he had won the race for the Smokle rocks? What matter that his followers had spent the past hour arguing the manner in which the wonderful Sharps carbines of the pony-soldiers were to be divided?

In truth, no matter, now.

Sitting his Apaloosie stallion among the granite boulders from whence he had expected to lead his warriors down upon the last of the white invaders, the giant hostile shrugged. He hunched his scarlet blanket higher against the chill of the rising river wind. The resilient shift of his thoughts demonstrated that remarkable elasticity of adjustment which Bell had so often marked and admired among the red men.

Wuska. Yonder came his long-chased prey to be sure. Worn down. Beaten. Ready for the kill. But then, alas. With them also came the cursed Red Wolf Nez Perces. And that louse-picker, Lawyer. With the empty-headed Lucas. Those fools. Riding up like heroes at the last minute. Robbing the Palouses of their rightful victory. Spoiling the carefully spread hostile tales of a planned Nez Perce treachery upon the soldiers. And the real pity was that he, *Kenuokin,* warchief of all the Palouses, had been within minutes of achieving the greatest Indian victory of them all over white soldiers!

But now? *Iki!E'sa?* Was it, after all, that bitter? Like gall? Should a real chief feel that way, in the end?

No. There was more to it than that. He had inflicted on the soldiers their most humiliating defeat. Their bad history in his country had as yet no parallel to it. *Aii-eee!* The name *Kenuokin* would put the cold sweat down their pale backs for a long time to come. *Kape't.* It was enough. *Wuska.* Let that be the end of it.

It was time to go home.

Turning to his waiting subchiefs, Kamiakin gave the word and the sign. There were no dissents, save from the glaring Malkapsi. The other subchiefs, in turn, grunted the retreat order back into the packed ranks of charcoal and ochre-blazoned faces. *Kape't, wuska.* It was time to go home. *Kenuokin* had said it.

When, with the lowering gray of the eight-o'clock northern dusk, the tattered Colville survivors filed past the Smokle

Creek rocks to enter the broad, granite track which marked the final fall of the Lapwai Trail toward the Snake, the Palouses were gone.

The Palouses were gone and in their places three solitary Nez Perce warriors sat their hunching cayuses on the skyline of the Smokle ridge, their slant eyes studying the march of the blue and gray-clad troops below.

Timothy and Jason and Lucas. Hesitating now that their work was done. Wondering which way to point their ponies. Watching in stony-faced silence the fading of the flag toward the west and Red Wolf Crossing.

In the minds of two of the watchers there was nothing but what their cherty eyes were seeing; the ragtag, broken passage of the ill-fated Colville column. But in the mind of the third were many things not seen with the eyes alone.

Timothy was seeing the empty places in that column. Captain Baylor dying with the dusk on Stedloe's butte. Lieutenant Gaxton dead in the hot sun of the Tohotonimme gorge. Sergeant Williamson holding his belly and bleeding to death while Ametsun Bell played his reed pipe in the lonely darkness. And Sergeant Demoix left with his mortal wounds and a loaded pistol somewhere along the morning darkness of the Lapwai Trail.

He was seeing, and hearing again, the brave but empty words of Colonel Stedloe in congratulating his troops on their survival, and in predicting, only Timothy knew how foolishly, that their stand against Kamiakin's rebellion would pave the way for the warless dissolution of the hostile's Yakima Federation.

He was hearing, too, those final words of the good, quiet Ametsun Bell. Telling him, Timothy, that his alone was the honor and reward for the saving of Stedloe's men. But telling him, too, that he must not expect this honor to ever come to him. Telling him it was not in the ways of the white soldiers to say that an Indian had led them out of the Palouse wilderness!

Timothy had nodded, then, knowing the gray-eyed chevron soldier spoke the truth. And he had nodded again when Ametsun had told him he was going to his home to the east, beyond the Shining Mountains, the lofty Big Horns. Going there with the girl, to make his peace with the army he had served so well. And going with Colonel Stedloe's promise of complete official backing, and the patient-eyed commander's hopeful prediction of full military pardon in the end.

But re-hearing and seeing all these fleeting things, the Nez Perce was seeing something else above them all. Something whose image had never left his narrow eyes. Something whose identity was even now being put to him in the guttural acrimony of Jason's dry words.

"Well, Tamason, there goes your pretty flag. Do we sit here all night chilling our buttocks with this Bitter Root breeze, or do we go after it?"

The sun-blackened leather of the chief's face held its chronic mask of blankness a long, three breaths. Then its wind-carved wrinkles were breaking to the deliberate fall of his words. There was nothing of bitterness nor of contempt in his quiet speech, but only the bare honesty of reality.

"It's a fool's flag, my brothers. And those who follow it with them, are fools. The red you see upon it is Indian blood. The blue is the empty sky they trade us for our lands. Those white stars are their promises, high as the heavens, bright as moonlight, cold and empty as the belly of a dead fish."

"Aye, maybe that's so, cousin." Jason's lead-faced seriousness acknowledged the accuracy of his chief's analysis, while at the same time challenging it. "But my belly, too, is cold and empty as a dead fish's. And the food is there. Where that flag is."

Timothy was quiet then, his gaze looking not at his waiting companions, but out across the desolate, thickening gloom of the Snake River highlands.

After a moment he waved his slender hand, turning his slat-ribbed paint with the gesture.

"All right, my brothers," was all he said, the deep bass of the agreement as soft as the nightwind stirring the young May grass. "Let us follow the flag—"

About Will Henry

Henry Wilson Allen (best known by his pennames Will Henry and Clay Fisher) was born in 1912 in Kansas City, Missouri. He worked as a gold miner, house mover, sugar-mill operator, small-town newspaper columnist, General Motors assembly-line laborer, stablehand in Hollywood, contract writer for Metro-Goldwyn-Mayer, television script writer *(Tales of Wells Fargo, Zane Grey Theater)*, and, since 1950, with publication of *No Survivors*, novelist.

Among his fifty-three books are *Pillars of the Sky, From Where the Sun Now Stands, The Gates of the Mountains, Alias Butch Cassidy, The Tall Men, One More River to Cross, Chiricahua, I, Tom Horn, Who Rides With Wyatt, Yellowstone Kelly, Mackenna's Gold, Warbonnet, Red Blizzard, Yellow Hair, The Fourth Horseman, San Juan Hill, The Brass Command,* and *Apache Ransom.*

Will Henry has earned a record five Golden Spur awards from the Western Writers of America, Inc. He was the first recipient of the Levi Strauss "Saddleman" award for career contributions to Western literature, and has earned the Western Heritage Wrangler Award and Outstanding Service Award from the National Cowboy Hall of Fame.

Two Will Henry novels, *From Where the Sun Now Stands* and *I, Tom Horn,* have been named as among the greatest Western novels of all time.

An estimated fifteen million Will Henry and Clay Fisher books have been sold by Bantam Books alone.

Eight motion pictures have been made from Will Henry's novels, including *The Tall Men, Santa Fe Passage, Mackenna's Gold, Journey to Shiloh, Yellowstone Kelly,* and, in 1956, the Universal film *Pillars of the Sky,* starring Jeff Chandler, Dorothy Malone, Ward Bond, and Lee Marvin.

Will Henry (the name he prefers, personally and professionally) is the most honored and respected of all Western writers and is widely regarded as the most significant author of historical novels of the West in American Literature.

Will Henry is one of our most respected novelists of the true American West, and PILLARS OF THE SKY is one of his most popular novels. Over the coming months, Bantam Books will reissue a number of other magnificent Will Henry classics.

Turn the page for a preview of the next outstanding frontier saga by Will Henry:

ONE MORE RIVER TO CROSS

A novel of an ex-slave
who carved a legend
out of the Western Frontier.

This book will be on sale in April 1991.
Look for it—and other Will Henry novels—
wherever Bantam Books are sold.

In the Arkansas Ozarks the times were uneasy that war summer of 1861. Since April and the cannons of Fort Sumter no man of the South who dwelled near the North could feel safe. While slavery was a fact of life below the Arkansas border, the Ozark hill country was much too close to the centers of Union loyalty for property owners such as Squire Huddleston to know true rest. Gathering his belongings, including his few slaves, hill farmer Huddleston left Siloam Ridge and went south. Riding with him upon the seat of the lead wagon was a small Negro boy of twelve. The boy's name was Ned. No man knew his father or his mother. Huddleston had bought him as a baby for four dollars and fifty bars of lye soap against a guarantee by the seller that the foundling would winter-through safely on a diet of raw cow's milk and warmed sugar water, a gamble which Ned repaid by thriving like a brown and happy weed amid the rocks and hard-scrabble of the homeplace.

From the beginning Huddleston understood he had

taken to shelter no ordinary boy. Unfailingly cheerful, instantly willing, lithe and handsome as a Nubian lion cub, the youth stood apart not only as an offspring of a shackled people but as an extraordinary individual by any judgment.

He had a magic hand with all animals, wild and domestic. Birds called to him and were answered. No fish hatched from mortal roe might elude the sorcery of his line, nor flee the hook and hackle of his home-tied flies. And he was like the animals: no white-tail buck trod more lightly in the thicket, no black bear hid with greater cunning in the bottom timber, no rabbit ran so well, no bobcat stalked the meadow's edge with greater stealth or keener cast of eye. Even with all the happiness of his foster home, it was the river's run, the ridge's crest, the wooded slope and grassy clearing where human voice fell not, nor clumsy booted foot, which were his true habitats. Within their spell he was secure, a natural child claiming nature as his only mother.

Adults liked the boy, favoring him for his alert, sunny spirit, and for his inherent wish to help all about him. For himself, Ned reserved two special loves—those of horses and of other children smaller than he, a twin devotion which he never changed, of failed.

He showed an early aptitude with firearms, and with all aspects of the hunt; by his tenth year he was steadily supplying game meat to leaven the otherwise monotonous menu of brined fat pork, grits and collard greens which was the daily fare of the Huddleston slaves.

Ned herded the farm's scant flock of sheep, tended and defended the band of scrawny chickens which gave eggs and an occasional fryer. He milked the cow, saw that the heifer stood to the bull, that the calf was not lost from the mother, nor taken by the catamount, the wolf, or the canny bear; he reported the labor of the mare in foal, the fleshing of the beef steers, the location and numbers of the half-wild herd of razorback pigs littered and ranging on Huddleston land. All of these things and half a hundred more he accomplished gladly and skillfully. In sum, he was of such use to everyone within the benediction of his instant smile or reach of his ready dark hand that when he was twelve his owner gave the boy his own name in formal declaration.

Thus it was that Ned Huddleston sat upon the driver's box of the southward-rolling wagon with the Squire of Siloam Ridge that long-ago day, outward bound upon the singular adventure that was to become the legend of Isom Dart.

The war went forward three more summers and a spring. Inescapably Ned became a part of it, serving as personal forager for his owner, who had taken a commission in a Confederate regiment. A forager in war is many things— cook, valet, mess boy, runner, jack-of-all-officers—but primarily he is a thief, his first duty being to beg, borrow or steal from the countryside whatever might be useful and return it to his camp.

The assignment might appear simple for troops based on their native lands, as were the southern forces; but the young Negro lad soon learned one of the truths of war: people who would offer their lives in a cause would not willingly give up a Confederate dollar's worth of personal property. They would *sell* the hoarded food or clothing—for Yankee money—but contribute freely no crumb or thread.

Ned pondered this discovery in his friendly, trusting way, and was soon to ponder it more painfully. He was captured five times in his first year of foraging. Three times he was severely flogged by irate Confederate householders, once badly beaten by a plantation overseer, once incongruously rescued by a Yankee major and a raiding squadron of Union Cavalry from being run down by a pack of redbone hounds set on his trail by the loyal southern landowners.

As the great struggle wore on and its tides of battle washed farther to the North, the boy found that stealing from the enemy was infinitely less dangerous than attempting to "borrow" from the southern friend. Billy Yank seemed by far better able to understand than was his Confederate counterpart, Johnny Reb, that war was war and that foraging was as natural to it as wet, cold, cannon fire, misery and hope.

But yet young Ned decided, it wasn't really the soldiers of either side who made survival difficult, it was the people who were too young or too old or too cowardly to get into the fight, who behaved meanly behind the backs of their brave soldiers. They were the ones who made all the talk about dying for the cause, yet they would beat you with a club, or fire a gun at you, or turn the foxhounds loose on you if you so much as tapped on their doors at broad noon and asked for a cup of water or shard of stale bread.

This strange selfishness made a lasting impression on Ned. So did the soldiers for whom he rustled and crept and stole, who claimed that in the name of war any act of theft or deceit or force was fair. It had no moral meaning. The only thing that counted was to survive, to somehow live through whatever menace loomed at the moment. Once safely past that moment, a man might tell himself that whatever he had done, or ordered others to do, had to be done. The only other choice was destruction, or defeat for the cause. If a farmer or townsman did not understand his patriotic duty to support his troops then he might have to be persuaded by a bayonet at his throat, or the throat of his woman or child, or by whatever naked ugliness was necessary, to surrender his chickens, eggs or milk, bread, warm blankets, good clothing or dry boots.

It was war. All things were fair.

Young Ned quite plainly did not see these forces at work in patriotic terms; nor did the still unbreakably good-natured Negro camp thief comprehend in any real sense the issues of the bloody fratricide which brought his master's southern white folks to kill and be killed by their northern friends and kinsmen. Had he been told that he, a slave, was the central if somewhat unadmitted cause of the terrible waste, he would have refused to believe it. "Me, suh?" he would have said to the by-then Colonel Huddleston. "My people to blame? Why, we ain't done a thing." And the Colonel would have smiled and patted him on his head and told him not to worry, that a "nigra" couldn't be expected to understand anything that complicated.

But even though Ned would not understand that the War between the States had been emotionally ignited by the issue of slavery, he had already learned another aspect of the white man's military reasoning which was to stay with him for the rest of his life: it did not matter what a man did, it was being caught at the doing which brought shame and punishment. A man or a mere youth like himself, might lie, cheat, steal, wound, even kill another man, or burn down his buildings, or defile his women, and it would be forgiven if it was brought off undetected. The entire idea was to do the deed and escape. Admit nothing. Always lay the trail away from the scene to avoid pursuit or capture. Sneak and thieve and deceive, but do not call it that. Call it war, and forgive yourself the trespass, because to the winner went the absolution, to the loser damnation because he had lost.

In the second summer of the war the rumor grew that Abraham Lincoln was preparing to issue his Proclamation freeing the slaves. Colonel Huddleston, with his command in the Confederate lines gathering for Second Manassas, called Ned to his tent. The Negro boy found his master in poor condition; his leg was mutilated to the hip by a charge of chainshot suffered in a forward skirmish some hours gone, and the surgeon did not believe the wounded man would survive. He was of no further military use and the brigade general had already signed his honorable discharge. A wagon train of captured Union blankets and medical materials was being sent back that same night. All southern wounded unable to walk or sit a horse were going out with the wagons, Colonel Noah Huddleston among them. It was of this fact the officer now apprised Ned. He then went on quickly to explain the particular urgency of the situation for his young forager.

"Lad," he began, "did you know the Yankee President, Mr. Lincoln, is said to be readying a paper freeing all the slaves?"

"No, suh," answered Ned. "I never. What's it mean, Colonel? What slaves Mr. Lincoln talking about?"

"All of them, Ned. That means you, too, boy."

The Negro lad shook his head. "Yes, suh, if you say, Colonel. What's it going to mean, though, suh, this here freedom paper?"

"It will mena, Ned, thàt if you can slip up through our troops and get to the river and on across it into the Union lines, you will be free."

"Free from what, suh?"

Huddleston, tooth-gritting pain aside, smiled wanly. Freedom was an empty word to the boy. He must be given another view of the term.

"It means, Ned," he tried once more, "that if you can get over the Rappahannock tonight you can do whatever you want to after that. You'll be free, just like a white boy."

Ned nodded and scratched his head. He was trying hard to help out the injured master. Clearly his leg had him fevered, was interfering with his mind's work.

"How am I going to do whatever I want, suh," he finally asked, "when fust off I got to do whatever you want?"

"All right, Ned," Huddleston said, the pain very great. "Since that's the way you understand things, that's the way we will have to do it. You will know the truth later, God being kind to you meanwhile. Bring me that pen and those writing sheets. Hurry lad. The hospital wagon will be by at any minute to put me aboard."

The officer wrote with great difficulty, but in a clear hand he stated he, the legal owner, freed the boy known in his own name as Ned Huddleston, and requested any who might find him by the road to give him aid and comfort to reach the North, where his freedom would mean something and he might have a chance to learn a trade and be a self-sustaining man of respect. The reason cited in the letter for freeing Ned was not Lincoln's forthcoming Proclamation, but rather the fact that in two hard summers of war the Negro lad had bravely earned the right to some better life away from the battlefield.

Huddleston knew, of course, that the honoring of his document would depend upon whim and pure chance should Ned be apprehended south of the river. But he affixed his name, rank, location of the family home and the dates of his commission, term of service and discharge, with the instruction that if Ned were captured he was to be returned to the Huddleston family in the south and under no circumstances punished for doing what his legal owner had ordered him to do—try to reach the Federal lines beyond the river.

Sanding the letter, the wounded officer sealed it in a vellum envelope and told Ned not to reveal it unless to save his life.

"Make yourself useful around here after they take me away," he told the boy. "Let on like you mean to stay and forage for the troops as before. I've already told my friend Major Gainesford that he can have you. Go to him and behave as you would with me. But, Ned, come tonight, you go. You understand that, boy? You take out and hit for the river."

Ned frowned. There were too many shades of meaning and maneuver here for his uncomplicated nature. Again he shook his head. "You want me to serve the Major but to skin out the minute he turns his back? Then shag over the river, suh? Who am I going to serve yonder?"

"Nobody," explained Huddleston wearily. "You'll be free."

"No suh," Ned denied. "You can beat me when you're well, or set the dogs on me, whichever, Colonel. But I ain't never going to leave you. I ain't never going to serve no Yankee Gen'ril, nor no other man alive, less it's you, suh."

"I don't want you to serve any other man, Ned. That's what the letter says." Lying on the cot, he propped himself up on his elbow. "I hear the wagon coming. I want your word, Ned. You do what I have told you, boy. You have my name, and it's a proud one. Now you're free, as well, if you can get away to the North. You do it, you hear? After the war, I'll try to find you. Meanwhile, you go north and make a life for yourself up there." The officer put a cold hand on the arm of the Negro lad. His fingers gripped and tightened, and Ned put his other hand to Colonel Huddleston's. "Ned," the latter said, "you're my boy the same as you were white, and you got to do what I tell you. Good-bye."

Ned was crying then and he fell back into the tent shadows as the ragged and filthy work troops came into the shelter and took up the Colonel and bore him out to the wagon. When the vehicle had rattled on, Ned came out of the tent to watch it until it disappeared into the trees.

Then, as he had done all his life, he did what he had been told to do.

Unable, however, to find Major Gainesford immediately, he wandered around camp helping where he could until another Negro lad, older than himself and a fellow-forager, told him that his own officer had been killed that same afternoon in a cavalry brush at Raccoon Ford.

"You mean," asked Ned, feeling his stomach grow small with dread, "that Major Gainesford done got kilt?"

"Well, I allow you know he was my master," replied the other. "So ain't that what I said?"

Ned then told the other youth his own similar dilemma, but nothing of the freedom paper in his shirt. When both boys later heard that a terrible fight was forming up along the banks of Bull Run, not far away, they decided to flee the Confederate camp together. With both their masters gone, it seemed to the two lads that crossing the river and seeking asylum with the Yankees now made considerable sense.

"Lookit yonder," directed Ned, pointing. "Twilight's shut down hard along the river. Them bottom shadows twixt the willers and the bank ought to hide us safe as two charcoal cats."

"Sure enough," agreed Snakehead, a youth of lean reptilian look. "You take out fust, Ned; you're the sneakiest nigger I ever seen."

Ned bobbed his head in dubious accord. "Likewise the scairtest one you ever seen," he said, and slipped off noiselessly through the settling dusk toward the willow brakes of the Rappahannock.

The two Negro youths came to the river. It flowed silently through the summer night, seeming far wider than by day. A great restless moving of troops was going on in the darkness which shrouded both banks. The boys shivered with the fear that a southern patrol might step upon their hiding patch of reedy brush before they could quit it. They lay close as common flesh, and each could feel the heartbeat of the other, wild and fast, like a bird or rabbit. At last, as there came a lull in the calling back and forth of the Confederate pickets, Snakehead stirred.

"I reckon we had best go, happen we mean to go," he whispered. "Ain't no Rebs near. You nerved-up yet, Ned?"

"My knees and teeth ain't," answered the other boy.

"That's all right," assured Snakehead. "When you is in the water that shaking will make you go like a speckled trout."

Ned started away from the brush heap. Both boys crawled belly-down. They were nearly to the stream

...head thought he heard a footfall off to their ... or one instant he took his eyes from the silhou- ...d beacon of Ned's buttocks humping along in front of him. When there came no second footfall, he looked back but could not see the other youth's rump. Writhing to the right, then the left, then forward along what he thought was their path toward the water, his desperate hand reached through the pitchblende gloom of the bottom- land, but he felt no touch of his friend's flesh. Forgetting everything. Snakehead stood up against the starlight and called out Ned's name, hoarsely, urgently. An answer came, but not from Ned.

"Hold!" challenged the Rebel picket. "Stand or be shot!"

Snakehead could see the picket now, up against the maples in the little bend above the brush clump. He could see, as well, the murky forms of several other gray-clad troopers moving in the starlight behind the first soldier.

Snakehead was not afraid, but he whirled in confu- sion. Where was Ned? Had he made it to the water? Was he hiding in the cattails of the bend, breathing maybe through the hollow stem of one of the tails, like any slave knew to do?

"Sing out!" said the picket. "Friend or enemy?"

Only one word would come to the mind of Snake- head, that was "nigger." That was all he was. He wasn't friend or enemy, he was just a nigger. He would tell the southern soldier boys that and it would be password enough for them.

Snakehead did not call out, however. He just started toward the pickets unthinkingly. He thought to grin and tell them who he was—Major Gainesford's forager—and that he had legitimate affairs down here by the river. But then he remembered that the Major was dead and that these boys would know that—maybe—and they might get hard with him for lying to them. They might even say he was trying to run away, and they could shoot him for that. Snakehead stopped moving. As he crouched and half-turned away, the voice fo the picket rang out again, and then the shots: one, three, five, seven of them. Snake-head felt only six. The last one missed and sang onto the surface of the river only an arm's length from where Ned lay half-submerged in the reeds. It skipped and skittered like a thrown flat rock over toward the Yankee side, from where the Federal pickets fired at it nervously and yelled for lanterns and a scout patrol.

The Confederate troopers laughed at them and called them blue-bellies. Then Ned saw the Confederates go through the starlight to the huddled form of Snake-head; he saw the first picket lean down and strike a match, heard his companions ask tensely who it was they had brought down, heard the first man say the word Snakehead had not said, "nigger," and that was all.

For an hour Ned lay in the reeds in the ebbwater of the river, and then he remembered with a start the letter given him by Colonel Huddleston. He was glad then. That paper gave him strength. It made him like a white boy, the Colonel had said; he had only to show it to anyone, and they would know he was Ned Huddleston, and help him on his way.

He arose from the muddy water, cleansing himself in its current. He didn't need to cross the river, nor explain to the pickets who he was. He wasn't like Snakehead, a nobody. He was Ned Huddleston, Colonel Huddleston's boy, and he had the paper to prove it.

Those southern boys hadn't killed Snakehead be-cause he was a Negro. They had shot at him because he had failed to answer their hail. They hadn't known what color he was. Snakehead had died for nothing, but Ned didn't need to die like that. He had only to go up the bank and show the nearest Confederate officer his paper. Then everything would be right.

In only a few minutes he found a tent with lantern light and voices to announce it as an important meeting place of officers. He went toward it and was barred by the

...ut he raised his voice to the soldier be-
...s the same as a white boy now.

...e soldier seized him and dragged him, still drip-
...g water, into the big tent.

"Begging your pardon, Gen'ril, suh," he addressed
the white-haired officer at the crowded map table within.
"This boy says he's got an important paper to show."

The slight man in the long gray cavalry coat and
high jack-boots came around the desk. He looked at Ned
and put a slender, fine-veined hand on the Negro lad's
sodden shoulder. Ned looked up at him unafraid. "Suh,"
he said, "I'm Ned Huddleston, Colonel Huddleston's
boy, suh."

"Yes?" said the sad-faced officer. "I believe you."

"Yes, suh, thank you, suh."

"You have an important paper for me, boy?"

"General, sir," interrupted one of the gilt-encrusted
staff, "we must get on, sir. General Jackson is waiting to
go forward to cut off Pope, and General Longstreet is
wanting to know about moving on your right, sir.
Please!"

"Colonel Malvern, I am doing my best, sir. Precisely
as this small lad. It is the same war for all of us. The
paper, boy."

Ned dug into his muddy shirtfront, brought forth
the precious envelope. The gentle officer took it from
him, extracted from within it the limp mass of Colonel
Huddleston's letter. He unfolded the missive, studied it,
passed it to the impatient colonel on his right. "What do
you make of it, Malvern?" he asked quietly.

"Suh," said Ned uneasily, noting the looks exchanged between the high officers, "that there is my freedom paper. Colonel Huddleston, he done writ on there
that he was setting me free, that I wasn't no slave no
more, that I was his boy same as had I been white. Ain't
you see that there, Gen'ril, suh?"

Colonel Malvern handed the paper back to his superior. The latter took it and looked at it once more. Then,

with a deep sigh, he held it down for Ned to see. The Negro lad squinted and peered, and reached forth to turn the paper in the officer's hand, examining the hidden side. He felt his heart stop beating within him.

"It's not legible, boy," said the white-haired general.

"Suh?" said Ned, puzzled and afraid.

"You can't read it any more," said the officer. "It has been spoiled by the water."

Ned tried to stand straight, but his shoulders drooped. He knew what had been said, and what the running ink spelled out for him. He would not see the other side of the river that night, or the next. He was not free as poor Snakehead lying in the summer mud. His name was nothing again. He was just a nigger now, like all the others.

He let the sodden paper drop, the tears shining against the dark wet of his face. The officer reached out and touched him. "Don't weep, lad," he said. "I believe you."

The boy blinked upward, awkward in the lamplight and the restive silence of the listening staff. "What, suh?" he asked hesitantly.

"I said that I believe what you say, Ned Huddleston," answered the officer. He bent and picked up the ruined letter from the floor. Brushing the dirt from it, he returned it carefully to its envelope, gave it back to Ned.

"Keep it with you," he said. "Carry it next to your heart, where you had it." He paused, his patient glance finding the boy's frightened dark eyes. "*You* know what it says, Ned," he told him softly. "That is all that counts."

With the quiet words, Robert E. Lee went back to his waiting officers and the map table and march orders which would send Stonewall Jackson and J.E.B. Stuart racing hard around the Union flank of John Pope to fall upon the great Federal supply base at Manassas Junction, fatal stage for the Second Battle of Bull Run, called Manassas by the South.

* * *

The kindness of "Marse Robert" was a brief candle in the night of Ned Huddleston's war. It lit the boy's spirit for a moment, but great men cannot stay, and Lee was gone with daylight. Ned's fortunes returned to those of camp forager for the Confederate army, and his life was to follow one regiment after another, now cavalry, now infantry, now artillery, as the South was driven back upon her last defenses.

In the process Ned became something more than thief and scavenger. During those final days when the great armies of the Confederacy were but rotten shells and food was the very name of survival in the field, all men became something different. The gallantry was gone. The great heroes, Jackson, Albert Sidney Johnston, Jeb Stuart, all were dead. The cause was now a curse and men sought to avoid it. Murder, arson, rapine and pillage were the secret military order of the day. Soldier lived in terror of soldier, and the people feared their own army as a plague.

Ned Huddleston lasted out this desperation because of the pride Squire Huddleston had given him with his name, and with the freedom paper. He was able to live because his master had said to him, "You are my boy, Ned; same as you were white." That was the grandest thing. A man could walk a long road mighty tall with those words in his memory.

The lonely Negro youth was sixteen years of age in that final spring of the war. Over six feet in height, he was as indestructible as a swamp oak fencepost. The bright handsomeness of boyhood was now a tightened mask of suspicion and vigilance. Eyes that once shone, now glittered. The wide smile, in the past so friendly, would gleam as quickly, but with a set configuration of the lips which wise men would read as anything but reassuring. Yet one warmth did remain to him, and it was not the gift of Squire Huddleston but a thing of his mother-blood, his birthright: his will to be of help to anyone who seemed in need of help. It survived, untouched by war, in the freed slave's broad breast, setting him apart from his fellows, making other men uneasy in his presence. No matter how menacing his outer form, good still lingered in the heart of Ned Huddleston. And men have always misunderstood such good, or simply feared its truth.

With the April of Appomattox and the Confederate surrender, Ned, as so many camp-followers of the lost cause, turned westward. Somewhere out there toward the sunset, men said, a new land waited, and a new life.

And something more. Out there beyond Red River, past the Sabine and the Neches and the Trinity, where the winds of Texas wandered—out there, somewhere, freedom waited.

ELMER KELTON

☐	27713	THE MAN WHO RODE MIDNIGHT	$3.50
☐	25658	AFTER THE BUGLES	$2.95
☐	27351	HORSEHEAD CROSSING	$2.95
☐	27119	LLANO RIVER	$2.95
☐	27218	MANHUNTERS	$2.95
☐	27620	HANGING JUDGE	$2.95
☐	27467	WAGONTONGUE	$2.95
☐	25629	BOWIE'S MINE	$2.95
☐	26999	MASSACRE AT GOLIAD	$2.95
☐	25651	EYES OF THE HAWK	$2.95
☐	26042	JOE PEPPER	$2.95
☐	26105	DARK THICKET	$2.95
☐	26449	LONG WAY TO TEXAS	$2.95
☐	25740	THE WOLF AND THE BUFFALO	$3.95